Krissi was born in Yorkshire and now lives in Dorset with her husband Bob. After her career in estate agency and now with her family grown and flown the nest, she spends her time indulging in her loves of baking, walking, the odd G&T and, at last, her passion for writing.

For my mum, Doreen (1923–2021), who passed away last year and was full of enthusiasm for my writing and an avid supporter.

Krissi Morris

FOREVER AND A DAY

AUSTIN MACAULEY PUBLISHERS™

LONDON • CAMBRIDGE • NEW YORK • SHARJAH

A CIP catalogue record for this title is available from the British Library.

ISBN 9781398456365 (Paperback)
ISBN 9781398456372 (ePub e-book)

www.austinmacauley.com

First Published 2023
Austin Macauley Publishers Ltd®
1 Canada Square
Canary Wharf
London
E14 5AA

It may seem crazy to thank the characters in my books but somehow they would not let me go and I have to confess that their stories are not over yet, as you will discover.

Special thanks however must go to my sister Elizabeth who is the Dean of the Cathedral in Bendigo, Australia for her invaluable help with the intricacies of the Church and its clerics.

Thank you too to the team at Austin Macauley Publishers for all their help and support.

Finally, once again, my grateful thanks to Clair Bossons for her suggestions, corrections and patience.

Chapter 1

"Arrrrrggghh!" screamed Molly wildly puffing and panting. "I hate you, I hate you, I… hate you…" she gasped as the pain seared through her body again, her eyes rolling backwards with the effort of it all. Alistair, totally confused, attempted to hold her hand not knowing any other way to help. He looked at Lucy for answers as Molly yelled once more.

"I don't understand," he looked pleadingly for help at Lucy as he patted Molly's hand.

She snatched it away.

"Don't touch me; just don't touch me. This is your fault entirely." Her head fell back onto the pillow, tears now streaming down her contorted face; as she clutched his hand digging her nails in, Molly let out another yell.

Lucy smiled at Alistair, "Don't worry, this is quite normal for mothers who are giving birth. I've heard much worse; believe me." She turned to Molly, "Come on, Molly. I can see the head, not much more now, one more push and your baby will be born." Molly began short fast puffing, her face bright red as she screwed up her eyes with the exertion.

Alistair stared unconvinced. He had never heard Molly like this before; it was frightening. Actually, that wasn't quite true; he let a smile slide onto his face at the memory of Molly last year frantically packing saying she was leaving him all red-faced and flustered.

She had shouted and cried, blaming him, and to be fair, it was his fault. That was a long time ago now, he had been stubborn failing to see Molly's point of view, but that was in the past.

Now they couldn't be happier. Another scream brought his mind back, only to realise that it was himself making the noise this time as Molly's fingernails dug into his flesh leaving red weals on his arm. He turned to look at Molly just as Lucy safely delivered their squirming, crying baby into the world.

"It's a boy!" declared Lucy taking care of him as quickly as possible and placing him between Molly's breasts, forming a bond that would be impossible to break.

Alistair kissed her forehead smoothing her hair back, a wet strand stuck to her face, and he gently lifted it. "A boy, darling; isn't that wonderful? I love you so much." He kissed her again. "He's just perfect."

"He is so tiny." Molly kissed his sticky head; her face wreathed in smiles as she looked up at Alistair. Her face suddenly crumpled and contorted as she began to frantically puff once more. Lucy retrieved the tiny bundle handing him to another midwife.

"Here comes the next one, Molly; give me a big push now; that's it, keep going, keep going; that's it; nearly there." Another baby slid out into the world all flailing arms and exercising his lungs letting everyone know that he had arrived.

"It's another boy, Molly," said Alistair excitedly turning only to see Molly's head flop to one side, her eyes dropping shut. "Molly are you alright?" he looked to Lucy for help filled with fear, "What's happening? Is she alright, Lucy?" He jumped up patting Molly's hand as a cold sweat slid down his back. Molly lay totally still with her eyes closed. Lucy quickly checked Molly who was breathing; she had passed out from exhaustion.

A few moments later, her eyes flicked open once more, and Alistair allowed himself to breathe as the fear he had held slipped away. Molly gave a faint smile.

"What happened? Are the babies alright?" she asked looking from Alistair to Lucy and back again as she tried to sit up.

"Yes, here you are. You have identical twin boys," she handed the babies to Molly and Alistair pulled out his phone to take pictures.

"I must look awful," said Molly, "… please Alistair, you mustn't show those pictures to anyone." She kissed each baby in turn grinning up at Alistair. "What are we going to call them?" She looked up as he was now taking a video; she grimaced attempting to smile at him.

He was overjoyed with pride and pleasure at his increasing family, "I don't know, but you look wonderful to me." He clicked away again. "It was easy to come up with girls' names, but I was thinking maybe Oliver and Elliott with middle names George and Trevor after your dad and mine. What do you think?" He traced a finger gently over the heads of both his sons, leaning in to kiss Molly.

"Perfect," she said, "just perfect."

* * *

Once home, the next few weeks passed in a blur for Molly, she had so many visitors, all very welcome but exhausting when all she wanted was to be left alone and rest. It seemed that every time the babies went to sleep, the phone would ring or a rap on the door and her nap disappeared along with her longed-for peaceful five minutes. She felt like no one actually wanted to help her; they would turn up with more flowers and chocolates, expect her to make the tea and entertain them! And as soon as one baby woke up, so did the other, and the visitor would disappear saying, "Well, I had better leave you to it!" Only Lucy understood. Lucy was her best friend, and she admired the way she was always nice and calm, never a hint of panic.

What would she do without her?

"Don't get me wrong," wailed Molly as she recounted her thoughts to Lucy. "I love to see people, but you know what I could really do with?" asked Molly as she sat feeding Oliver.

Lucy peered around the kitchen door, kettle in hand, "Go on, what?"

"Someone to vacuum the house or cook me a meal," she sighed, turning from Oliver and staring at Lucy. "Even Alistair walks in asking, 'What's for dinner?'" They both grinned before bursting into laughter with each other.

"Men always think that motherhood is easy because after all what do you do all day other than feed and change the babies, and of course sit around watching TV?" joked Lucy.

Molly shook her head, "If only," smiling she lifted Oliver gently up to sitting to enable her to pat his back to bring up any wind, "… so," she asked turning an enquiring eye in Lucy's direction once more "who does the shopping, washing and ironing, cleaning the house, cooking the meals and a million and one other things? Oh, yes, I nearly forgot, and that's after suffering a sleepless night with two mouths to feed." Molly began to laugh as tears filled her eyes and tumbled down her face. "If that's not enough, I look a mess, no makeup and I live in sweat pants," she blubbered. Lucy came to her rescue.

"Give Oliver to me, and I will change him; Elliott is asleep, so put your feet up and drink your tea," smiled Lucy. Molly gratefully handed her little squirming bundle over to Lucy and gratefully sank back onto the sofa. She drifted off into a blissful sleep. She dreamt she was relaxing on a sunny warm beach, a gentle breeze blowing, a book in her hand and a cocktail by her side.

Suddenly, a loud noise woke her up; she sat startled for a moment trying to think where she was and what day it was. The noise, it turned out, was her mug of tea falling and smashing onto the tiled floor. Tea had splashed everywhere, and Molly hung her head, shoulders slumped, at the thought of cleaning up the sticky mess. Everything was quiet, eerily quiet; she stood up looking around fear gripping at her heart. There was no sound at all nothing.

"Lucy," she called out; still no sound; the house was empty. Molly dashed into the bedroom and found the cots both empty, dread-filled her core her heart thumping so hard she clutched at her chest. It was then that she spotted a note, now covered in tea, picking it up, tea dripped onto her sweatpants. "Am taking the twins for a walk down to the sea," it read. "Have a bath and get dressed up," Lucy had left a couple of kisses on the bottom. Molly smiled to herself, letting out the breath she had been holding, her heart slowed.

She didn't deserve her really, grateful for such a good friend, with all the moaning she did, but she also knew that you can only moan to your best friend.

"Lucy," she said out loud turning the radio on, "I love you; what would I do without you?" She twirled around, cleared up the broken mug and headed for the bathroom.

An hour later, Lucy was back just as Molly put the finishing touches on her makeup.

She felt better than she had for weeks. She pulled out the tongs to tame her bubbly hair, staring at herself in the mirror. Oh no, were there some little lines appearing by the side of her eyes? She examined them more closely, shook her head as if she could shake them away before bouncing out to see Lucy.

"Wow, you look better," Lucy grinned as she surveyed Molly, no sweatpants in sight.

"Oh, Lucy, I feel much better, like my old self again. How are the boys?" She peered into the pram, both asleep, "… thankfully, Alice is picking up Jessica today," she glanced at her watch, "… they should be here soon, and I must express some more milk. Then you can tell me why I needed to dress up," she looked quizzically, grinning at Lucy.

"Well…" she hesitated.

"Yes…" said Molly as she turned the pump on filling the first bottle.

"I thought that you could do with a treat, so I spoke to Alistair. He has booked a table at that place you both like in Wareham. Bertie is coming over, and we will look after the children so that you two can have a romantic evening out." She finished with a flourish.

Molly gaped in amazement, stunned into silence.

"… But, all three of them? Are you sure? I mean have you any idea how hard that is?" she stuttered.

Lucy laughed, "I am a midwife, remember; I think we can cope for one evening. Jessica adores Bertie; he's like her second daddy and is looking forward to it; honestly, no need to worry. Please. Just go and enjoy yourself." Molly gave in, relieved and pleased to escape for a few precious hours.

"Thank you sooo much," she said. "I owe you one."

The door opened and in came Alice with a wriggling Jessica.

"Hello, dear," said Alice absentmindedly; then taking a second look at Molly, "… you look lovely; what's the occasion?"

"Lucy and Bertie have offered to look after the children this evening so that Alistair and I can have a night out, isn't that wonderful?" she bent down to pick up Jessica who was pulling at her skirt trying to get her attention.

"That is nice dear. You know that George and I would love to, but I think it might be too much for George these days," she patted her hair turning to Lucy. "I'm sure that you young ones will manage, Lucy dear, and of course, if you need us, we are not far away." She gave a little smile, "I must be going anyway. George will be wanting his tea." Alice picked up her bag and gave Molly a peck on the cheek before leaving.

Molly and Lucy couldn't help but chuckle after she had left.

"I think that Jessica is more than enough for Alice, and if I'm honest, I'd rather you looked after them anyway," she hugged Lucy. The babies began to squirm and wake each other up. "Here we go again," she shrugged at Lucy picking up Elliott. The door burst open and in walked Alistair with a huge bunch of flowers and a big grin.

Chapter 2

Alice marched into the snug as disgruntled as she had been when she left Molly. She pulled off her jacket, dropping it untidily onto a chair, looking for George. She found him fast asleep on a sun chair on the terrace, legs stretched out, and his newspaper had fallen into an untidy heap on the floor. This blissful sight did not quell her frustration; in fact, she was now cross with George too. She snatched the paper from the floor attempting to fold it muttering under her breath about lazy husbands with nothing better to do.

George, awakened by the kerfuffle, lifted his head sleepily, opening one eye to look at Alice. A fly buzzed around him, and he lazily attempted to swat it away with his hand.

"Hello, dear, you are earlier than I expected," he threw her a little smile. Alice was in no mood for placation.

"Clearly." She flopped down onto the other sun chair. "It's obvious to me when I am not wanted," she snapped.

"What are you talking about dear? Tell me what has happened; I'm sure things are not quite as bad as all that." He struggled to sit up, turning in order to give her his full attention.

"You know nothing about it I just feel that I'm being side-lined and well…" tears squeezed from her eyes, and she swiped at them for being so… just so there. Her face crumpled as tears threatened to turn into a deluge. She fumbled for a tissue carefully dabbing her face; she had taken extra care to put makeup on today. George came to her rescue.

"You sit there my dear, I will be back in a minute," George clumsily pushed himself up out of his chair with a huff putting his glasses back on.

Alice couldn't get rid of the thoughts crowding her mind vying for attention. She wanted to shout at George to tell him that a couple of pills were not going to sort this one! If things were that simple she would have sorted it herself by now. She sat back in her chair; the sun had moved around and was flooding the terrace with warmth. It seeped slowly into her bones. Alice loved this place, her garden, the brook that bubbled along its boundary, the family of ducks on the bank. The trees were heavy with blossom at this time of year and the church fete that was always held in her garden, all began crowding in needing to be dealt with. Now things had moved on to the next generation she felt left out, wanting to tell them that she was not too old to help.

George returned carrying a tray, and to her surprise, it was not pills and a glass of water but sherry and a packet of sea salt crisps. She couldn't help herself but smile at him even though she would have rather had a grumble.

"Here you are, my dear. Let's just chill out for a while and not worry about a thing."

He kissed the top of her head placing the tray on the table between them. He sat down, opened the crisps handing them to her and sat back, hands clasped over his generous belly.

Alice stared at him for a moment, nothing ever seemed to fluster him. He could be annoying sometimes that way. Alice picked up her sherry taking a gulp, it felt good.

"George…"

"Yes, my dear," he put his sherry down, a smile dancing on his lips. He lifted his eyebrows in the way that always made Alice tingle inside. Her battle that had been waiting to leap out to cause chaos and Alice only too willing to do it justice, suddenly it all disappeared.

"I've been thinking that maybe we should put our holiday on hold…" she glanced over at George but he made no comment. "It's just that with Alistair and Molly having twins and dear little Jessica too that maybe they might need our help and if we disappear halfway around the world… Well, it might just not be the right time." She gave him her sweetest smile picking up her sherry to take another satisfying sip. George let out a small sigh placing his empty glass on the table. He shuffled in his chair attempting to make himself more comfortable, Alice had seen this little act so many times she could wait. A blackbird landed close by and began to sing, Alice watched him she was in no hurry either.

"I think we need a top-up, my dear," George pushed himself up to retrieve the now near-empty bottle of sherry. He topped up both glasses, cleared his throat and sat down again. "I can see where you are coming from and in many ways I agree with you, however, don't you think that we should let the young ones live their own lives? They don't want us hanging around interfering…" Alice shot her head up.

"I would never interfere," she felt hurt at such a suggestion and tried her hardest to quell the images that flashed up of all the times that she had actually interfered, but this was different.

"Now Alice, I'm not saying that you have or would but do you remember when you had Christopher and Alistair? If I recall the last thing you wanted was your mother trying to tell you what to do and all I'm saying is that it is their lives now and we should get on with ours."

He could be annoyingly right thought Alice as she struggled to come up with an answer. She had felt put out when Lucy was going to look after the babies; after all, she knew what to do but... she finished her sherry... she had been tired just looking after Jessica so maybe it would be better to leave them to it, they knew where to find them if they needed them.

"You're right George, as usual, I just felt superfluous and well... that's all really."

"I know my dear, but we can have our time now like we always wanted. Let's finish this sherry," he picked up the bottle tipping it at an angle to see how much was left and draining the last drops into Alice's glass. They sat quietly watching the mad happenings in the garden. A drake was chasing a duck, a pigeon was picking up bits of twig and two doves were bobbing up and down at each other. Alice smiled with contentment placing her glass on the table. She put her head back and drifted off to sleep, the sherry having done its job.

Chapter 3

Sandra heard her flight called and dragged herself up to walk to the check-in gate. This was not a trip she wanted to make. She was miserable. Miserable for many reasons not least because she was leaving Spain. She glanced over her shoulder at the clear azure blue sky her heart aching already. Her plane climbed away up above the clouds. Sandra tried to relax a feeling of foreboding overtaking her. She clutched her bag pulling her jacket tighter around her, why anyone would choose to live in the cold, wet UK she couldn't imagine. Still, it was a duty visit and she would just have to hold her head up, get on with it and make the best of it.

She sat staring out of the window watching the clouds turning grey and slowly darker as the rain began to spatter across the window.

The 'fasten seat belts' sign came on and her mood descended along with the plane.

Waiting at the carousel was torture, *why is everything in this country such a problem?* She asked herself letting out a long sigh. Her cases retrieved she struggled out to the taxi rank.

After hesitating at the cost of a taxi cab to Dorset she changed her mind and headed to the hire car booth instead.

Once on the road, Sandra ran through her mind over and over what she would say to Molly and Stella. Stella would understand but Molly, she was always black or white no room for anything in-between. Molly would ask and ask questions until she was satisfied. Her eyes began to droop and she yawned, the miles stretching out ahead of her. She decided to pull into the services and get a coffee and something to eat it had been a long time since breakfast. She browsed the shops looking for something suitable to buy her grandchildren but there was nothing, just boring bits and pieces and it was pointless buying chocolates as neither Molly nor Stella would approve. What a dilemma.

"Oh, well, I will just have to go with no presents," she said out loud before realising she was talking to herself. She felt rather foolish and her throat was still parched. Her hand flew automatically to her neck and looking at her watch she decided to have another coffee before setting off once more.

The drive down to Dorset seemed to take hours and Sandra felt torn between seeing Molly first or Stella? The car seemed to make the decision for her as she pulled up in Trentmouth outside the vet's. She sat in the car re-applying her lipstick and combing her hair.

She opened the boot lifting out her case before thinking better of it pushing it back in again, Pulling herself up to her full height she locked the car and headed to the barn next door.

"Mother!" exclaimed a clearly surprised Molly. "What are you doing here?"

"Well, that's a nice way to greet your mother when I have come all this way to see you," she understood her daughter's surprise but was still taken aback not to be greeted with a hug and a kiss. "Can I come in?" she asked rather haughtily. Molly opened the door wide looking over her shoulder.

"No, Enrico? Or should I say Eric with you?"

"Always the cutting remark Molly and no, Eric is not with me." Sandra waltzed into the sitting room and sat on the sofa. Molly followed her.

"So what are you doing here Mother? Not run out of money again so soon have you?"

Sandra could not blame Molly for her hostility even though it hurt her that her daughter's opinion was so low. Sandra had caused a lot of grief and had not exactly left on happy terms the last time she was in England. It shamed her to think that she had put Eric before her family and had not listened to them when they were only trying to help. She deserved nothing less than the contempt that Molly was now throwing in her direction.

"Actually, I am here to see my grandchildren, you can't deny me that surely?" she turned a pleading look at Molly.

"I suppose not, but the boys are fast asleep and Jessica is at nursery. Alice will be bringing her back soon a cup of tea?"

"Please." Sandra sat contemplating her next move. What she couldn't do was to tell Molly the real reason she was here, not yet anyway. She looked around the barn. Molly had turned the old store into a lovely home. She admired the range and recognised the rocking chair from the farm. Her mind immediately whisked her back to those days. She had never really taken to farming, all that dirt under her fingernails, and the smell. She wrinkled her nose at the memory, but Trevor had loved it, she never imagined that he would agree to move to Spain and they had been happy at first. Molly reappeared carrying a tray.

"Sorry, I've only got biscuits, no time for baking with three children to look after," she sat down opposite her mother. The hostility was palpable, Sandra gave an involuntary shudder. She picked up her cup of tea.

"You have a lovely home here Molly, you should be proud," she sipped her tea surreptitiously eyeing her daughter for any softening of her approach. Molly said nothing. "I mean who could ever have imagined that it could look like this." Sandra glanced all around feeling hot knowing that she was blushing in front of her own daughter. "Whatever happened to your dad's old Morris Minor Traveller? Your dad loved that old rusty heap, but he wouldn't part with it." She attempted a chuckle.

"Look, mother, you didn't come here to talk about Dad's old car so why are you here?" Molly stared unblinking at her. Sandra knew that this was going to be harder than she had ever imagined. She put her cup down trying to pump up her courage. She could hardly blame, Molly; it was her own fault. She had left on bad terms when she was last in the UK.

Enrico's little secret had been discovered and to cover her own embarrassment she knew she had been unforgivably rude. Now she wanted to put things right.

"I came to see my daughters and all my grandchildren, of course. Can't I do that anymore? I'm trying to make amends here Molly and you're not helping." Her resolve was failing and the last thing she wanted to do was tell the truth right now. "I miss you all, it's only natural." Molly appeared to soften.

"Well, you have to admit it was a surprise to see you when I opened the door, not a phone call, or a card for months. So let me ask you again, why are you here Mother?" Sandra opened her mouth to speak and closed it again gulping like a drowning fish. The door burst open and in walked Alice a squirming Jessica trying to escape. Sandra was pleased and relieved. She never imagined that Alice Warren would come to her rescue. Alice had always looked down her nose at Sandra thinking that she was not good enough to be part of the family or at least that is what it felt like to Sandra.

"Oh," exclaimed Alice, "… um hello Sandra. What brings you here? I'm so sorry you must think me awfully rude, how nice to see you. How is Spain and um Eric?" she asked looking around the room. Molly had swept up Jessica swinging her around and trying in vain to shush her. Jessica was squealing with delight. Sandra looked at the happy, homely sight with envy, why had it never been like this when her children were small?

"I'm very well, Alice; nice to see you too," Sandra forced a smile that didn't reach her eyes. She fought hard not to give her a look saying, "Go away."

"I hear that you are planning an extended holiday. I love Spain actually it's my home now so I decided to pop over to see all MY grandchildren." Molly must have sensed the atmosphere as she turned to look at them both.

"Alice, thank you so much for bringing Jessica home for me it's a big help. Would you like a cup of tea?" asked Molly innocently.

"Thank you, dear, but I must get back as George will be home from his football practise by now. He does love it and it is certainly proving to trim his waistline." She chuckled heading for the door. She turned just as she was leaving, "Same time again tomorrow?"

"Yes please Alice, thank you." Alice left with a flourish.

"Molly… I could do that for you, you don't have to rely on Alice all the time," said Sandra, a hurt tone in her voice.

"Why? Are you staying somewhere? Not with me obviously; we have two bedrooms and three children." Molly could be very matter of fact giving no room for manoeuvre to Sandra at all.

"No, of course not, I was rather wondering about the cottage at the farm." Molly let out a real belly laugh.

"Mother, you forced us to sell the farm, remember? It belongs to Bertie and Lucy now and they have let the cottage long term." She sounded triumphant and Sandra began to wish she hadn't come back at all. This was going to be a lot harder than she thought possible.

Chapter 4

The day of the opening of Bertie's café was fast approaching. He stood in the middle of the dining area looking around; he nodded his head with satisfaction. The wood burner stood in pride of place warm and inviting, the sofa plumped and ready with cushions, Lucy had draped some fairy lights along the beams, all that was missing were some original seascapes, and he would have to look into that. Lucy slid her arms around his waist and Bertie lifted his, snuggling her into him. He kissed the top of her head.

"I think it's all ready for tomorrow I hope I haven't forgotten anything," he said as he surveyed the room. It had taken almost eight long months to get to this day. Planners, health officials, highways, fire officers, his own course for hygiene; it seemed to go on and on. The rafters made for an open feel to the place, light-flooded in making the atmosphere cosy and welcoming. He had always hated dark nooks and crannies in cafes. The cold cabinet was full of cakes from fruit to chocolate, lemon drizzle, Victoria sponge, lavender and coffee cake.

His store cupboard was bursting with every kind of herb and spice he thought he could possibly ever need. There were dainty vases of fresh flowers on all the tables and blue gingham clothes, a touch he wasn't sure about but Lucy had insisted on. He took down the blackboard and picking up the chalk began to write his first menu. He had reluctantly gone ahead with his organic vegetarian and vegan menu. He had wanted it to be completely vegan but, as usual, he was overruled by, she who must be obeyed, his wife Lucy. He had chosen to go for sandwiches, Panini's, muffins, toasted teacakes, salads, and quiche and of course Dorset clotted cream teas. He would keep it simple for now and see how it goes. It needed to go well as he had sunk all his savings into it and Donald, Lucy's dad, had put a lot of money into it too. He couldn't let anyone down. They took another look around and headed for the door.

"I'll just pop and see Mum before we go," said Lucy. Bertie nodded and followed her next door. The café had originally been the village shop and Lucy's mum Tricia had run it until the fire that had caused considerable damage last year and Tricia was now sadly living with Dementia.

"Hello, Dad," she kissed his cheek. "How's Mum?" she asked looking at his weary face.

Lucy was quite worried about him as he had sunk into a depression since the fire, given up volunteering on the Swanage railway and hardly seemed to go into his shed anymore. His shoulders were slumped, he hadn't shaved and he was looking decidedly scruffy around the edges.

"Same as always," said Donald. "I'll put the kettle on you go and speak to your mum."

Lucy wandered into the sitting room feeling shocked at the sight of her. She had seemed quite with it a few months ago at the wedding but now she just sat staring into the fireplace. Tears stung her eyes. Bertie squeezed her arm but said nothing. He watched her kiss her mum and sit down attempting to make conversation.

"Hello, Mum, how are you today?" Bertie felt his heart tighten for her, she looked so sad. They drank their tea and invited Donald to bring Tricia to the opening the next day even though they knew that he wouldn't. Tricia became very frightened when they went out and Donald felt safer at home. They drove back to the farm almost in silence wondering what may happen next for poor Tricia.

* * *

Bertie turned the sign to 'Open' and unlocked the door. It was a beautiful spring morning. The sun was still lukewarm in the sky struggling to warm the earth. He had done his best with the garden in front of the café but it still had some dead winter foliage and as yet only a few primroses braving the day. He made a mental note to tackle the garden, maybe put in some pots and a seat; colourful window boxes might help too. He scanned the road but there was no one in sight. Stepping back into the warmth of the café Lucy put her arms around his neck planting a kiss on his lips. She had taken a week off work to help him get started. Their eyes met searching each other.

"What have I done? What if no one comes and it's a failure? It was a mad idea, people want bacon butties not egg and mushroom rolls, and coke not speciality coffee." He dropped his arms defeated.

"Stop it, Bertie. It will be fine, you have been open…" she turned to look at the clock, "… five whole minutes," she grinned at him, "… give it a chance." She kissed him again.

"The hundreds of leaflets we put out with the opening day offer are bound to bring people in, you'll see and I could do with a coffee myself, why don't you practice on me?" He threw her a smirk. "… not that kind of practice." They both laughed and hugged.

"Right, let me see what I can do." He donned his new black apron with the logo 'Bertie's Café' emblazoned across it and set to work making his first coffee.

"Why don't you do a today's special, say coffee and cake for example, on the blackboard and stand it outside? That might attract some attention from passers-by," smiled Lucy sipping her coffee, "hmm… this is good."

"What do you think if I string some bunting along the front? And I was thinking of getting a bench for under the window and maybe a dog hitching post," quizzed Bertie.

"Great and…," there was a clanging of the doorbell and in walked the local vicar, Suzanne Martin. "Hello, Suzanne, you are our first customer so what will you have? On the house of course," beamed Lucy.

"Oh, thanks. I will have a cappuccino and a toasted teacake, please. I haven't had breakfast yet as I have walked Axis and was about to go on my rounds. It all looks wonderful and it is so warm and cosy, I'm sure that it will be a success," she smiled at them both as she glanced around. "I was wondering if you would be interested in a stall at the church fete this year. I can't let you have teas and cakes as that would step on the toes of the WI but you could do sandwiches and light lunches, what do you think?"

Bertie stood motionless as his brain whirred "Can I think about it and let you know?"

"… Of course. I have other ideas too, for the church fete I mean, but I have to run them past Alice and the church committee first," she grinned, "… wish me luck."

The doorbell clanged as two more customers walked in.

* * *

Molly put the twins into the pram covering them with a soft blue and white crochet blanket that Alice had made. Jessica was safely in the nursery so she had a couple of hours before feed time again. She slipped her jacket on and headed for the café. Although Trentmouth desperately needed a café she was worried that Bertie's choice of food might limit the clientele. She had been careful not to voice her opinion.

There was a strong breeze this morning coming up from the sea, the gulls were screeching and circling above her head, the air was crisp making her shudder. She chastised herself for not inviting Alice to join her on Bertie's opening day, she could do with some support as her Mother wanted to join her 'for a chat'. Molly couldn't imagine what that could be about. Sandra had visited Stella and finding she couldn't stay there either she had resorted to a Bed and Breakfast in Wareham. Not the Priory this time. Sandra had been in England for a few days now and Molly was becoming suspicious, had she lost the villa? And where was Enrico? Or should she call him Eric now that the truth was out? She wanted a chat of her own.

She lifted the pram up and over the steps up to the café it was quite difficult and she was huffing and puffing when she opened the door, it clanged. The warmth hit her like a comforting blanket and Molly immediately breathed in deeply, the smell of coffee vying for attention along with the delicious smell of toasted teacakes.

"Molly!" Lucy called bursting the bubble of tranquillity that had surrounded her. "It's great to see you. We are rushed off our feet, isn't it marvellous? Sit over here and I will get you a coffee. Can I see the twins? Aw they are so sweet." Lucy just couldn't stop talking and Molly smiled knowing that feeling of sheer joy when she opened her veterinary practice that first day. She sat by the window so that she could see Sandra arriving and if she stretched far enough she could just see the sea. She pulled the blanket away from Oliver and Elliott so that they wouldn't get too hot, feeling proud of her little family. Lucy returned with her coffee and a muffin sitting down opposite her.

"I'm so glad that you made it, George and Alice have promised to come in today and Isabel and Maggie are calling in later too. Oh Molly I'm so relieved, I have been worried but I know it's only the first day, and well, Bertie has driven me mad with his panic every five minutes," they both chuckled.

"It looks great; honestly, I envy you in a way, following your dreams no matter what. Oh and can I suggest a slope instead of the steps, I really struggled with the pram and anyone with a wheelchair would find it difficult too." She sipped her coffee hoping not to offend her.

"Funny you should say that as Bertie is planning to do that on Sunday when we are closed and he wants to turn the front from a garden to tables and chairs ready for the summer. If Alistair is free maybe he could help?" Molly thought about her husbands' desk job, and although it sounded easy enough, she wasn't so sure if he would be up to mixing cement.

"I'm sure that he would be delighted to help," she smiled, "… this coffee is delicious by the way you will be taking business away from the garden centre," she grinned.

"Oh, I don't know about that, they are too far away for us to have an impact and anyway people go there for the plants and all the other things they sell. We can't compete and we are not trying to actually, we are more your walking fraternity and day trippers," the door clanged and in walked Sandra, "… oops my cue to leave you to it," she kissed Molly on the cheek and smiled at Sandra.

"Hello, Sandra, what can I get you?"

"Hello, Lucy, just coffee oh and one of those whatever Molly is having," Molly rolled her eyes at Lucy by way of apology for her rude mother.

"Coming up," smiled Lucy as she returned to the counter clearing a nearby table on her way.

"Why are you always so rude to people?" seethed Molly through her teeth. Sandra shot her head up in surprise.

"I don't know what you are talking about I was civil considering they practically stole the farm from us." She huffed. Molly couldn't believe it, nothing had changed.

"Mother, you are impossible, I don't know why I bothered agreeing to meet you this morning," pushing her chair back she stood to leave.

"I'm sorry Molly, please sit down it's just that you don't know the strain I've been under and I came to apologise to you… and Stella of course," Molly sat down again wondering if that could ever be true but prepared to give her yet another chance.

"Okay, I'm listening," Molly said. Lucy arrived with her coffee placing the muffin with a fork and napkin beside her.

"Thank you," said Sandra. Molly threw Lucy a quick smile mouthing her thanks too.

Sandra stirred her coffee keeping her eyes down. Molly began to fidget and the babies stirred.

"Look Mother come on out with it. I will have to be going soon – feed time – I don't want to rush you but you were saying something about an apology?" Molly gently rocked the pram the last thing she wanted was for the twins to wake up now.

"I can come home with you and help if you like. I can change nappies or whatever you wish me to do." Molly saw the pleading look on her face and realised that her mother was not going to make any of this easy for herself or Molly. With a huge sigh, she pulled on her jacket and made for the door.

"Finish your coffee and can you pay for mine too? I'll see you at home." Molly manoeuvred the pram down the steps. The wind was whistling up the road from the sea making her shiver, it was turning into one of those brisk spring days that could blow your washing off the line. No matter how hard she tried Molly couldn't guess what it was her mother wanted to say but she knew better than to think there actually was an apology forthcoming.

She pushed the pram up the hill and indoors just as Elliott let out his first tiny cry throwing his arms around and bumping Oliver on the nose. He woke up and let out a cry too.

A distinctive odour wafted up from the pram. *Who said that having twins was easy?* She asked herself as she shook her head. The door opened and in walked Sandra, it always irritated her that her mother walked straight in. The farm had been different but this was her home, Molly shrugged attempting to get rid of the ill-feeling gnawing at her.

"Let me help, please," said Sandra. Molly really did need help so she gave in for once feeling gratitude towards her.

"Could you change Oliver while I feed Elliott... please?" she added without feeling.

It wasn't long before peace reigned. Molly leaned back in her rocking chair eyes closed.

"I used to feed you girls sat in that chair," proffered Sandra, "... they were happy days. I was always worried that girls should keep away from farm machinery and animals. I know I was silly now but I had no experience you see. I expect you girls thought that I was paranoid and stupid." Molly didn't open her eyes she had drifted back to the days when their father had taken them around the farm when Sandra was out. It was their secret and Molly loved it. She sniffed as her eyes stung at the memory of her dear dad. She had loved him and always blamed Sandra for keeping them away from him.

"I suppose I can understand that but we were fine with Dad he was proud of the farm and wanted to share it with us." Molly changed breasts, Elliott looked satiated. She burped him and handed him over to Sandra and began to feed Oliver. "So are you going to tell me what this is all about?"

Chapter 5

Suzanne, the local vicar, only had a few house calls to make this morning. It was a small parish, and in some ways, she was grateful so that she could find her feet gradually. She could manage the workload on her own and that suited her just fine. Her first call was to Doris, even though Suzanne knew that Doris did not like her, believing that women had no place in the pulpit. She took a deep breath and rapped on the door. She couldn't hear a sound, relieved she turned to leave just as the door opened.

"Good morning, Doris, how are you today?" Suzanne bestowed her best smile onto Doris.

"Oh… it's you, I suppose you had better come in," Doris left the door wide open and Suzanne followed her. "… Cup of tea? I was just going to have one myself." She shuffled away towards the kitchen.

"Please… let me do that for you Doris," she watched as Doris, with difficulty, made her way down the hall. Suzanne made a quick surreptitious scan of the cottage. It was neat and tidy. A black cat was curled up in an armchair. It opened one eye to survey her and closed it again. Suzanne couldn't help but think of the wicked witch of the west as Doris always dressed in black and now she had a black cat too. Scary, she grinned.

"I can do it. Sit down in the parlour I won't be a minute," Doris called over her shoulder cackling as she disappeared into the kitchen. Suzanne felt even more nervous now as no one 'cackled' these days except... she shook herself trying to get a grip.

"Thank you," muttered Suzanne. She sat in the chair opposite the fire hoping that she didn't choose the wrong one to sit in as that would only antagonise her further. The tiled fireplace was from the fifties, it stuck out into the room and Suzanne wondered if there was an inglenook hidden behind the wall as the chimney breast was much deeper than normal. A single bar was lit on a very old electric fire throwing out a miserable amount of heat. She rubbed her hands together deciding to keep her coat on. The wallpaper was covered in faded old English roses, cobwebs hung in the corners of the room like lace curtains and some of the tiny windows were cracked.

"... And what do I owe this pleasure then 'vicar' you trying to get me to come back?" she asked peering over the top of her half-moon glasses, without any feeling whatsoever.

Suzanne wondered if this was a mistake but Alice had assured her that Doris was actually a sweet old lady. That image had completely gone and all Suzanne could see was the old lady from Hansel and Gretel!

"Only if you want to Doris, I just thought that I would come and say 'hello' see how you are and if there's anything I can do for you," Suzanne began to fidget knowing how cantankerous Doris could be.

"Hmm… well, I am fine. I keep in touch with the Bishop, of course." Doris picked up her cup of tea noisily slurping it. Suzanne stared at her own cup of dark treacle purporting to be tea with dismay but took a sip gulping down the horrible brew trying vainly to shake off the image of a crafty old witch with a poisonous cauldron that was now filling her head.

"How long have you lived here Doris? Is that a picture of your husband?" Suzanne pointed to a fading sepia picture of a man in uniform.

"Questions, questions," Doris sounded irritated. "All my life. I was born in this cottage and I will die here," she slurped once more, "… we got married when he was on leave from the army, much to my mums disapproval at the time… he was seriously injured in the war and despite his efforts to work he never really recovered and died in his forties…"

Doris disappeared into the past and a tear trickled down her face. "Ah… well, that was a long time ago, but I still miss him. Haven't you got somewhere else to be?" asked Doris turning to look at her. Suzanne knew that her audience was over and got up to leave.

"Nice to see you, Doris," she put her cup down gratefully. "I'll see myself out and thanks for the tea." Doris only nodded her head returning to her own cup of tea once more.

Suzanne stepped out into the fresh air taking in a deep breath. It was actually warmer outside she mused, in more ways than one.

She began to walk back to the vicarage her thoughts turning to Alice and the conversation she was about to have in the afternoon. Suzanne wanted to make a few changes.

She had been here nearly a year now and had continued the traditions carefully, not wishing to cause any upset but that had afforded her the opportunity to see what worked and what could be improved. She smiled to herself as that sounded quite a good way to approach the subject with Alice. Suzanne had her head down against the bracing wind trying to protect her from the force of it lost in her thoughts when suddenly a voice penetrated her subconscious.

"Suzanne… hi, do you fancy a coffee?" She turned in the direction of the sound to see Hugh. He was standing in the doorway to the vet's. She liked Hugh, a lot, and kept hoping that he would ask her out but so far he had not and she began to wonder if she was imagining the looks he gave her and she had returned making her tingle from head to toe. Molly had filled her in about the day he was left standing, literally, at the altar. Her heart broke for him that was any vicar's worst nightmare. He was so lovely and she couldn't understand any girl running away from him. She threw him a beaming smile and turned in his direction, crossing the lane.

"Sure, yes, I'd love one," she felt herself blush as she swept past him her arm touching his and there was that delicious tingle again. She licked her lips immediately chastising herself for being inappropriate. They sat in his office and he regaled her with stories of his patients and their owners. Suzanne nodded politely desperately trying to come up with a change of subject, not that she didn't like animals far from it, she loved her dog Axis but… she couldn't help feeling that he was nervous.

A lull in the conversation afforded Suzanne with her opportunity. "How is your mum?"

She hasn't been to Dorset for a while.

"No, and she does keep asking me if she could possibly come for a visit. She's lonely, oh I know she has her little job but she is always wanted to know what is happening here so I suppose I could ask her down again." He glanced over at her and Suzanne tried to read his expression.

"Does she attend her local church in Richmond? It's as good a place as any to meet people and make new friends," quizzed Suzanne.

"She used to but after my wedding, that never happened; by the way, she was too embarrassed and stopped going. I escaped down here and I guess I left her to handle the fallout." He shuffled his feet and tapped the table. Suzanne felt for his misery and shock.

"Well, why don't you invite her again? I'd love to see her and I know that Emma really got on well with Alice," smiled Suzanne squeezing his arm. Big mistake as there was that rush of heat again sending her hormones into overdrive. She had an instant flash of happy families, two children running around the garden and Emma, the doting Grandma. She shook her head dragging herself back to the here and now.

"Are you alright?" he asked reaching out touching her arm and making her decidedly hot under her dog collar.

"Fine but I must go." She stood up to leave then a thought flittered into her brain and turning she said, "I had a coffee at Bertie and Lucy's new café today, do you fancy having lunch there one day, you know to give them some support?" she twinkled her green eyes swishing her golden curls at him. He flushed bright red.

"Yes," he almost shouted as he leapt up rather hastily, "… I mean yes, what a good idea and I'll call Mum." He plunged his hands into his pockets. Suzanne smiled sweetly and left.

That's got him she grinned to herself as she marched up the road trying to switch her brain into Alice mode.

* * *

At precisely 2 o'clock she knocked on Alice's front door. Alice let her in all smiles and warmth. Suzanne enjoyed her visits to Alice whose hostess skills were legendary as Alice always had a yummy homemade cake on offer and loved having visitors to fuss over.

However hard she tried not to, she felt rather nervous today.

"Suzanne, please come in. Can I take your coat? The kettle's on we'll go into the snug. George is out this afternoon it's his day for walking football in Wareham. How are you, my dear?" Suzanne struggled out of her jacket wondering which statement or question to answer first. Alice was a lovely lady but she did rather overdo it sometimes.

"Thank you, Alice; it is lovely to see you and yes I'm fine. I take it that George loves his football."

"Not really dear, but doctors, orders mean he has to exercise and trim some of that weight off. My fault really, we went on a cruise after my stroke and well the food was fabulous, and of course, you can eat all day long, so George did rather put on weight and now he's trying to get it off again." She paused for breath, "… Anyway you don't want to listen to me prattling on, I will bring in the tea you take a seat, won't be a minute." And she gracefully swept out of the room. Suzanne was left twirling madly as if a whirlwind had crashed into the house filling every space, sucking out the air and just as quickly flying out again. She sat by the window in a daze attempting to get her head back in gear. Alice was not the easiest person to talk to, she was used to being in charge and telling other people what they should do, but nicely.

"Here we are," declared Alice pushing the door open, tray in hand. Suzanne jumped up to help her. She placed the tray onto the cricket table that they kept by the French doors ready for teatime in the summer. Suzanne, a wave of nostalgia flowing over her wondered if she should abandon her ideas for today. *Coward*, she heard a voice in her head say realising with a sigh that this was much harder than she had imagined. "Now Suzanne dear, help yourself to lemon drizzle cake and scones. There's plenty of jam and cream, tea?" She smiled sweetly lifting the teapot as Suzanne nodded.

"Alice you shouldn't have gone to all this trouble, I'll have some lemon drizzle cake please, thank you. I'll be joining George at football if I'm not careful; honestly, a biscuit would have been fine."

"Nonsense my dear, you're as thin as a beanpole." She handed Suzanne a cup of tea in a rather nice China cup and saucer decorated with tiny blue forget-me-nots. No mugs for Mrs Alice Warren. Suzanne took a bite of her cake as Alice asked her a question. "Now what is it you want to talk about today?" Suzanne shot her eyes up just in time to see a smirk on Alice's face as she lifted up her own cup and saucer. *Little minx* thought Suzanne.

"Actually, Alice I want to talk to you about the summer fete and other events on the church calendar," Suzanne paused. "I have been thinking of perhaps making one or two changes." She drained her tea.

Alice gave a little jolt to her shoulders her eyes wide and staring. She quickly regained her composure saying, "I don't think we need any changes Suzanne dear, things have worked very well for the past thirty years that I know of so you don't need to worry about that at all." Suzanne swallowed knowing that she was trying to close the subject down and she would have to be stronger.

"I am tasked with increasing the congregation Alice and one way is to bring our events up-to-date to attract new people and younger ones too. So, with that in mind, I have some ideas to run past you."

"Oh, I see well that sounds different if it's my advice you're looking for I'm sure that I will be able to keep you on the right track Suzanne," she smiled ever so demurely, "… more tea?" she lifted the teapot and poured out another cup.

"Please… thank you. The thing is Alice if we just consider the fete for a minute. Last year you added a dog show and Molly and Hugh had a stall and brought hens and ducks. That was inspirational and a big success, some new people with children came along, that's what I'm talking about diversifying a little encouraging people who may not normally come to the fete."

"Oh, I see what you mean, that was rather a good idea of mine wasn't it?" she puffed out her chest sitting straight-backed with pride.

"Yes, and we need to introduce other things too. I had in mind a jazz band in your summer house, a hot dog stand, hoopla, maybe a beer tent too. Invite other charities along to hold a stall maybe the scouts and guides. Everyone needs funds Alice don't they?" Alice shot her head up and her mouth dropped open. For a moment, Alice appeared to be stunned into silence.

"… But… but thousands of people might turn up. What about my beautiful garden? And I'm not having hordes of people traipsing through my house looking for toilets. No, it's out of the question." Alice pulled a face as if she was imagining hundreds of people making muddy footprints across her sitting room. Suzanne picked up her pen writing 'toilets' on her pad.

"I will look into the cost of hiring portable toilets Alice and then no one will need to go into the house at all." Suzanne tapped her pen on her chin hoping that Alice's reply meant that she approved of the other changes she wanted to make and if she approved or not Suzanne was going to make the changes happen.

"I'm not sure about this at all. The fete has been successful all these years and I don't see the need to change it, Suzanne. In fact, I'm sure that George would agree with me when I say that we don't wish to hold the fete in our garden ever again. We are getting too old and my mind's made up, you'll have to find somewhere else to hold the fete." She crossed her arms throwing a look of disdain mingled with satisfaction in Suzanne's direction heaving a satisfied sigh.

Suzanne was at a loss, their chat had not gone as she planned at all and Alice's hostile reaction was far more than she had bargained for. Puzzled for a moment her mind racing she was left with only one choice.

"If that is what you wish Alice, I'm sorry you feel like that but we need to move forward with the times. I respect your decision and I will find another venue. We can discuss it at the next parish meeting. I do have other items that I want to run past you. I value your input very much, you have been a significant figure in me settling into church life here."

Alice softened opening her arms to pick up her tea.

"I do my best, and of course, any way I can help, I'm at your disposal but… I doubt you will find anywhere else to hold the fete it's been a tradition for so long at our home." She reached over helping herself to a scone piling on the jam and cream.

"Thank you, Alice. Perhaps we could move on to other matters, especially the church hall. The new kitchen and toilets are excellent you did a good job with those but we need to install a ramp for prams and wheelchairs, the heating is hopeless, the floor is in poor condition and I fear that if we wash the curtains they will drop to bits..." The afternoon wore on and Suzanne only managed to discuss half of her list but the thing that nagged at her most of all was where on earth she could hold the next fete. A decision needed to be made soon, very soon or the village would have no fete at all.

Chapter 6

Suzanne walked back to the village feeling despondent. She needed to talk to someone but who could she confide in? She thought about each member of the parish council dismissing them all in turn except possibly Lady Isabel but that somehow seemed disloyal. She opened her garden gate and stopped, staring at the way spring had suddenly arrived and her garden was a multitude of colours and scents. The birds were singing on the tops of their voices all vying for attention, she decided to make a cup of tea and sit on the bench under the apple tree and pray for guidance. The phone was ringing as she slipped off her jacket and she snatched it up hoping for a friendly voice.

"Hello, Reverend Suzanne Martin speaking…" she paused.

"Hi, sis… what are you up to this weekend? I thought I might come down and see you."

Suzanne was relieved to hear Freddie, her brother on the end of the line; her prayer had been answered before she had even asked, making her chuckle.

"Well, apart from all the services at the church of course, I am always busy at weekends but I would love you to come down I want to run something past you."

"Great, I might come Friday actually as I want to see Bertie's café now that it is up and running. There was a time when I thought it would never happen and maybe ask Maggie to lunch..." he paused. He had met Maggie the previous summer when Suzanne was inducted into Trentmouth Church. She ran the Trentmouth Manor estate for her aunt Lady Isabel and they had seen each other a couple of times since. It was obvious to Suzanne that that was his real plan for visiting but right now she didn't care she needed her big brother.

Suzanne poured out her tea and retreated to the garden. She needed to sit in quiet contemplation to go over the events with Alice and the situation she now found herself in. In a way, it was the right decision for Alice to make, her garden really wasn't big enough for what Suzanne had in mind but she didn't want to offend Alice either. She let out a long sigh and sipped her tea pondering her next move. The land next to the church hall was overgrown and sadly had been used as a dumping ground by the general public. There were all manner of things sticking out of the bushes and Suzanne had been putting off clearing it for fear of what she may find and even if she could achieve this momentous task it would not be in time for the church fete. She decided to call an extra meeting of the PCC and hoped that some suggestions would come forward from its' members. Suzanne let her head drop back, closing her eyes, it really was a lovely day, she could hear the birds singing, bees buzzing, the sun warmed her and she nodded off.

"Suzanne... Reverend Martin... where are you?" Suzanne couldn't be sure if she was dreaming or if someone was actually calling her name. She stirred, struggling to sit up wondering what time it was and what day it was. She heard her name being called again and dragged her eyes open.

"Ah… Suzanne, there you are. Lovely day for it, a snooze I mean, I have come to talk to you." Suzanne roused herself with a shake of her head and looked up to see the Bishop looking down at her. She jumped up, was she going to be sacked? The Bishop never visited without an appointment and he had caught her asleep. She was mortified.

"Oh, Bishop, hello, come inside and I will put the kettle on and yes it is a lovely day I was just hmm praying for guidance and here you are. How fortunate…," she leapt to her feet and began to walk towards the house still feeling more than a little disorientated.

"Tea would be lovely and maybe some cake if one of your parishioners has been baking for you. I am always receiving such kind gifts. It upsets my wife sometimes as she thinks that they are currying favours or worse still think that she can't bake…," he chuckled.

He heaved his heavyweight up the steps and into the drawing room where he fell into the nearest chair. "You have made this place very homely, my dear, very homely." He nodded to himself glancing around the room.

"I won't be long Bishop and I'll see what I can do. It will be biscuits I'm afraid as my parishioners know that I like to keep slim," she bit her lip realising what she had said, the Bishop needed to lose more than a pound or two and she hadn't meant to insult him on top of everything else. She scuttled quickly out of the room her face feeling hot, dashing into the kitchen and splashing cold water over her eyes and neck. A few moments later and now quite calm Suzanne returned to the drawing room carrying a heavy tray placing it in front of the Bishop.

"Thank you, my dear," he helped himself to two heaped spoons of sugar and two bourbon biscuits settling back into his chair. Suzanne couldn't sit still afraid of why he was visiting her and not the other way round. She tried to keep her hands from shaking as she picked up her tea. "Now tell me how you think you are getting on," said the Bishop between mouthfuls as he peered at her over his spectacles. Suzanne cleared her throat.

"Well, I... think... I... am doing well," she hesitated as thoughts of Alice flashed through her head, surely Alice had not complained about her to the Bishop? "There are a few new faces in the congregation and I have one or two ideas for increasing our fund-raising efforts." The Bishop nodded picking up another biscuit signalling for her to continue, "... there are some repairs needed at the church hall and eventually I would like to tackle that piece of waste ground, put it to better use..." She looked at him once more, and he nodded, "... so ..." she hesitated but thought that it would be better for her to tell the Bishop about her conversation with Alice rather than let him find out some other way, "... so, with that in mind I saw Alice today and after a long chat she has decided not to let the church have the use of her garden this year as I have plans to increase what we do to encourage a wider and younger crowd to come along. I thought that would make it more attractive and therefore more profitable don't you think Bishop?" she held her breath daring to hope that he hadn't heard from Alice or that he would not see her point of view.

"Just so Suzanne excellent in fact…" He placed his cup down pressing his hands onto the arms of the chair to raise himself up, "… carry on and keep me informed as to progress."

He walked towards the door leaving Suzanne not knowing if he had spoken to Alice or not.

She was puzzled. Suzanne closed the rectory door leaning against it in relief. She hadn't been sacked and possibly had been praised? The Bishop appeared to be happy, and on reflection, the Bishop hadn't actually said why he was there at all! That's what makes him good at his job she smiled. Suzanne almost danced back into the drawing room collecting the tray on her way through. With renewed vigour, Suzanne sat at her laptop to write her sermon for Sunday and plan her menus for Freddie's visit.

* * *

Friday dawned with Suzanne in a panic for Freddie's arrival. Despite her best efforts, work had conspired to keep her from shopping, her fridge was bare. She had managed to book an extra PCC meeting at short notice for this afternoon and with a crisis looming at the village hall after complaints about the floor as it was crumbling in one corner, the last thing she needed was a visitor, even though she badly wanted to lean on him. She pulled herself up straight giving herself a strong talking to. *Now come on, you know that God has called you to this position so he must have faith in you to carry out his work.* "Who am I kidding?" she asked her reflection in the mirror. "I never knew it could be this hard and damn it I'm lonely here in this big house. So what am I going to do about it?" she asked with more confidence than she felt. Suzanne let out a long sigh as a tear attempted to squeeze itself onto her cheek.

She grabbed a tissue sniffing and wiping away the annoyance. A crash outside the front door shook her back to the here and now as the door flew open and Freddie stood there a big grin on his face.

"Hi, sis... thought I would make an early start," he said dropping his bags onto the floor.

Suzanne couldn't hold it in any longer as she rushed towards him throwing her arms around him the tears began to flow and she gave into them and hugged him, her body shook with sobs letting all the anxiety overtake her. At that moment, nothing else mattered.

* * *

Freddie held her tight his hand smoothing her hair. He kissed the top of her head rocking her slightly from side to side.

"Shush... shush... whatever it is it can't be that bad," Suzanne sniffed pulling away from him.

"I'm just being silly, I'm sorry Freddie. Let me make a coffee, that wasn't the welcome I was planning for you, honestly, but I am so pleased to see you." She turned to walk into the kitchen and Freddie followed pulling out a chair and sitting at the kitchen table.

"So... are you going to tell me what this is all about?" he quizzed leaning on the table and fiddling with a mat. She looked at him, tears threatening once more.

"Well… I don't know where to start really. Alice has withdrawn her garden for the village fete, we have had complaints about the state of the land next to the parish hall plus the repairs needed at the hall itself, the floor is quite rickety," she sat back sipping her coffee, "on top of that I sometimes wish I had never left the BBC." She paused gulping down her fears, "I have no one to discuss everything with and I can't help it but I have to admit that I am lonely at times." Axis laid his nose onto her lap and she absently fluffed his ears, he licked her hand.

"Right… well…" he drained his coffee cup. "… Let's take it one at a time and I think we will need a refill. Have you any biscuits? It's a long time since I had breakfast," he grinned.

Suzanne jumped up grabbing her visitor tin of goodies from the shelf and switching the kettle on once more. "… And there's something I want to discuss with you too." She turned her head quickly to look at him raising her eyebrows.

"I'm sorry Freddie I didn't mean to be so selfish, I am supposed to be here for others not blubbing over them," she tried to laugh as her face cracked once more.

"Hey, come on sit down, and start at the beginning; tell your big bruv what the problem is."

Chapter 7

Sandra stared at her daughter, disbelief on her face, when did she become so cruel? She was flustered momentarily, pushing her chair back and scraping the floor she stood to face her.

"I might as well go back to Spain," she snapped. "I can see that I am just an annoyance to you, Molly; you never used to be like this." She bent down to pick up her bag, "… If you're not interested in your own mother… well that's that." She made to flounce out of the door throwing her dyed blonde hair back over her shoulders. Drama had always been her speciality, and she usually got her own way. Molly's mouth dropped open as she stared after her.

"I'm sorry Mother, please come and sit down. It's just that things have been in turmoil since Dad died." She paused, "… Then Enrico, selling the farm… anyway what did you want to tell me?" Molly had made an effort to look concerned and Sandra was grateful not that it was going to make her task any easier. She hesitated, should she spill the whole story and risk further alienation, not to mention humiliation, keep quiet or just come clean and see what happens? Either way, she would have to tell her daughters sooner or later, she had prevaricated long enough. She took a deep breath.

"I don't suppose you have any… 'proper' coffee?" said Sandra pulling a face. Molly let out another sigh and took down the coffee pot, switching on the kettle. "I can't get used to this instant stuff… it doesn't taste right does it?" No reply from Molly. "And… would it be too much to ask for a splash of something stronger?" she pleaded. Molly still didn't reply but took a bottle of brandy from the shelf adding the merest drop. "Thank you," she cleared her throat feeling better and more courageous for what she had to say.

"Are you going to tell me now? I don't mean to push you but the babies will be waking up soon." Molly slipped into a chair opposite with a look that could have been interpreted as bored, worried or maybe slightly concerned, Sandra couldn't tell but knowing it was now or never she put her coffee down.

"I don't know where to start really but I came back to tell you what has happened. Oh, I know that I could have telephoned but thought it better to come and see you… face to face so to speak… I do want to make amends," she searched Molly's face for a reaction but as usual Molly never let you know what she was actually thinking. She pushed on, "Enrico, I mean Eric and I have split up…" She paused.

"Is that it Mother? I am pleased naturally but you needn't have flown over just to tell us that. I thought that it was something important." She made to stand up but Sandra's hand flew out to take hold of Molly's arm.

"No… that's not all," Molly sat down again looking alarmed.

"Please don't tell me he hurt you? I never trusted his smarmy ways, he was always shifty-looking, I thought, and…," Molly stared at her Mother, "… what?" Sandra had held on to her grief for too long tears began to trickle down her face she rummaged in her bag for a tissue. "Mum? What is it? Please tell me." Molly leaned over towards her mother took hold of her arm with a gentle squeeze. Sandra blew her nose.

"I miss your dad. We had a… good marriage. I admit I never took to farming and it was me who dragged him away from the farm to live in Spain. I loved it but your dad only put up with it for me. I knew that. He longed to come back to you two girls especially when the grandchildren came along. He would keep asking about when we could come back he missed the farm, I knew he was lonely and bored if I'm honest but… well…" For the first time hearing it out loud, Sandra felt dreadfully guilty and embarrassed, especially in front of her daughter. Molly took in a sharp breath making to say something but Sandra stopped her.

"… Hear me out, please Molly," Molly relaxed again. She never took her eyes off her mother and Sandra was beginning to feel that she could go through with this after all. "… When your dad became ill and we came back, I admit that I was rather cruel to you Molly, accusing you of having lots of men around and then making you leave the farm…" Molly snatched her hand away standing up.

"You certainly were. You have no idea what you put me through I hated you." Molly began to pace the kitchen, "Is this all what you came back to say?" She snatched up the bottle of brandy unscrewing the top, in a fit of pique, glugging far too much into a glass. Sandra watched her screw the top back on holding back waiting for her to calm down. Molly fiddled with the glass then instead of drinking it she pushed it in her mother's direction, "Here, you need it more than me." She flopped down on the chair once more, "… Go on. I'm sure that's not it."

"No. This is dreadfully embarrassing Molly. I went back to Spain because… well for one thing I felt that you two had your own lives now and didn't want me around and I truly love Spain. I have a good circle of friends and a good life…"

"… But what about Stella and me and your Grandchildren? We thought that you just didn't care about us only yourself!" Molly looked flabbergasted and Sandra couldn't blame her.

"You are probably right, certainly at the time and for a while I was happy. I tried not to think about you all and what you might be doing. I realise I have missed so much and that's one of the things I wanted to say." Sandra took a deep drink on the brandy and spluttered as it hit her throat. "Can I have some water and… and another coffee please, Molly?" Molly duly obliged tutting but saying nothing. "Anyway there was a bar by the beach and I met Enrico… he was charming and handsome," she smiled to herself at the memory, "… And he flattered me, paying me lots of attention. Oh I knew he had to be fifteen even twenty years younger than me but he made me feel young and… and desirable."

"Oh, pleeease, Mother, spare me the details. There are some things I just don't want to know. I think I need a drink but I can't, not when I am still breastfeeding. Shouldn't you be telling all this to Stella too?"

"I… thought that I should tell you first," she stammered.

"Oh, I get it, if you can get it passed me Stella will be a pushover. I suppose what you are leading up to is that you have sold the villa and want to move back to Dorset, be part of our lives; well, it's not going to be that easy." Molly was in full flow and Sandra had to stop her before she went too far.

"Molly stop, as lovely as that would be, I know that I can't just step back into your lives but yes, I would like to visit more. I have not sold the villa and much more importantly I am trying to apologise and finish what I came to say."

Sandra could hear one of the twins begin to make noises just little snuffling sounds, she felt exhausted and turning to Molly said, "you must take care of your children I'll go but can I see you again, soon? I have more to tell you." Sandra turned not expecting much response; Molly took hold of her arm.

"Okay. I would like to hear the rest but with Stella. She is coming over on Friday as she has a wedding cake to deliver to The Priory. Why don't you come back then? Come for lunch."

* * *

Sandra spent an agonising few days trying to put her thoughts in order ready to face Molly and Stella, but an invite to lunch… Well, that was a first and she wasn't going to mess it up. She had spent far too much time in England already not to mention the money it was costing her. She sat on a bench by the river watching the ducks squabble and fight over the crumbs that some nearby children were throwing into the water. She glanced at her watch, still two hours before her appointed time not daring to turn up early. She let out a long noisy breath, looking at her watch again.

"Oh, dear, that sounds ominous. Anything I can help with?" said a kindly voice to her left. Sandra turned to see a beautiful young woman, the sun glinting off her stunning hair, *that didn't come out of a bottle* she thought.

"Very nice of you to ask dear but I don't think that you would be able to help me. No one can." Sandra turned back to look at the river just as a huge pleasure boat turned the bend heading for the quay. It was packed full of holidaymakers on a day trip from Poole.

"Oh, dear, I can't cope with all those noisy, happy people today," she got up to leave.

"Come and have a coffee with me in the Granary, my treat. You look as though you could do with one." The young woman smiled at Sandra as she battled with fleeing the scene, even though the sound of a coffee was awfully tempting.

"I… I don't know. I should be going," Sandra hesitated to twist her fingers round and round looking about her for a reason to escape.

"If it makes you feel any better I could do with a coffee myself and you can talk to me." She pushed her hair over her shoulder revealing a dog collar, something Sandra hadn't noticed before. The young woman stood up rather expectantly saying, "Come on… before all these holidaymakers head for the balcony," she pointed to some empty tables that hung out above the river affording a splendid view. Sandra followed her.

They settled at a corner table, having ordered coffee and some shortbread. Sandra felt distinctly awkward, stirring her coffee not wanting to reveal anything to this very young woman who could hardly have any experience at all. Distracted by some loud screams from excited children on the quay, Sandra turned to glare at them, not that anyone noticed.

"Do you have children? My name is Suzanne by the way, pleased to meet you," she smiled warmly at Sandra waiting for a reply. Sandra put down her coffee.

"Sandra… and yes, I do have children, two daughters, in fact, grown up now with children of their own. I'm meeting them for lunch today. I was merely passing the time of day here on the quay till it is time to meet them." She picked up a shortbread taking the merest nibble and dabbing her lips with the paper napkin, attempting to show complete nonchalance either way to this 'vicar'. Sandra had never had much time for the church, or the people who went along for that matter far too heavenly minded to be any earthly good she used to say. Suzanne broke her shortbread in half and began to eat it as she surveyed some children paddling from the opposite bank of the river. A watchful mum had a picnic laid out on the grass as the children, whooping and splashing, were frightening the squawking ducks away. Sandra viewed her from the corner of her eye, with the smile of one who has conquered an adversary.

"So what's actually troubling you, Sandra? It's clear you are wrestling with something to do with your daughters I am guessing." She smiled just a little at Sandra picking up the crumbs on her plate. Sandra eyed her with suspicion but she was desperate to confide in someone and as she would never see her again Sandra tentatively began.

"Well, yes. It's a long story and I really don't want to bore you… shall we have another coffee? I could do with one," Sandra signalled the gangly youngster who had served them earlier and ordered two more coffees before turning to Suzanne. She opened her mouth and before she could stop herself the whole sorry tale tumbled out including the debacle with Enrico, selling the farm, her estrangement from her daughters, her regrets and finally the real reason she was over here. "So you see, there is nothing you can help me with, I feel such a fool, maybe I should just go back to Spain and keep quiet after all." Sandra sat back in her chair rubbing her forehead wondering why she had bothered to confide in Suzanne. How could she help her?

"So Sandra, tell me, is that what you really want to do? Go back to Spain I mean and not tell your daughters the truth?" Her eyes were searching Sandra's face for an answer.

Sandra gulped, it sounded like a good option but then she risked never seeing Stella and Molly again not to mention her precious grandchildren. No, for once in her life she had to be brave, if they told her to go then so be it but at least they would know the truth. Suzanne sat quietly waiting to watch Sandra's every move. Finally, Sandra pushed herself forward.

"I am going to tell them and face the consequences. Thank you for listening and helping me; I'm very grateful." She stood to leave picking up her handbag, turning she asked, "… You are a real vicar, aren't you?" then let a smile spread across her face.

"Yes. Yes, I am Sandra your secret is safe with me." Sandra looked at her watch and hurried out of the restaurant without glancing back. She stumbled over the cobbles to get back to her car. There was a man looking suspiciously like a traffic warden, notebook in hand, lurking by her car.

"Hello, officer, I'm not over my time am I?" she cooed gently patting her hair attempting her best demure act of innocence.

"No, not this time, luv," he pushed his pen back behind his ear closing up his book he threw her a smile, "… just watch it in future." He strolled around to find his next victim and Sandra slipped gratefully into her car and drove off. She ambled along the lanes back towards Trentmouth knowing that it was showtime she had to come clean no matter what happened next.

Chapter 8

Oliver and Elliott lay gurgling and smiling on a rug as Sandra arrived giving her the perfect distraction with just the excuse she needed to prevaricate still further. She knelt to tickle and talk to her latest two grandchildren avoiding her daughters for a bit longer. Molly prepared to feed and change them ready for an afternoon nap as Stella set about making lunch. They all chatted about this and that bringing their Mother up to date with the various goings-on.

Stella's online business had taken off much quicker than she had expected and she had already employed two people to help her cope.

"I can't believe it actually, business was already good but if this carries on I am considering asking Tony to give up his job and join me!" she chuckled.

"Surely not, Stella, I mean a man in the kitchen? I wouldn't have thought that he would go for that no, not at all, you surely can't be serious?" Sandra tutted as she fidgeted with her cutlery.

"Mother…" Molly scolded throwing her a warning shot. Sandra picked up her coffee downing it in one gulp.

"Sorry, Stella, you know best, of course." Her cheeks flushed pink as she tried to get over her embarrassment *why could she never get anything right?* She wondered.

Stella cleared her throat, "Tony is a genius at marketing and talking to reps and… he loves paperwork which I do not. So I had in mind for him to take the orders, organise deliveries, payroll, the VAT you know all the background stuff."

"Yes. Yes, I'm sorry Stella I didn't think." There was a moment or two of silence as Stella turned her back and placed the food onto the table. It was to be a simple lunch of asparagus tart, salad and new potatoes followed by strawberries and cream. Molly took the children for a nap and they settled down to lunch together.

"So," said Stella eventually, "you have something to tell us I believe. Molly has already filled me in with the story so far but I gather there is more you want to tell us." Sandra placed her knife and fork down onto her empty plate.

"That was a lovely lunch. Thank you, and yes, there is more to tell," she coughed, pulled out a tissue and dabbed her mouth. Molly and Stella were both staring at her with bated breath, arms folded and leaning on the table. Sandra took a deep breath.

"When Eric and I got back to the villa, he was better than ever, so attentive and he began talking about the future, our future and hinting that he might be about to propose."

"What!" gasped Molly, "… you are joking Mother, please tell me you are joking?"

"I was flattered, I can't deny that and I was beginning to think that I had found a new life partner," Sandra's thoughts drifted back to Spain remembering the afternoon when they lay soaking up the sun by the pool. She sat staring into her memories for a moment letting out a long-held breath. Molly jumped up and reached into the fridge for the cheesecake she had made that morning together with a jug of cream and the bowl of strawberries placing them onto the table beside the chocolate cake that Stella had thoughtfully brought them to have with coffee.

"Anyway, it was just after that that Eric began talking about investing the money from the sale of the farm into a new building project. He had found a big old house down near the harbour and wanted to convert it into high-end apartments. At first, I thought that this was a brilliant idea a good investment for my money. I visited the site, everything looked good to go but something caused a niggle in the back of my mind. I couldn't put my finger on it and decided to do some research of my own." She paused as Molly placed a slice of cheesecake in front of her, "Thank you," she smiled picking up her fork.

"Don't tell us it was just another big fiddle Mother and you fell for it. I don't know if I want to hear anymore." Molly scraped her chair back on the stone-flagged floor picking the kettle up to make coffee.

"Well, not quite, but it was one of those complicated Spanish affairs where the property is owned by a number of family members and they all have to agree. However, some of them knew nothing about it and did not want to sell. So I talked to Eric and said that I didn't want to go ahead with it and… well, he just lost it saying that I didn't trust him, it was all above board and I was being silly."

"Oh, Mum, how awful for you. What did he say then?" said Stella patting her Mother's arm always the more sympathetic of her two daughters.

"Well, let's just say that we had an almighty row and he left. He just cleared out all his things and left." Stella and Molly both heaved a sigh of relief as they looked from one to the other sitting back and relaxing.

"Just to be clear Mum, you didn't give him any of your money did you?" enquired Molly.

"No, I didn't thankfully and I haven't seen him since," Sandra looked forlorn, sitting nervously twisting her handkerchief. Molly and Stella glanced at each other and shrugged.

"So what now Mum?" Molly queried. Sandra felt touched as finally, Molly sounded like a concerned daughter something she had longed for.

"Well, the main reason I came over, apart from telling you what has happened, I have thought long and hard about the money I received from the farm and… the truth is… the truth is that your dad always wanted you, girls, to have the farm. I was wrong to make you sell it and I'm… I'm sorry." Molly and Stella looked at each other but said nothing. It might have been a shock; Sandra wasn't sure. She looked at her two girls waiting for them to say something but they didn't. She pushed on. "Anyway, I have decided; in fact, I have already made the arrangements…" she paused. It was Molly who jumped in first.

"I suppose you are taking a world cruise or… or… something. You forced us to sell the farm and now you want sympathy from us. How could you do this to us Mum?" Molly turned away in disgust flashing her eyes at Stella for support.

"Come on, Molly, let's give her a chance eh," the whistle from the kettle broke the silence and Molly got up to make the coffee.

"If you will just give me a chance you two, I am trying to tell you that I have set up two trusts in each of your names. The money is for all of my grandchildren when they are older to pay for university or whatever when they are 18…" she stopped for breath staring at each other in turn waiting for a reaction. They appeared to be struck dumb which caused her to laugh. "You two… if you could see your faces," she started to belly laugh, and in turn, Molly and Stella laughed too.

"I've never seen you like this before Mum. I have wondered where our real Mum had gone for a long time," said Molly still laughing. Sandra dabbed her eyes and stood up; her arms open wide to hug her girls.

"I am so sorry, so sorry for all the upset I've caused. Please forgive me." "Of course," they chorused in unison.

"That is a wonderful gesture for the children and is much appreciated. Thank you so much," cried Stella, "… but what about you, what are you going to do now? I mean are you staying in Spain, moving back here or as Molly said 'going on a world cruise.'"

"Well, to begin with, I hope to have a coffee, with a splash of something in it… please," she looked up at Molly hopefully, "… then I am going back to Spain but I intend to make frequent visits back home if I am welcome that is." They all started chattering at once; Molly found the brandy and topped up everyone's coffee.

Sandra finally left leaving Molly and Stella still in shock from the day's events. If anyone had asked them to come up with a storyline for their mother it would not have been generosity! Sandra had always lived her life for herself, whatever she wanted she somehow always managed to achieve including whisking their father off to Spain. They had to admit that in her sixties their mum was still a good looking woman, she had always looked after herself, she wasn't known for getting her hands dirty around the farm and had tried to keep her girls away from anything she considered 'unhygienic'. They supposed that she would meet someone else eventually but this time someone who was not after her just for her money.

"You know I still can't believe it," Molly sat on the couch curling her feet up under her and Stella sat beside her.

"I know. It is the best gift ever. I just wonder what will happen to Mum now, she seems determined to go back to Spain and I think she's probably doing the right thing." They both sat quietly for a moment "You know what? I am going to try and take the girls there this summer for a holiday, go and see this villa and what makes Spain so attractive to Mum."

"Good idea…" there was a loud rap on the door. Molly turned to look at Stella "I wonder who that could be?" she opened the door to find Hugh leaning on the door jamb covered in blood. "What on earth has happened to you?"

"I need your help, next door," he nodded his head towards the surgery. Molly put on her shoes turning to Stella.

"Can you look after the twins?" and without waiting for a reply she was gone.

Chapter 9

Suzanne, intrigued by Freddie hinting that he wanted to talk to her about something, sat mulling over their conversation. In the end, probably due to her fragile state, he had not actually told her anything at all but done his brotherly duty encouraging her at every turn. She missed him very much and pondered on her own situation. She had been thrilled to be offered the church in Trentmouth without considering that it was so small and insignificant in the greater scheme of things. She had jumped at it believing that she could change the world, well, Trentmouth at least, never ever thinking that it could be so hard. She sniffed but refused to let tears get the better of her again.

She had arrived in Trentmouth knowing no one, that wasn't as daunting as she had imagined but Doris had left the committee joining a different parish without even giving her a chance. Alice had withdrawn the use of her garden for the church fete; the church hall needed urgent repairs, the waste ground next to the church hall… well, and to cap it all Hugh did not appear to have any interest in her at all despite the frisson of electricity she felt every time she met him and was sure he felt the same.

"Now come on…" she told herself, "stop this, you are just feeling sorry for yourself.

Get out there and meet some parishioners, see what is going on in the world. The answers will come if you look for them instead of wallowing in self-pity."

Suzanne decided to change into her walking gear, pulling on jeans, a sweatshirt, and hiking boots and packed a rucksack with water, an apple, cereal bar and notebook and pen.

She stuffed a waterproof in too although there was a cloudless sky outside, the weather could change very quickly as she had discovered before. She grabbed her camera put the lead onto Axis and set off towards the sea and the coastal path that she knew and loved so well.

It was a beautiful day as she climbed happily up towards the top of the hill, where from this vantage point, you could see for miles in all directions and there was a welcome bench overlooking the sea waiting for her. She stopped to take some pictures of early celandines, coltsfoot and violets. She leaned over an old dry stone wall where sheep were bleating in the field keeping a close eye on their young. Lambs were running, jumping and gambolling over each other having such fun and Suzanne clicked away at them with her camera smiling to herself.

Reaching the seat she flopped down opening her bag for her water, retrieving her notebook she opened it up to a blank page and let her mind wander over the situation that she now found herself in. Axis rested his nose onto her lap and she absentmindedly ruffled his ears giving him a biscuit.

She jotted down each problem on a separate page and began to think of all possible solutions and even some impossible ones too. The most urgent problem was where to hold the church fete. She wrote down the vicarage garden, the parish hall, she even considered asking Lucy and Bertie about the farm knowing that it was too far out of the village to be practical. She could do nothing about the church hall without much-needed funds or the land without serious help. Then she remembered the web page and of course the parish magazine and decided to write a plea for help and or ideas from the villagers and see what came from that.

Feeling energised she re-packed her bag and they set off once more for the village passing ancient earthworks and a tumbledown cottage where brambles had made their home and an old wrought iron gate hung from a crumbling stone pillar covered in lichen. A smile found its way onto her face and she began to feel more like her usual confident self, the wind and sun healing her soul. It wasn't long before she reached the cobbles, of the now-abandoned jetty, taking a detour she wandered onto the beach to watch the waves crashing onto the shore.

"Penny for them..." Suzanne, startled out of her daydream, turned to see Maggie walking towards her.

"Hi, I was just watching the antics of the gulls, it's so beautiful here. How are you? I haven't seen you for a while." She smiled.

"No. Sorry. Do you have time for a coffee? We could go to Bertie's place they have the most delicious cakes." She implored Suzanne.

"Love to..." She followed Maggie back up the jetty and into the village. It was warm and cosy in the café with a few mums with pushchairs all talking animatedly and laughing.

How wonderful, thought Suzanne, *I wish they were in my church.*

"I will get these," Maggie said walking towards the counter, "which cake do you fancy?"

"They are all scrumptious but I think that I will try the lavender…" she paused, her finger crooked on her chin.

"Sounds lovely, make it two," smiled Suzanne. Order placed, Maggie made her way back to the table tucked in by the window and sat down opposite Suzanne.

"I'm glad that I bumped into you as I wanted to have a chat with you about something. If you have time that is?" Maggie picked at her cake eyes cast down shuffling in her chair.

Suzanne tried to hide her smile as she was sure that she knew what was on her mind.

"Of course, you can talk to me anytime, my door is always open," she smiled hoping that that sounded encouraging. She took a forkful of her own cake in an attempt to relax them both.

"How are things going? At the church I mean and of course your new job. How is that going?" Maggie sipped her coffee and glanced at Suzanne over the top of her mug instantly steaming up her glasses. She pushed them up onto her head creating mayhem with her bubbly curls. Suzanne thought for a moment knowing that that was not her real question but decided to go along with it explaining the difficulties of being new and a woman! How she needed to grow the congregation somehow and lastly the church fete having no home and it may have to be cancelled. Maggie sat quietly listening. She pulled on her lip deep in thought then sucking in a deep breath she looked at Suzanne.

"Fancy another coffee? I do, I am thirsty for some reason," and without waiting for an answer she nipped over to the counter ordering two more coffees. Once sat down again Maggie paused looking deep into Suzanne's waiting gaze. Maggie was older than Suzanne, how much she wasn't sure but she guessed in her early thirties thinking she must ask Freddie.

She gave an encouraging smile.

"Well, I have to say that I had no idea that things were… were so… so," she gesticulated with her hands making circles in the air "the thing is, I might be able to help you in some small way, maybe…" she paused again.

"Great. Fire away, I'm open to all suggestions although I usually have to pass them by the PCC and the Bishop sometimes but I'm willing to listen. What did you have in mind?"

Maggie stirred her coffee again as if she were collecting her thoughts before she put her spoon down lifting her eyes to look straight at Suzanne.

"The thing is, I will have to speak to Aunt Izzie of course but I wonder if it might be possible to hold the church fete up at the Manor… no promises but I can sound her out if you like?" Suzanne couldn't help herself she gasped in pleasure.

"That would be wonderful, just wonderful Maggie oh I do hope she says, 'Yes,' I don't know what to say." She relaxed back in her chair with a grin that threatened to split her face wide open.

"I have a few other things I want to talk to you about too but if you don't mind I need somewhere… a bit more… private." She pushed her chair back picking up her jacket.

"No problem, come back to the vicarage with me and we can talk as I have something to run past you too." They left the café waving to Bertie as they closed the door and wandered up the road chatting about nothing, in particular, passing the vet's. Suzanne shot a look across the road to catch a glimpse of Hugh but he wasn't in sight.

"Has he asked you out yet?" asked Maggie. Suzanne shot a look in her direction, horror on her face, heat rushing around her veins and flooding her body and mind with embarrassment.

"What… What do you mean? Who Hugh? No, he probably has a girlfriend a guy like him. No, he wouldn't ask me out, no. No." Suzanne was completely flustered, her mouth running away with her. Maggie chuckled.

"Seems to me that you might like it if he did I'm sure he likes you I have seen the way he looks at you when you are not looking. I think you should take the initiative and ask him for coffee or something." She casually remarked glancing sideways at Suzanne.

"I did, actually, I invited him to lunch at Bertie's when it first opened. It was lovely but… he didn't ask me out again so I thought that maybe I wasn't his type or something and he only came along to be polite. So…" she shrugged her shoulders "I don't know."

They reached the vicarage and Suzanne clicked the wrought iron gate open, it squeaked and creaked making her shudder "I must get someone to do something about this gate for me and soon," she rolled her eyes at Maggie, "… you don't know a handyman do you?" They both chuckled and headed towards the door brushing by the lavender with their legs. The heady scent wafted upwards and a crowd of tiny honeybees flew up in a cloud of hysteria before swooping down again to search out the hidden treasure of nectar.

"This is a beautiful old house but it must be a nightmare to look after with everything else you do Suzanne." She followed Suzanne down the hall her heels clicking on the parquet floor. "A bit big for one person isn't it?"

"I suppose it is but traditionally vicars always had a large family and servants so a big house was definitely required. Come into the kitchen and I will put the kettle on, unless…" she half turned to Maggie "I do have a bottle of Chablis in the fridge…" she grinned, a twinkle in her eyes.

"Sounds like a deal to me," Maggie grinned back "I could do with a drink, I have had such a busy week and it's not often that I get the chance for a glass of wine." Suzanne immediately felt guilty; she should have asked Maggie to come to visit before; after all, she is Freddie's girlfriend.

"Oh, do tell me more. I haven't any cake or chocolates I hope you don't mind?" She collected two glasses and the wine from the fridge placing them onto the countertop.

"Don't your parishioners bring you cake? They used to inundate the old vicar all the time."

"Hardly…" she laughed "actually I told everyone not to bring me cake I don't want to put any weight on," she smoothed her hands over her hips before picking up the tray. "Let's go into the snug, it's lovely and warm in that room by the window." She walked across the hall and into a small room she called her 'snug' putting the tray down on a table by the window.

This room afforded a great view over the garden and across to the Purbeck hills beyond. They settled companionably. Maggie took a deep breath.

"You know, I hope you don't mind me saying, but if you accepted the cakes from people they may warm to you more and be willing maybe to volunteer and help you with other things… and of course, you would have some cake to offer visitors." Maggie shuffled nervously sipping her wine. Suzanne was aghast that she may have inadvertently offended her parishioners causing one or two to be frosty towards her.

"I… I never gave it a thought, how stupid of me Maggie. I am pleased you told me but I have no idea how I am going to resolve that one." She flushed and not from the wine. "I am grateful though that you mentioned it. Anyway, you wanted to talk to me about something so fire away." She quickly topped up their glasses desperately wanting to divert the conversation away from her and onto much safer territory.

Maggie put her glass down "Well, actually, I do have a couple of things to talk to you about. Aunt Isabel wants to turn Trentmouth Manor into a wedding destination. It's going to take a lot of work and our aim is to have it up and running for next year." She paused taking a moment to sip her wine before continuing, "… and we have already approached Freddie to be our architect and help with the designs. There is so much to think about, and of course, we do have a chapel on the grounds and that's what I want to ask you about really. It hasn't been used for many years and we wondered if you would be able to come and look at it and give us your professional opinion." She rushed on "we don't want to step on your toes by taking weddings away from you obviously, however maybe you could conduct the weddings in our chapel. What do you think?" She sat back her eyes clearly quizzing Suzanne's face.

"Wow. Well, I'm not sure about all the protocol here. I will have to speak to the Bishop but before then I would be delighted to come and see the chapel and take it from there.

The whole venture sounds exciting. It's what Trentmouth needs to attract more visitors, bring the place to life, very exciting. Would you have rooms too for guests? Or am I getting ahead of myself here."

"Actually, yes, at least a bridal suite to begin with as there is almost no accommodation in Trentmouth at all, amazingly, considering we are a seaside village."

"True. It certainly needs shaking up a bit and that's what I want to do. Thanks for the tip about cake Maggie. I am so sorry that I don't even have a few nibbles. Something I must rectify tomorrow. Now, you said you had a couple of things you wanted to talk to me about."

She smiled.

"Yes. Well, the second thing is much more personal and I don't really know how to say it. It's just that Freddie and I have been seeing each other quite a bit and I like him… a lot."

"Yes," said Suzanne "he talks a lot about you too, I had rather guessed. So what is the problem?" she quizzed.

"He doesn't talk about himself much or about his life in Oxford, I know very little about you both… sorry. Sorry, Suzanne, I shouldn't have asked, you must think me very rude and think it's none of my business," she got up to leave, "… sorry …" Suzanne grabbed her arm.

"Hey, it's fine, look do you need to get back? If not let me make something to eat and I will fill in a few gaps for you. What do you say?"

"I'd like that and no I don't have to rush back anywhere."

Over lunch, Suzanne tried to put Maggie in the picture about the awful accident that had killed their parents and how Freddie, being her big brother, thought that he needed to look out for her. Suzanne had still been at school and Freddie was doing his finals, he had persuaded the authorities that he could look after Suzanne as they wanted to take her into care. However, they had agreed to a trial period with supervision and, in the end, had agreed that he could be her guardian until she was eighteen. He now worked for a notable firm in Oxford and loved his job although it was his ambition to set up on his own one day.

"… Was?" Queried Maggie looking concerned.

"I suppose I should say 'still is' but it's hard to start up on your own what with finding premises not to mention the costs involved. Still, one day, I'm sure that he will achieve his ambition. I hope that has filled in some missing bits for you, you can always ask him yourself… I believe he is coming down again this weekend?" Suzanne smiled sweetly hoping to draw out some information from Maggie too. She liked Maggie, she was good for Freddie but he had never mentioned their relationship to her and she would never pry.

"I have an idea…" Maggie enthused, "as Freddie will be here on Saturday why don't we have a get-together? You could invite Hugh and the four of us could go out for dinner or I will cook at my cottage, what do you say?" Maggie looked expectantly at Suzanne excitement in her eyes but Suzanne wasn't so sure. After a few moments of prevaricating, Suzanne stood and paced the room before turning to Maggie.

"Look that is very kind of you and I appreciate the offer but I couldn't possibly ask Hugh to join us and I am not spoiling the evening for you two. No, you go ahead with your plans I will be happy here… promise." It was a wonderful idea but after having lunch with Hugh and no further mention of going out again Suzanne was firm of the opinion that Hugh was just not into her. She felt sad about that but determined not to let Maggie see she turned on her best smile saying "would you like a cup of tea?"

Maggie looked at her watch "actually I should be going. Let me know if you change your mind about Saturday," she collected her jacket and made her way out leaving Suzanne feeling sadder than ever.

It took a lot of effort for Suzanne to concentrate on her sermon for Sunday, that blank page would not go away but the more she tried the harder it became. Closing the lid of her laptop she dragged herself out to the kitchen, finding a glass she drained the last of the wine into it taking a large gulp letting out an enormous sigh. Axis gave her a sideways look, ears up ready for action. He stretched and yawned loping out of his basket, he shook himself making Suzanne smile.

"Come on then, let's go for a walk see if I can find inspiration from somewhere." They set off together down the village towards the sea. She looked cautiously into the window of the vets, hoping not to be seen but too late Hugh had spotted her.

"Hey," he called, "… time for a cuppa?" he waved a mug in the air, a grin firmly in place.

"Of course," she smiled hoping to hide her now hot face at having been caught out. She crossed the road and noticed the bandage on his hand. "What happened to you?" She put her hand out in comfort quickly retreating it again telling herself off for such an outward show of affection.

"I was clearing up after an operation and accidentally cut my hand, Molly came to my rescue but honestly, it looks worse than it is and I promise that no animal was hurt in the making of this incident." She couldn't help herself beginning to laugh and immediately chasing her blues away, wondering what all the fuss was about. Hugh was a good friend and nothing more. They sat on the bench in the sunshine sipping coffee with Axis at their feet just chatting amiably. Inspiration came flooding into Suzanne's head.

"Must go, thanks for the coffee. See you Sunday morning?" she quipped.

"Yes, actually, my mum is coming to stay and she insists we come along." He grinned.

"Great. It will be lovely to see Emma again. Bye," she waved cheerily heading down to the coast at quite a pace almost dragging Axis wanting to make her escape before things became awkward just friends or not.

Chapter 10

On Saturday morning, Hugh and Emma decided to wander down to Bertie's to have coffee and a toasted teacake as they watched the world go by. It was very busy, the usual mums missing, replaced by walkers and weekenders. They managed to find the last available table up in the corner.

"I like sitting here actually," exclaimed Emma. "I can keep an eye on what is going on," she grinned. Lucy had served them apologising that she couldn't stop to chat saying she would hopefully be back later to join them.

"This is a lovely warm cosy café Hugh it reminds me of The Cherry Tree back home."

"Cakes look good too. Do you know who makes them for Bertie?" She gave him a quizzical look.

"Err… no idea Mum. I know Bertie is an excellent chef but it might be Lucy who bakes. Why don't we ask her? Oh, and why do you want to know?" He grinned suspiciously "If you are thinking of offering to bake for them, you can't, you are supposed to be on holiday," he teased having learned many years ago that what he thought had no effect whatsoever. He threw his hands up in the air just as Lucy came towards them.

"No, not at all, I was just curious as they are good." She turned to Lucy, "you are awfully busy in here today just you and Bertie?"

"… Afraid so, trouble is you never know how busy you will be. Is everything okay can I get you something else?" Lucy asked looking flustered and a little out of breath.

"No, dear, thank you. Did you make all those delicious looking cakes?" Emma glanced longingly towards the cold counter.

"Some, when I have time and Bertie does too. We could do with more cakes and time.

"Oh, please excuse me…" She disappeared with the tray of crockery.

"Come on you," Hugh grinned "then you can tell me what that was all about and don't try to pretend you are not planning something." They retrieved their belongings weaving their way through the crowd, waving to Bertie as they went. The air was cool outside; a light wind blowing up from the sea, Emma tucked her arm through his as they wandered towards the beach. "Right now, are you going to tell me what you are thinking?" They wandered onto the beach settling down on the stone wall that had once been part of the jetty, now long abandoned and crumbling into the sea.

"Well," started Emma cautiously, "I have given things a lot of thought." She paused to turn and look at her son, "… but I won't do anything you don't approve of, you know that don't you and if you think it's a bad idea so be it." She searched his face and Hugh couldn't help but smile.

"Come on out with it, nothing you say could surprise me. So what is it?" he smiled encouragingly although he had a good idea already what she was about to say hoping that she would say it for herself.

"I have found myself getting more than a little lonely since you moved here," she turned anxiously. "I'm not blaming you, Hugh, after the wedding fiasco and well you know…?"

Hugh nodded "It's just that now your move is permanent I wonder what you might think if I sold my little house and… and moved to Dorset?" she paused squeezing his arm "I wouldn't want to cramp your style in any way I would find my own place and maybe I could work for Bertie in his lovely café," pausing for breath she stared into his eyes. Hugh suspected that was what she would say and had even thought of it himself. It made sense really as he worried about her in Richmond all alone. Ever since that awful day; he had escaped the pitying looks and comments but poor Emma could not. She put a brave face on for friends and neighbours trying her best to act as if she had guessed and therefore pleased about it but in private it broke her heart. He took hold of her hand.

"Look Mum, if it makes you happy then I'm happy too, it would be good to have you down here near me, I have missed your cooking." She pulled away to look at him gently cuffing his shoulder and grinning.

"That's settled then I will start making plans as soon as I get home," she stood, renewed vigour written all over her, "… and we had better start walking up into the village, we mustn't be late or Alice will be cross. So nice of them to invite us to lunch," she grinned.

Hugh got to his feet brushing the sand from his trousers.

"That's true but I must warn you not to say anything about your plans or Alice will have you all organised and moved before we get to dessert!" They both laughed and set off back up the steep slope towards the village. They wandered up the cobbled street with renewed interest taking in each cottage as they passed by.

"I wonder how much a lovely place like that would cost?" she asked gazing at a delightful thatched cottage with a neat garden bursting with hollyhocks, lupins and ox-eye daisies in front of it.

"Forget it Mum you couldn't even afford the garage," he joked. "But I will try and find out some prices for you, that's why I am renting Bertie and Lucy's cottage as everything is out of my reach. It is a beautiful part of the world but beyond mere mortals price range," he sighed heavily. They continued on past his veterinary practice and as they walked by the vicarage Hugh couldn't help himself but look for Suzanne. He didn't see her but there was a car on the drive that he hadn't seen before, he knew it didn't belong to Freddie but his curiosity was piqued.

"I wonder who that car belongs to? I don't think I've seen it before, bit flash a sports car and it's a Mazda." He strained his neck to see if he could see any further but without success. "Perhaps I should go and check that everything is okay... as we are passing the door."

"Leave the poor girl alone Hugh, she is entitled to have visitors without you poking your nose in. It could be a couple wanting to get married, a parishioner, a friend, who knows?"

"You like her, don't you?" Emma turned to him beaming that look that only mothers have.

"Well, yes, of course, everyone likes her, well except for old Doris but we are mates, I hope. It's just that I haven't seen that car around here before. Anyway, we must walk a bit quicker I should have bought flowers or a bottle of wine or something for George and Alice I have only just thought of it now I feel guilty going to lunch without a gift." He ruffled his hair absently rubbing his forehead between thumb and fingers trying to think of a solution, knowing it was too far to go home he suddenly remembered Bertie's café wondering if they sold wine.

"You carry on Mum I am just going to nip back to Bertie's I've had an idea," he quickly ran down the road dashing into the café out of breath. "Bertie I don't know if you can help but do you sell wine?" he gasped.

"No, sorry mate, can't help you there," Bertie stood hands on hips "are you that desperate, you look done in?" Hugh quickly explained and Bertie thought for a moment "tell you what I do have a bottle of sherry that I keep for making trifles you can have that and I know that Alice loves her sherry."

"Thanks, mate, you're a lifesaver. How much do I owe you?" He asked as Bertie handed over the sherry.

"Nothing mate I don't have a licence to sell alcohol but you have given me a brilliant idea so thanks. Call it quits," Hugh turned to leave and for one horrible heart-wrenching moment he stopped dead as he saw Suzanne having lunch with an unknown man, sitting heads close together deep in conversation.

Chapter 11

The next day was Sunday and Hugh reluctantly accompanied Emma to church. The last thing he wanted to see was 'that man' sitting looking adoringly at Suzanne or worse he couldn't bear the thought of the opposite with Suzanne doing the same to him. He dragged his feet up the road, shoulders down, silently turning over every possible scenario in his mind getting nowhere except he knew he liked her, really liked her and now it was too late.

His mum had been a regular churchgoer up in Richmond ever since his dad had passed away, she helped with the flowers even tea and coffee on a Sunday morning.

"I think you will slot into this community very easily, Mum," he said suddenly feeling love for her. It had not occurred to him how lonely she might be up north with no family around. He had fled as quickly as possible taking the first job he could regardless of where it was and working for Molly tucked away in Trentmouth had been his salvation.

"Why thank you, darling. What on earth made you say that? Not that I mind, of course."

Smiling as she glanced at him. "You look worried, dear; you don't normally mind coming to church with me. What's the matter today? I bet I can guess but tell me anyway."

"Oh, nothing really." He scuffed his feet in the pebbles, hands in his pockets. "It's just well, after seeing Suzanne yesterday with "that man," I am finding it hard to face her today.

"Stupid really as she can see whomever she likes, it's nothing to do with me." He shrugged letting out a heavy sigh.

"Hmm, well it's obvious you like her very much so why don't you tell her? Ask her out or cook a meal that usually starts things off… if you want to, of course."

"I wish it was that easy. It's just that, well… she is a vicar and I don't know what the protocol is and I suppose I don't want to make a fool of myself. We're good friends and I would hate to lose that if she wasn't interested in me. Anyway, come to think of it, why am I discussing my love life or lack of it with my mother?" he nudged her and they both laughed.

* * *

George was standing at the church door welcoming people in and Alice was handing out hymn books. Hugh, overtaken by a sudden panic attack, could not bring himself to enter the church instead he turned to his mum.

"I have some urgent work to do at the office Mum, you go ahead and I'll be back in an hour to walk you home." He kissed her cheek retreating quickly before she could argue with him and made his escape. He trudged back down the lane feeling morose and he had to admit stupid too. *"I'm a bloody idiot,"* he told himself *"why can't I just ask her out like any other girl and now it's too late."*

"Hugh… hi what are you doing going into the office on a Sunday, anything I should know?" The sound of Molly's voice broke into his reverie he was so absorbed in his own thoughts that he hadn't noticed her pushing the pram up the road. Alistair was carrying Jessica in a papoose, they were the picture of perfect love and happiness. How he envied them.

"Actually, I wasn't supposed to be here at all," he rubbed his wrinkled forehead. "I've left Mum at the church and thought that I would make myself a coffee and sit here for a while."

"Everything is fine by the way, no problems in the office." He looked down at his feet unable to find enthusiasm for anything.

"Look mate, come to us, I have some beers in the fridge, you look like you could do with one," Alistair said throwing a glance in Molly's direction for her agreement.

"Yes, do; we were just about to have coffee ourselves and I have some of your favourite lemon drizzle cake… if you like," she sounded pleading and with no better plan in mind he re-locked the office and sauntered over to them.

"Wow, it must be bad," Alistair exclaimed slapping him on the shoulder "you definitely need a beer and I have a bottle of single malt hidden away if you fancy a chaser." Hugh had to smile at that following them into the barn that was now their home. Molly took care of the children and Alistair rescued Hugh by taking him into the small courtyard at the rear of the barn together with the promised beer and single malt. They chatted about football, the stock market, business in general and even the weather!

"Look, it's none of my business but if you want to talk I'm listening if not… have another whisky," Alistair topped up their drinks just as Molly appeared with her coffee and homemade cake. Hugh looked from one to the other.

"How did you do it?" He made a circle with his arm enveloping everything in sight gulping down his whisky.

"What? What in particular? We need more info," Molly chuckled as she squeezed Alistair's hand.

"You have a lovely home, three gorgeous children, and the perfect happy marriage… I want to know how you did it?" he searched their faces for answers.

"Well…" started Molly "the first two we can agree with you straight away but the perfect happy marriage takes a lot of hard work and it is a long bumpy road. Truthfully it is a never-ending road you have to both want to make it work every single day. What's brought this on Hugh? I've never seen you like this before." Molly reached over gently squeezing his arm. Alistair picked up his faithful whisky waving it at Hugh, he shook his head.

"I have to collect Mum soon from church so I'd better not, wouldn't mind a coffee though if it's no trouble, Molly?"

"Of course not, back in a tic," Molly left them to it giving Alistair the chance to jump in.

"It has to be a woman mate and that road is never easy believe me. I thought you were off women after… you know." He slugged the last drop of his whisky just as Molly returned with a tray of coffees and some biscuits to soak up the alcohol. Hugh gratefully took advantage of both.

"The thing is… the thing is… the thing is I admit I'm lonely and I admit that I do like Suzanne… a lot, but well, yesterday I saw her in the café head to head with a bloke and it just… well, freaked me out," blurted Hugh feeling more stupid by the second it was his problem and he shouldn't have involved them. "So I suppose I retreated and stayed out of the way this morning, you know so that she wouldn't see me and if I'm honest so that I couldn't see him in case, well in case he stayed over," he felt himself getting hot under the collar and very uncomfortable unloading himself like this. "It must be the whisky talking, sorry to embarrass you and me come to that." Hugh jumped up "I must be going, sorry again."

"Hey Hugh, sit down you have plenty of time before you need to meet Emma," Hugh reluctantly sat down again picking up another custard cream pushing it into his mouth so that he couldn't say anything else stupid. Molly let out a sigh "Hugh, let me try and see things from Suzanne's point of view. She's been here nearly a year and anyone can see that you two have been hedging around each other ever since you set eyes on her."

Hugh shot her a startled look "I haven't been that obvious have I? Oh, God; what might people think; even my mother has noticed; what am I going to do?" At the mention of Emma both Molly and Alistair burst out laughing making Hugh turn bright red and start to laugh too. "I'm an idiot, sorry but I don't know what to do."

"So let's look at the facts, as we think we know them. She likes you but you haven't made any moves on her so from her point of view she might think that she has imagined your interest and just want to be mates."

"Yes, but…" Molly held up her hand and continued.

"What do we know about this man? Nothing, nothing at all, we don't know his name, why he is in the village," she counted the points on her fingers in order to make a forceful statement "Did he stay over? Was he in church this morning? In fact, all we know is that Suzanne had lunch with him yesterday and that could be quite innocent," she caught her breath fixing him with a stare.

"Bloody hell Molly you are right and I am such a fool but I still don't know where to go from here?" he slapped his forehead and jumped up walking around the courtyard. "What if he really is a new boyfriend and I've let her slip through my fingers?"

"There's only one way to find out mate, you need to talk to her, be her best friend and ask her out before it's too bloody late." Alistair sounded exasperated even though his advice struck Hugh with an idea and he was grateful. The sound of the church bells brought him back to the here and now he stuck out his hand.

"Thanks, mate, and now I really must go before Mum wonders where I am." Hugh rushed back up the lane towards the church just in time to see his mum shaking hands with Suzanne at the church door.

"Sorry, Mum, I lost track of time. Morning Suzanne," turning his attention to Suzanne and smiling, his heart pounding so loudly he thought that everyone would hear it.

"We missed you this morning Hugh but Emma tells me you had something urgent to do at the surgery, not a sick animal I hope?" she smiled at him and Hugh felt even more guilty.

"No, nothing like that, there was something I just had to do. I have been wondering though, about something and would it be alright if I might pop in sometime... and have a chat?" he shuffled his feet anxiously. Suzanne smiled.

"Of course, I don't have my diary with me but I think tomorrow when you close the surgery should be alright. Why don't you call in then?" she smiled so innocently that Hugh could only think of himself as the biggest fool on the planet. "See you tomorrow."

Hugh and Emma walked silently along the lane back towards the farm and the cottage.

"There was no single young man in the church today looking at Suzanne if that's what you are wondering Hugh, so stop beating yourself up and talk to me." His mother knew him too well. They had grown close since his dad had died and his brother had taken up that job in the USA. She had been a rock to him after he was abandoned at the altar, taking care of things when he was too shocked to even think straight.

"Suzanne is a lovely girl and is just as lonely as you stuck in that big house all on her own. I think that Freddie is coming down again next week; oh and Maggie was in church with Lady Isabel," Hugh half-listened to her prattling on formulating a plan in his mind. He just couldn't wait for Monday at 5:00 to arrive until then he had things to do.

Chapter 12

Monday morning Molly was still feeling concerned for Hugh, after their chat yesterday, desperately trying to think how she could help without interfering. She was deep in thought when Alistair made an announcement.

"I think that I will have to hire an assistant very soon Molly, I have so much work coming in and I'm finding it hard to keep up with the paperwork. What do you think?" He stared at her over the top of his coffee.

"Hmm I suppose if you think so," she considered asking Alice for her thoughts about Suzanne but quickly let that thought go, Alice was not known for her discretion and was famous for matchmaking as she knew only too well. Still, she had to think of something.

"So I've interviewed this gorgeous twenty-something-year old with a fabulous figure, she's no good at paperwork but hey who cares, she would look good in the front office. So I thought that I would offer her the job, give her a nice fat salary, alright?" Alistair let out a chuckle, he was attempting to feed Jessica but she had other ideas of what to do with her food and most of it was on the floor.

"What darling, you've found a new assistant?" she turned her attention to Alistair who was grinning at her, spoon mid-air with Jessica trying to reach her breakfast.

"I give in, where were you? No, I haven't taken on a new assistant but I am thinking about it."

"Oh, why is that? You haven't mentioned it before," Molly had now turned her full attention to him and their daughter rescuing the spoon and filling her open mouth with porridge, honey dripping from the spoon landing on the floor.

"The thing is you know my new client the one I told you about who is in the timber industry?"

"Yes, I remember he's made millions and doesn't know what to do with it, that right?"

Molly took over feeding Jessica who was now contentedly eating her breakfast. Alistair picked up his toast spreading it thickly with marmalade continuing.

"More or less, I mean to be fair I wouldn't know where to start with a truckload of timber but yes he has done very well and wants to invest some spare money. So what I need is another Bertie who I could train up and run the office when I see clients." He crunched into his last mouthful of toast picking up his mug of coffee.

"Right, that sounds like a good idea and by the way, no gorgeous twenty-something with a fabulous figure," she chuckled, "… in case you thought I wasn't listening." Alistair laughed leaning in for a kiss as he picked up his briefcase and keys ready to leave.

Molly thought about visiting Alice once more, Lucy was far too busy working full time at Poole maternity hospital and every spare minute helping Bertie at the café. She suddenly felt aggrieved for Lucy, not that she was ignoring her best friend but more it was finding time to see each other. Then of course she could always call in on Suzanne under some pretext and try to find out what she thinks of Hugh. Deciding none of these scenarios would work she set off on a good old fashioned walk down to the beach, with three children under the age of three was not going to be easy but then it was her own choice she grinned.

Passing the café she could see that it was quiet this morning so ventured in.

"Morning Bertie is Lucy in today?" she gave a wave as she struggled with the heavy pushchair, noisy grumbles emanating from within. Bertie came round the counter to help her and they sat by the door for an easy escape.

"She is due in any minute, coffee?" Bertie disappeared behind his counter immediately grinding beans, steaming milk hissing into life. Molly sank down grateful for the coffee and the chance to talk to Lucy, hopefully… she didn't have long to wait. Lucy burst in through the door colliding with the pushchair.

"Oh, Lucy, I'm so sorry," she jumped up to greet her friend and rescue her from the large contraption now whizzing forward into the legs of another customer. "Oh, I'm so sorry," feeling more embarrassed and wishing she hadn't ventured out that morning as she caused mayhem. "Please let me get you another coffee and I'm sorry again," the customer was appeased accepting a second coffee.

"Molly, hi," Lucy dropped onto a chair next to her "I'm sorry I haven't seen you lately but with work and the shop… well, you know how it is I don't have to tell you. And how are these gorgeous children of yours?" Lucy popped her head into the pram to admire two sleeping boys. Jessica was now on her mother's lap reaching for a toasted teacake knocking a spoon onto the floor with a crash. "Sorry, Molly, but I must help Bertie," she stood up pulling off her jacket, "… catch up with you later."

"You look peaky Lucy are you alright?" inquired Molly.

"Just a bit tired that's all. Anyway, we must get together soon." She made to move away but Molly stopped her.

"Why don't you pop round later, when you've finished? I miss our girlie chats," implored Molly putting on her best pleading face before collapsing into grinning at her.

"Okay, around 7:00?" Lucy smiled as she moved across behind the counter collecting her apron as she went.

Molly spent the rest of the day preparing for her evening with her best friend. With the children bathed and into bed and Alistair promising to take a long overdue visit to see his mother, wine chilling in the fridge and even a box of chocolates ready to indulge in; Molly stood back checking her watch for the umpteenth time. Seven came and went and Molly began to think that Lucy had forgotten her completely so when 7:30 clicked round Molly picked up her iPhone pressing her number. A rather breathless Bertie answered the phone.

"Molly, sorry I'm in an ambulance on the way to Poole hospital, Lucy collapsed at work," he panted.

"Bertie I'll get Alistair and I'll be there as soon as I can, what is wrong with Lucy?" she shrieked, pain searing her in two for her best friend.

"Molly, slow down let us get to the hospital and I'll call you later when we know more okay?" he clicked off without waiting for a reply. Molly sat tears streaming down her face as she called Alistair. He raced home and within minutes his arms were around her smoothing her hair holding her tight.

"Have you heard anything more from Bertie?" Molly shook her head dabbing her eyes and blowing her nose yet again. Her voice croaked.

"I saw her this morning, she said she was tired and I thought she looked peaky but Alistair I didn't think she was ill not like this anyway." She sobbed again.

"I know, I know, let me get you a coffee with a drop of brandy. Come on sit down."

He led her to the couch before heading to the kitchen and switching the kettle on. The phone rang and Molly was on it like lightning.

"Bertie… what's happening? Is she alright?" Molly gasped.

"She… she lost her baby. I didn't even know she was pregnant oh Molly why didn't she tell me?" Bertie sounded distraught and Molly ached to go to him and Lucy. "They have just taken her to theatre for a D&C. They tell me it's routine in these situations and that she will be alright but will need a good rest."

"I'm sorry Bertie but I didn't know either, I thought she looked pale this morning but she never gave me a clue. Look shall I come over now and then at least I can bring you home again later when we know that Lucy is alright."

"Yes. Yes please, I'm still in A&E, they told me to wait here."

Molly put the phone down and between sobs and blowing her nose she filled in Alistair. She grabbed her coffee quickly gulping it, her keys and jacket making for the door.

Alistair hugged her once more kissing her gently.

"Don't worry and drive carefully… oh and Molly call me," he too was distraught "I want you home again safe and sound."

Molly drove as quickly as she dare, mindful of her own shock and tiredness mixed with worry turning over in her mind that she hadn't noticed that Lucy was even pregnant!

Making her feel guilty, not that she could have done anything, but still… the thought did nothing to appease her sense of sheer worry.

Poole was quiet and she easily found a parking space. It was now dark, the lights from the hospital shining out lighting up her path as she picked her way to the A&E doing her best to put on a brave face for Bertie. He was waiting for her by the door to A&E his eyes were painfully red sunken into his ashen face. Her heart went out to him and without thinking she just raised her arms to envelope him in an embrace, he sobbed and sobbed his shoulders heaving with pain. Molly rubbed his back holding him tight. Eventually, his sobs subsided and Molly waited for him to blow his nose before they sought sanctuary inside the hospital.

"I don't know what happened. We were clearing up after we closed and Lucy said she felt a bit queasy, the next thing I knew, she had fainted. I thought that was it and I tried to give her a sip of water but then she started to clutch her stomach and screamed in pain. She looked up at me; fear in her eyes said, 'the baby, I think I am losing our… our baby.'"

I said something stupid, and she burst into tears telling me to send for an ambulance. He gulped turning to stare into his coffee swirling it around and not really drinking it.

"Why didn't she tell me she was pregnant? She has been working so hard in the café as well as her full-time job. I should have realised there was something wrong but you know how it is one day flows into another sometimes." He fell silent returning to his coffee and his thoughts. Molly struggled for words.

"She didn't confide in me, Bertie, so I don't know maybe she was waiting for her twelve-week scan…"

"But she could have told me, it's… my baby too," he choked, tears squeezing onto his cheeks trickling down towards his chin. He swiped them away.

"I know and I'm so sorry Bertie. I wonder if we or you would be allowed to see her before I take you home."

Twenty minutes later, they climbed into Molly's Land Rover and set off for Trentmouth. It was almost dark with just a hint of light encircling the clouds as they drove over the railway bridge towards Purbeck. All was quiet including Bertie. He sat twisting his hands deep in thought.

Finally, Molly broke the silence "Lucy will be alright, she will probably be home tomorrow but she will need a lot of rest… I'll help all I can you know that… maybe I could get Alice to do some babysitting," she ventured. Although she was not very hopeful as Jessica could be a handful on her own and then the twins… "Look I'll see what I can sort out tomorrow just let me know how she is and when she's home. She just needs peace and quiet for a bit not more worry about the café."

The next day Molly popped in to see Hugh before setting off to visit Lucy after safely depositing Jessica with Alice although she had to keep the twins with her. She quickly filled in Hugh with what had happened to Lucy. Fortunately, Hugh had a quiet few minutes and he sat looking pensively at Molly.

"I have an idea, I will have to have a word with my mum first but you know she works in a café serving drinks, making scones and so on; anyway, long story short she has put her place up for sale and is planning on moving down here so… she might be able to step into the breach for a week or two and work for Bertie!"

"Hugh… that would be wonderful I am just on my way to see them now. Let me know what she says and what a surprise that she is moving to Trentmouth… you are pleased aren't you?" she asked as Hugh who was holding his chin one finger on his lips looked pensive.

"Yeh; Yeh it's just that… well I did want to talk to you about the business but it can wait, today is not the time. Look let me call Mum and I will call you later, then perhaps we can sit down and talk."

Chapter 13

Hugh sat staring at the clock as it slowly ticked around towards 5:00 when he was due to see Suzanne at the vicarage. He felt a little anxious, even though it made no sense, desperately trying to keep his mind on the job. He had to admit that he always ended up stumbling over his words whenever he met her and couldn't help the hot feelings inside finding it so hard not to touch her and want to take care of her. He shook himself trying to remain focused on his job today.

There were relatively few customers leaving him plenty of time to update the website and conduct a search on his idea for Suzanne. He glanced again at the clock only ten minutes left when the door opened, the buzzer making him jump, he looked around the corner of his office to see Miss McPherson with her dog, Charlie. He smiled at her, despite his misgivings;

Miss McPherson was not one to hurry. She always wanted to chat and Hugh had the distinct impression that she was flirting with him and he had no idea how to put her off. He strode into the waiting room.

"Hello, Miss McPherson, what seems to be the trouble with Charlie today?" he enquired whilst stroking the little dog and feeling around his head and ears.

"Felicity please," she smiled coyly turning pink.

"Felicity; so what has Charlie been up to?" he wandered back to the examination room carrying little Charlie, for such a small dog he managed to get into many scrapes.

"I'm not sure but when I touch his back paw he yelps and he keeps gnawing at it."

"Come on fella let's have a look at you," Hugh gently felt around his paws quickly finding the sore spot. He looked at it more closely. "It looks as though a splinter has imbedded itself into his paw. Hmm, shouldn't be too difficult to remove it. I do have some gel to numb the area enough without causing him any distress. It shouldn't take long, would you like to sit down Miss M... hmm Felicity," he shot her a smile and she retreated to the waiting room. Hugh attended to his patient returning him with his paw minus the offending splinter back to Felicity. She thanked him profusely as she paid the bill with her credit card then she stuttered.

"I was wondering Hugh... hmm that is I was wondering if you might, that is if you are not doing anything else if you might like to have a coffee with me at Bertie's one day?" She stammered turning bright red shuffling her feet and looking quite uneasy. Hugh, taken aback, couldn't think for a minute then deciding not to hurt her feelings and wanting to get away as quickly as possible, took a long look at her. She was probably about the same age as him but painfully shy and dressed as though she was a throwback to the 90s.

"That would be lovely, how does Saturday about 10.30 sound?" he allowed just the touch of a smile to cross his lips.

"Great, see you on Saturday," she exclaimed as she hurriedly disappeared carrying poor Charlie under her arm.

Hugh looked at his watch. He was late, very late. He grabbed his jacket turned off the computer, locked up and dashed up the lane towards the vicarage. This was one day he did not want to be late and rather than risking telephoning Suzanne and finding she was busy, he jogged up to her door, half out of breath, and pulled the long mental handle that rang a bell deep inside the house. He could hear her footsteps on the parquet floor hurrying to the door.

"I'm sorry I'm late, emergency I'm afraid a dog with a splinter in its paw…" he stopped his mouth dropped open, she was stunning dressed in an apricot coloured dress that fell softly around her knees her hair loose over her shoulders. "I… hmm, may I say you look beautiful, am I allowed to say that? It's just that I usually see you, you know in your… your hmm working clothes," he kicked his toe against the doorstep. *"Shut up, you idiot,"* he thought.

Suzanne let out a laugh.

"Come on in," she said completely ignoring his stupid outburst. He was relieved and quickly followed her into her study. "Would you like a cup of tea? I have a lovely cherry cake that Alice made." She smiled beguilingly at him. He looked into her sparkling blue eyes that never failed to light up when she saw him, he didn't deserve it he knew as he had consistently found he could hardly speak whenever he saw her and always ended up looking at his feet.

"I hmm… yes please, sounds good to me," he sat in a comfortable armchair by her desk fidgeting. Turning his attention out into the garden he could see that Suzanne had been busy, the borders were a plethora of flowers, geraniums, delphiniums, foxgloves, roses and more, half of them he didn't recognise, full of every imaginable colour. The doors were open and the air hung with a heady scent wafting in making him feel soporific.

Suzanne pushed the door open with her derrière struggling with a heavy tray. Hugh jumped up.

"Here… let me," he took the tray placing it onto a low table noticing that there was only one cup and saucer. "You're not having one?" he glanced up at her surprised feeling that he should have declined her offer of tea, the cake sounded too tempting for him as Alice made the best cakes apart from his mum, of course.

"No; actually, I'm going out this evening… to dinner… with a friend," she looked down and Hugh noticed her killer heels for the first time, not her usual little flats that she wore.

Pink turning red crept up her throat. Hugh wasn't sure why exactly, women were difficult to understand.

"Oh," he took a deep breath wondering if he should go "I mean, great, you should have rung me and cancelled I can go now if you prefer?" He stared at her, the object of his affections thinking about the sports car he had seen on her drive the other day. *Was this the friend?* He thought.

"No… no, I would never turn away a parishioner that's what I'm here for." She had forced a laugh he knew sitting uneasily at her desk. He wanted to apologise for making her feel uncomfortable but didn't know how, his mind had gone blank. He took out a handkerchief wiping away the beads of sweat that had appeared on his forehead his throat constricted.

"What did you want to see me about Hugh? You said that you had an idea and wanted to run it past me if I remember correctly." Her professional smile had returned it was now business and Hugh was gutted.

"I just thought that you lived in this big place all alone and wondered if you maybe ought to have an alarm system? And a panic button by your bed and by the front door, you know for security in case… well, in case you know." Hugh dried up, after all, it was none of his business what she had or didn't have, but goddam it, he cared about her. The sound of crunching gravel drifted in through the open doors, her 'friend' had arrived.

"That sounds like Gary now," declared Suzanne signalling the end of their chat "I will give your suggestion some thought Hugh and get back to you." She rose to turn a sweet smile in his direction. The bell jangled somewhere rather impatiently.

Hugh couldn't resist wanting to find out more "Gary…? Is he the one who you had lunch with at Bertie's the other day, drives a sports car?" He wanted to kick himself, ashamed for asking but the words were out of his mouth before he could stop them.

"Why? Yes, Gary Braithwaite, he's a producer at the BBC. I used to work with him," her eyebrows raised as she gave him a quizzical look. The bell clanged an urgent clang, jangling his nerves, the moment lost; they both made for the door. Face to face with his rival Hugh looked up and down at this smart guy with his smart suit smart car and shiny smart shoes and to make matters worse he was carrying a huge bunch of flowers. They stared at each other momentarily, Hugh felt inadequate, scruffy even, in his old trousers, loafers and battered blazer he kept for work.

"Hi," said the even smarter Gary Braithwaite. "Hello, gorgeous," he turned on the charm to Suzanne handing her the flowers. Hugh pushed past him seething.

"Hmm… I'll catch up with you later Suzanne," he hurried down the path, hearing this, this guy asking Suzanne who he was?

Chapter 14

Trentmouth Manor had never been so busy, resplendent with colourful bunting, balloons and twinkling lights. The church fete turned out to be a fabulous success in no small part due to Suzanne and Freddie who had as usual willingly agreed to help, Maggie the obvious attraction. The grounds were filled with the usual stalls, WI teas, Hugh with his dog show, Miss McPherson with her dad's honey, all the competitions, flower arranging, cake and vegetable displays. Suzanne wandered around smiling till her face hurt. Gentle jazz playing in the background, children with ice cream running down their arms and dripping off elbows, mums with wet wipes trying to catch them, even Doris had taken up residence in her usual spot in the WI tent harrumphing at every opportunity. Suzanne couldn't be more delighted.

She spotted Lady Isobel and wandered over to her.

"Thank you so much for letting us use your meadow, Isobel, and what wonderful weather!" The day had started out overcast and Suzanne spent the morning panicking staring up at the sky hoping and praying that the sky would turn blue, the people would turn up and her first fete would not be a failure in any particular order.

"Wonderful. We have had several enquiries about weddings too. I have to admit I had my misgivings in the beginning when Maggie first mentioned it to me, and of course, I didn't want to step on poor Alice's toes but I tend to agree that it has all turned out rather much for the best." Isobel smiled surveying the crowds milling around "when Rufus died I thought that that was the end of my life, especially socially, but I am busier than ever and so pleased to have Maggie running things. Oh look I can see the Bishop heading our way I think I'll leave you to it."

Isobel sashayed away her skirt swinging in the breeze around her knees as she acknowledged smiles and waves from visitors. Isobel was far too young to be widowed still in her fifties and sadly they had not had any children. Rufus had been a successful businessman and MP till he died suddenly from a heart attack when attending Parliament. He had been made a Sir for his services to industry and his company later became the subject to a buyout by his Directors, leaving Rufus able to take up his seat in the House of Lords. This had suited Isobel and she had turned her efforts into running the estate with the help of her niece, Maggie.

Suzanne turned to see the Bishop with his poor wife trailing along in his wake.

Clarissa, his wife, tiny by comparison trudged meekly behind him, eyes down unsmiling.

Suzanne had yet to have a conversation with her. It was impossible to get her on her own and she often wondered what she was really like.

"Ah, there you are, Reverend Martin, excellent day, you have certainly surpassed expectations. Yes, a great credit to this parish but then I had faith in you. I knew you couldn't fail." He beamed pulling his handkerchief from his pocket to mop his brow.

"Thank you, Bishop; would you and your wife like a cup of tea? I'm sure you could do with a sit down," Suzanne gestured towards the WI tent.

"That would be…" began Clarissa.

"No, no thank you, we are busy visiting every stallholder first to encourage people along to the church too. Come along my dear," he said to Clarissa moving away. Poor Clarissa looked forlorn proffering a weak smile in Suzanne's direction.

Suzanne had no chance to tell him that flyers were being handed out to do just that as well as inviting people to come along and join in the new breakfast club, mums and toddlers group and proposing an idea for a church band looking for volunteers. Things had come a long way in a year but it would keep for another day.

Suzanne wandered over to see Maggie and to have a cup of tea herself. The tea tent was very busy. She looked around to see Alice chatting to Freddie, she collected a cup of tea and a slice of fruit cake before making her way over to join them. Freddie jumped up to find an empty chair and Alice shot a beam of delight at her.

"May I join you?" she asked not wanting to disturb any private chat that Alice may have been conducting.

"Of course my dear I was just asking Freddie about his work and so on. He appears to be down here in Trentmouth more and more these days," she let a tiny smile touch her lips.

Suzanne knew instantly that Alice was really trying to find out about Freddie and Maggie and hoped that he had given nothing away. She needn't have worried as Freddie was as keen as she was not to let the secret out, not just yet anyway. Freddie returned carrying a chair sporting a huge grin.

"How is it going, sis? It looks brilliant to me I never knew events like this still went on in the sticks." He sipped his tea throwing her a cheeky grin.

"Actually, better than I imagined myself, to be honest, and there is still more to come."

"The dog show is back by popular demand and I have already had ideas for next year."

"Really," declared Alice eyes opened wide, "what may I ask?" Suzanne couldn't help but chuckle.

"Sorry, Alice but you will have to wait for the next PCC meeting. Anyway, I must go and check with Hugh it's almost time for the dog show."

"See you later," called Freddie after her as Suzanne raised her hand in acknowledgement "I'll make dinner tonight," he trailed off. Suzanne could see Hugh talking to Molly behind their table with animal toys gaily dangling from a stand and lots of excited children shouting and pushing to get a view of the baby chicks and ducks in their pen. Hugh spotted her coming over and raising his hand checked the time, rushing out to cross the field.

He called and waved to her.

"I am on my way," and he was off at a jog towards the arena where people were already gathering with their canine friends. Suzanne walked over to talk to Molly.

"Hi, Molly, is Hugh avoiding me? How are the family by the way?" she enquired turning to smile at Molly regretting her mouth opening before her head woke up to catastrophe.

"Growing fast already, you must pop in and see us soon," Molly smiled with her head on one side as if she was about to say something else.

"I will. I will but it has been quite hectic with the fete and everything. I must get back to my pastoral visits soon," she flushed as she really wanted to enquire about Hugh knowing that Molly had definitely heard her. Hugh undoubtedly had been avoiding her recently and Suzanne assumed it was because of Gary but needed to know for sure. "Is um… is Hugh alright? I haven't seen much of him recently." She struggled to meet Molly's eyes.

"Yes, as far as I know, and no, he hasn't been avoiding you at least I think not. I understand you have had a recent visit from someone from the BBC a producer or something.

Tell me about him, I'm dying to know all about it," she enthused trying to keep an eye on the chicks at the same time as some children were trying to touch them.

"Nothing to tell really and I understand that Hugh has been seen out with Felicity," she countered a note of sadness in her voice. Molly swung her attention back to Suzanne her eyes raised looking as if she wanted to say more but managed instead.

"Not jealous are you?"

"Gosh no of course not, I must be going and I promise to come and see you soon," she exited quickly not giving Molly time to reply and asking God for forgiveness for her blatant lie.

Chapter 15

Lucy had reluctantly agreed to visit Molly as in truth it was easier for her to travel, as Molly could hardly drag three little ones out to the farm. She drove into the village melancholy pulling her down, it was her first time out after her miscarriage and she really didn't want to see other people's healthy babies but Molly was her best friend and she missed her. The world looked different somehow she noticed the leaves on the trees and the flowers in the hedgerows. The world had moved on without her causing Lucy to feel even more depressed than she was already.

Molly opened the door with her finger placed over her lips dragging her out to their tiny courtyard garden. Waiting on the table in the sunshine were two glasses, a bottle of white wine probably Chardonnay, Molly's favourite, and a plate of gooey chocolate brownies. Lucy couldn't help herself but smile. Molly knew her so well, truly her best friend.

"Thank you, Molly; you always know just what I need," they hugged each other for a moment. "I've missed you and our chats, sorry Molly."

"No need. Let's have a drink and you can bring me up to date with all your news before I tell you mine," she grinned conspiratorially. Molly poured out the wine handing one to

Lucy, they clinked saying 'cheers' Lucy started to feel more like her old self with each sip of delicious cold wine trickling down her throat.

"Where's Jessica?" she asked suddenly realising that the normal noisy Jessica was not around.

"Playschool, and Alice will be collecting her later so that we can have some time to ourselves. I will miss them when they go on their travels, not long now. I still can't believe that they are going on this trip around the world but I suppose why not?"

"Oh, yes, I had forgotten about that, three months is an awfully long time, I don't know how George managed to persuade her to go. She will miss the children and all the gossip," they both laughed. Molly topped up the wine pushing another brownie towards Lucy.

"Now come on, you can tell me all about it and I mean ALL about it," Molly looked straight at her as if into her very soul. Lucy heaved a huge long sigh knowing that she should have confided in Molly before but…

"Banged to rights, as usual," a tiny smile touched her lips "I wanted to be sure this time and even though the test was positive I thought that I would wait until my first scan… you know how excited Bertie gets and I… I wanted to be sure, really sure before I told anyone." Molly just sat quietly listening making no comment so Lucy pressed on "I carried on working even though I was tired and starting to get morning sickness, Bertie didn't notice," a small huh escaped her lips "anyway, I was going to tell you that evening but I crumpled up with a searing pain and I knew, at that moment I knew that I was going to lose my baby," tears emerged on to her cheeks turning into rivulets as they coursed down to her chin. Lucy pulled out a tissue wiping them away, "… sorry," she said.

Molly launched into action grabbing a box of tissues hugging her sobbing friend, making no comment just rocking her gently as if she were one of her own babies. Lucy let her tears fall the one thing she couldn't do was confide in her mother as now that she had dementia it was difficult to hold any sort of conversation. Her dad was in his own depths of despair and Lucy knew that she couldn't burden him, he had his own share of worries.

Minutes later Lucy blew her nose and drained her glass. Molly obligingly opened another bottle without criticism or complaint. The sun warmed the courtyard, bees were busy in and out of the petunias but no other sound could be heard it felt like a little bit of heaven to Lucy. How she wanted to curl up there leaving the world behind.

"So…" Molly twisted her glass round and round "what now?" That was the thing that Lucy loved most about Molly, she didn't offer her own opinion and never said "you should do this or that," she always asked you what you want to do.

"Well, the specialist said that there was no apparent reason for me to miscarry, which I knew of course, not that that helps either. However, I need a break and I have a few weeks holiday to come plus my sick leave so I am going to take the time to recover and then have a serious think about the future." Lucy took a third brownie, they were just too good not to, she bit into it the luxury of chocolate and the feeling of treating herself spreading through her like hot custard over sticky toffee pudding, yum, yum.

"I am pleased to hear it but knowing you I'm sure that you have tossed around your options…" a smile crossed Lucy's face "come on, out with it," Molly cajoled.

"Emma is a godsend, what with Bertie fussing me and wanting me to sit down with my feet up all the time; anyway, Bertie wants to offer her a full-time job once she gets moved down here and I have been thinking quite seriously that I should give up my career in midwifery, help more with the business," feeling more confident saying it out loud she pressed on "Bertie is creative and loves being in the café, paperwork not being his favourite job and… I do it now anyway," she chuckled, "so I think that I will take over that side of things and try to come up with new ideas for bringing in the customers," she took a deep breath "come on Molly tell me what you think."

"Sounds perfect to me, I like it and Emma has slotted right in she will be thrilled to work for Bertie I'm sure. I'm just worried about you giving up your career that's all, I know how much you love your job, are you sure that's what you want to do?" Ever the one to think about others smiled Lucy.

"Quite sure and I'm not giving up my career just changing one adventure for another and this one really is life-changing for both of us."

"Then I am truly thrilled for you," she raised her glass. "Congratulations, I love it and I'm also a little bit envious," they both laughed.

"The thing now of course is to hope for a brilliant summer, customers and new ideas to make our venture a success," they clinked again. "Now, your turn Mrs Warren," Lucy felt grateful that Molly didn't ask about trying again for another baby, she did not want to tell Molly that she may not get another chance to be a mum.

"Hmm, well, where to begin?" she looked thoughtful "Hugh wanted to chat to me about our practice the other day and the last thing I expected was that he wanted to buy me out…" Lucy couldn't help but let her eyes shoot up in surprise.

"How did that make you feel?"

"To be honest, at first, I was shocked I mean it is my business, I started it and well it still feels like my baby… oh sorry Lucy I didn't think," she leaned over squeezing her arm "fancy another drink," she asked waving the empty second bottle in the air.

"Coffee I think would be better," she grinned. Molly jumped up whisking the empties away heading for the kitchen. Lucy gazed around the little bit of heaven aptly named Molly's garden. It was an exaggeration but still heavenly warm with dappled shade crossing the patio bringing welcome relief from the overhead sun. She felt soporific, probably the wine or the sheer fact that she had finally talked to her best friend a problem shared and all that. Molly returned carrying a tray, two mugs a coffee pot and a plate of chocolate finger biscuits waking her from her reverie. Lucy let out a sigh.

"Please Molly, I will get fat!" they both burst out laughing but ate them anyway.

"So…" said Molly between crunching another finger and licking her own fingers to remove the melted chocolate, "… at first, I said, "no," but on reflection and discussing it with Alistair, we came up with a solution and to be fair since Jessica was born and then the twins I have hardly been in the office at all… and I know that's not fair on poor Hugh." She sipped her coffee and pulled out a baby wipe to clean her fingers pushing the packet in Lucy's direction.

"So I have agreed to sell him my half of the business and hopefully become his locum instead a bit of a turnaround. I'm still not sure about it though but as you say I'm not giving up on my dreams just changing one adventure for another."

"Touché," declared Lucy raising her coffee cup. They both chuckled. "It's funny how things turn out, isn't it? Not even a year ago I married Bertie, you only had Jessica, I was set for promotion and the café was only a distant dream, now look at us." They sat silently contemplating the changes, none of which were planned except Lucy and Bertie getting married and both their lives were about to change dramatically once again.

"I've been thinking," Molly placed a curled finger on her chin turning her attention to Lucy.

"Hmm… what have you been thinking? And please don't make it too complicated I am a bit squiffy."

"It's ideal for your café actually."

"Oh, no, I knew you couldn't resist it, your brain box is working overtime… again."

"You could say that. What you need are some regular groups coming in especially in the winter so what about you set aside one corner for say 'knit and natter' or regular talks with coffee on all different subjects like gardening, the sky at night, what to look for along the shoreline, or how about 'food for free' you know seaweed you can eat and…"

"Whoa stop, first of all, I haven't brought a pad and pen with me and even just those ideas will keep me busy for the next six months!"

"Sorry, I do get carried away don't I? So how about you and Bertie come to us one evening I'll make dinner and if you wish we can get our heads together and see what we can all come up with?"

"Great, I love you Molly it's a date. Now tell me more about your future plans."

Changing the subject as Lucy was struggling to keep her eyes open and had already forgotten Molly's ideas.

"Well, I do have a problem and it concerns Hugh and Suzanne…"

"Why, what do you mean?" immediately Lucy felt more awake giving Molly her full attention.

"I am in the awkward position of having both of them enquire about the other and both thinking that the other is not interested… and at the same time Suzanne is seeing some guy called Gary and Hugh has been out with Felicity a couple of times," she let out a sigh.

"Oh, dear," grinned Lucy "you are turning into your mother-in-law," beginning to laugh.

"It's not funny, I'm deadly serious. You don't really think I'm turning into Alice, do you?"

Chapter 16

"Geoorgge…" called Alice "where are you?" she popped her head around the door into the snug and spied him sitting on the patio fast asleep, the newspaper scattered on the floor. She tutted picked up the newspaper trying to decide if she should wake him up. Thinking better of it she folded the newspaper retreating to the kitchen to make a pot of earl grey tea. The phone rang and Alice quickly retrieved it not wanting to disturb George.

"Hello…" she trilled, "… yes that would be fine." She replaced the receiver as quietly as possible.

"What would be fine, Alice?" Alice gave a gasp of shock as she nearly leapt out of her skin clutching her chest.

"George you startled me, nothing dear… hmm wrong number. Cup of tea dear I've just made a pot?" she turned to go to the kitchen leaving George gaping after her but he didn't enquire further much to her relief as that was one secret she was keeping for now. Alice carried a tray of tea and banana bread through to the snug and onto the patio where George had taken up residence once more. She poured the tea and handed cake and a napkin to George, looking and feeling smug, as she had avoided letting out her secret.

"Okay, I give in you are up to something Alice and I want to know what it is… if you don't mind," he took his cake breaking a corner off whilst keeping his eyes firmly fixed on Alice. She chuckled.

"Alright it wasn't a wrong number but I can't tell you yet it is a surprise, so don't spoil it… drink your tea," Alice was desperate to tell George she had been planning it since the church fete and it had been killing her to keep quiet but keep quiet she must at least until the weekend, when all would be revealed. And Alice was convinced that George would be pleased and another member of the community too. She did her best not to grin but it overtook her face as she tried to return to a semblance of normality sucking in her cheeks as she did so and swallowing a giggle.

"You haven't forgotten that Isabel is coming to tea this afternoon have you, dear? Only we have some church business to deal with before we go on our travels."

"No, dear, but that does remind me I need to go into Wareham later and collect our various currencies and check that everything is in order. Not long now. Is there anything else you need my dear as I will be passing the supermarket and I could pop in for you?" He carefully refolded his paper before polishing off his cake, "… and I must collect our prescriptions too. I'm sure you have a list, Alice, did I forget anything," he smiled indulgently.

Alice calculated that he would be out long enough to see Isabel and finalise her own preparations. "No, dear, that will be fine," George harrumphed at Alice but she took no notice of his ill-disguised tantrum at wanting to know what she was up to.

Isabel arrived, they air-kissed, Alice ushering her into the snug where more tea and cake was waiting. "No, George?" she enquired looking around.

"No, and he will be out for some time, he has been fishing all day trying to find out what is going on," Alice twitched with delight at the prospect of pulling off a surprise for George. They settled down to first discussing church business as Alice was going to be away for such a long time and she was anxious that all her duties were taken care of and that Isabel knew how to contact her, in case of emergencies.

"I still can't believe that you agreed to go, Alice, I know it will be a wonderful holiday for you both but still… won't you miss seeing those adorable grandchildren and so many events happening whilst you are away," quizzed Isabel.

"Don't set me off again Isabel, it has been a dream of George's ever since he retired and I am the one who kept putting it off. It never seems to be the right time, always something happening and if I'm honest I still don't want to go, at least not for this long.

However, that's why I needed to enlist your help and I am delighted as I think that we can just pull this off. Let's have a sherry to celebrate."

"I don't normally drink sherry but yes please as it is a bit of a celebration, isn't it."

Alice bustled into the kitchen returning with the sherry and two glasses including a box of chocolates. "Alice, I have a feeling that there is more you want from me," she let a broad smile stretch across her face and Alice chuckled.

"Well, I have been thinking about it and I am so grateful to you for agreeing to have us up at the Manor. We will miss George's birthday, Alistair's, Alistair and Molly's wedding anniversary, not to mention so many church events. Thank goodness we will be back just in time for Jessica's birthday and the twins first Christmas otherwise I told George no can do."

They both laughed at that.

"Right now Bertie is organised with the catering, Emma is helping him by the way I must talk to you about Emma later, Maggie is doing a splendid job with lights, balloons, flowers, streamers, music and so much more. That little band of local jazz musicians was a big success at the fete and Suzanne kindly got in touch with them for me and they are booked so what have I missed?" asked Isabel.

"I think that is it except you need to invite us up for supper so that I can appear totally innocent," that tickled Alice as she fluttered her eyes a picture of pure innocence "Everyone is geared up to complete secrecy, let's hope that no one lets it slip before the day and that is when I will tell George all about Freddie," she let out a long breath "I do hope he is pleased when I tell him about Freddie, you know what he can be like if it wasn't his idea? I expect he will harrumph a bit and then be alright."

"I'm sure you're right and it is such a brilliant idea Alice and it has Maggie all hot and bothered," they both chuckle "so if that is all sorted can we talk about Emma?" Isabel placed her sherry glass onto the coffee table sitting comfortably in the wing chair. She glanced out of the French doors across the garden towards the little stream which would eventually meander down to the sea. Ducks were pecking around the grass, quacking and chasing each other furiously over some titbit or other. The garden was a riot of colour with lupins, hollyhocks and foxgloves all swaying gently above marigolds, carnations and roses.

"I do love your garden Alice…" she said wistfully turning away from the meditative scene just as Alice topped up her glass, "… thank you, Alice. Although I may have to ask Maggie to come and collect me. I will be in no state to drive after drinking two glasses of sherry."

"Nonsense my dear George will take you home now, Emma?"

"Yes, Emma. I like her very much she seems to have settled quite quickly into life here. She has sold her house you know and is hoping to buy the thatched cottage with all the sunflowers in the garden. I understand that Hugh is going to stay up at the farm, I suppose he doesn't really want to move in with his mother, although I understand that she would love to have him."

"She was telling me when I popped into Bertie's that she will be going back to Richmond soon to pack up and finalise the movers and I agree with you she will fit into our community quite nicely. I believe that Lucy is back working again in the café, so sad to lose her baby, I am not sure if she is going back to her job though." She sipped her sherry before picking up another chocolate and passing the box to Isabel "I always thought that Hugh and Maggie would get together but then when Freddie turned up… well, they are so suited to each other. Any sign of wedding bells? They are not so young and there is still time for Maggie to have children don't you think, Isabel?"

Isabel nearly choked spluttering her sherry "Alice you are incorrigible, I have no idea what their plans are but I am sure that you will be the first to know," recovering delicately dabbing her lips "So let me ask you who is on the guestlist apart from family? I know that Lucy will be helping Bertie..."

"Neatly changing the subject Isabel, yes and then I have insisted that they both join us as our guests. Freddie, of course, Hugh with Felicity, I never would have put those two together and Suzanne with this Gary fellow who I do not know much about but thought that I should include him..." she stopped talking for a moment and wandered into her own private space deep in thought "still I'm sure that it will all be fine. Emma is hoping to be back too and that's it. You will join us too of course?" Alice leaned over to squeeze Isabel's arm.

"Wouldn't miss it, Alice; give you a good send-off; and don't forget I want plenty of pictures and updates. George has put a lot of work into this trip and it sounds marvellous, wish I was coming with you... maybe one day."

"Yes, he has even bought an iPad although he is going to ask Alistair how it works," they both tittered.

"I don't know why I am chuckling as I have an old fashioned desktop computer and I even have trouble with that, I am impressed with George, are you going to have a lesson too?"

"I think I'll leave it to him, I have my camera, much more reliable. You were telling me about Emma, is there more to know?" Alice tipped her head on one side in query.

"Only that she attends her church in Richmond and whenever she is in Trentmouth she always attends our church. I was thinking of suggesting to her that she becomes a church member when she has moved in with a view in the future to encourage her onto the PCC... what do you think, Alice?" Isabel searched Alice's face.

"That sounds like an admirable idea, we need younger people, I know she's not that young nearly sixty I understand but in comparison to some members and we could do with some new blood." She paused pursing her lips, *was going away such a good idea am I being replaced?* She thought. Isabel must have guessed what she was thinking.

"We could never do without you, Alice. You are the one person who kept things going when old Sykes was struggling and getting muddled," she assured her.

"Thank you, Isabel…" she sucked in her breath, "… now would you like a cup of tea before George returns," she collected their empty glasses before walking to the kitchen. She stood by the sink clutching the worktop her knuckles white with worry wondering if she was being side-lined for a younger woman and what she might miss. She chewed her lip, is it too late to cancel?

Chapter 17

Lucy sat in the Sisters' office turning her envelope over and over as she sat waiting for her. It had been a long and hard decision as midwifery was all she had ever wanted to do. Her decision had not been taken lightly and not just because she had lost her own baby either convincing herself that her dreams had changed. Her dreams had changed no doubt about that, she was married to a wonderful man who adored her and whom she loved deeply, making her tingle all over whenever he touched her. They had a new business nothing like she had ever imagined or knew anything about if she was honest and she wanted to keep a close eye on her mum and dad too. However, she knew that she would miss it very much; all those new babies and helping mums to feed their little bundles. It was a thrill every single time helping a new life into the world. A tear trickled down her cheek and she let it, it flowed for every baby she had delivered and everyone that had been lost too.

The door burst open and a flustered Sister Jane bustled in, "Now Lucy," she sounded exasperated, overworked and tired. She sat down behind her desk with a thump, "… are you sure about this, it's not too late to change your mind and God knows we need you. You are an exceptional midwife and will be sadly missed." she took a deep breath looking more closely at her "Oh, I'm so sorry Lucy, I didn't mean to upset you and we are all so sorry about your own miscarriage. That's not the reason that you want to leave us, is it?" Sister Jane grabbed a box of tissues pushing them in front of her, Lucy pulled one out sniffing.

"No. No, it's just that I have been trying to support my husband with his new venture, work full time and take care of my parents and I just can't do it all. I know women are supposed to be good at multi-tasking but I am exhausted and it's a myth; by the way, women being good at multi-tasking I mean," she sniffed again, "… I have thought about this over and over and I might be giving up this career but I am joining my husband in our new café called Bertie's down in Trentmouth and it is going very well." She drew herself up to her full height, "… and it is very exciting. I have loved being a midwife and working with you here at Poole and as I'm sure you realise the department being transferred to Bournemouth hasn't helped."

She breathed heavily and sniffed, "… It would take me over an hour to get there." She stood up, holding the envelope out to Sister Jane "Thank you again, and I hope all goes well in the move to Bournemouth." Defeated, Sister Jane stood taking the envelope from Lucy. They hugged a farewell and Lucy walked briskly out of the front entrance and into the nearest coffee shop.

She sat toying with her coffee, her mind wandering round and round. It wasn't that she didn't want to work with Bertie; she was looking forward to it in one way but the loss she felt at leaving the hospital hit her more than she had anticipated.

She had known nothing else for over ten years and had truly loved it. The truth was losing her baby had been devastating.

She could admit this to herself but not to anyone else. All of her plans disappeared including little things like decorating the small bedroom, buying a crib, wandering around all the baby care shops. She blamed herself. She should have told Bertie and Molly, she should have made allowances and slowed down, admitted she was tired and not tried to do it all like some superwoman. So many 'should-haves' it was her own fault that she had lost her baby. A tear escaped blurring her vision, she sniffed lost in her own world a shudder shot through her body and brought her back to reality. Lucy took a deep breath, downed her cold coffee and left the café for home.

She headed straight to the shop where Bertie was waiting arms open wide ready to snuggle her; she fell into them luxuriating in his love. Lucy sobbed and sobbed. Bertie held her head close to his chest and swayed her gently from side to side, no words necessary, just kissing the top of her head.

Eventually, Lucy pulled away from him saying "sorry, I'm so sorry, so, so, sorry.

Please forgive me?" She sobbed again, blew her nose and dabbed her eyes.

"There's nothing to forgive, it's not your fault. Are you sure you want to resign and work here with me? I know it's not what you wanted to do." He tucked a wayward curl behind her ear, lifted her chin his lips pressed oh so softly on hers. She responded lightly at first then more searching for his unconditional love and Bertie didn't let her down.

Eventually, he pulled away lifting her chin.

"Lucky the shop is closed, shall we continue this at home?" he grinned. Lucy grinned back as they left hand in hand.

The sun was setting as they lay in bed satiated. Bertie held her tightly caressing her arm with one finger tracing a languid pattern as goosebumps spread through her body. She reached up for a kiss, her body on fire for more. They entwined making love again; less eager this time, more sensual and almost casual in only that way that two people are who love each other so totally.

Lucy woke suddenly to the sound of Bertie in the shower. She was cold and reaching out to gain some warmth from the space where he had lain. In a moment of clarity, Lucy knew that Bertie was her rock. She made a promise never to leave him out again. To always tell him what was bothering her… always to include him in all of her plans. They were together… a family. A tear fought its way onto her cheek but she swiped it away. *No need for that,* she thought, springing out of bed to join Bertie in the shower. Mistake! She laughed.

Bertie cooked dinner as Lucy opened a bottle of wine and prepared a bowl of strawberries for dessert.

"I forgot to tell you Molly has invited us to dinner one night. She has lots of ideas for our café you know; different groups and themes? I couldn't stop her once she started, and of course, I had nowhere to jot them down, so as it's easier for us to go there I said yes." She bounced around with delight. Lucy realised that Bertie had fallen quiet; she looked up to see him grinning at her.

"Welcome back, I do love you… so much," he dropped the ladle onto the worktop encompassing her around the waist and zooming in for a kiss. "We could try again you know, I'm up for it if you are." She pushed him gently away.

"As wonderful as that sounds, no, I'm hungry and did you hear what I just said?"

"Every word..." he dropped his arms defeated and returned to his cooking. "... it will be fun. I want to talk to Alistair anyway, the sly dog. He has a new assistant and from what I hear she is a stunner."

Chapter 18

Suzanne hurried to the phone wondering who could be calling at this early hour, to her delight it was Freddie.

"I have some proposals that I want to share with you Suzanne and I was wondering about coming down this weekend, what do you say?" Suzanne knew that this was just another ruse as Freddie wanted to see Maggie. She didn't mind, of course; in fact, she was rather pleased. She wanted Freddie to settle down and she couldn't think of anyone better than Maggie.

"No problem except that Friday night I am going out to dinner with Gary…"

"… What again!" He sounded surprised and even a little disapproving. Suzanne, anxious not to snap back took a deep breath.

"Yes, actually, he is very nice, good company and all that," she hesitated and that was all Freddie needed to throw in his considered opinion.

"Are you sure about this? I remember when you were at the BEEB you thought that he was a chauvinist and didn't have a good word to say about him chasing all the girls and dropping them as soon as someone new arrived." Suzanne said nothing, Freddie pushed on, "… or am I mistaken and that was someone else? I'm only trying to look out for you; sorry Suzanne, have I overstepped the line?"

"I… yes, well he is the same, Gary. He is a charmer no doubt. He knows he is wasting his time if he thinks that I will just fall into his arms but…"

"He is still trying it on… why don't you cancel? As I am coming to stay it's a good excuse."

"No," snapped Suzanne. Immediately regretting her rudeness, "… sorry Freddie. I know you mean well but I want to have dinner with him and it's not a date and… I'm sure you will be taking Maggie out anyway so…" she left the rest unsaid, feeling a bit used by her own brother but also not wanting to admit to being left on her own… again.

"You're right I am the one who should apologise. I really do have some proposals to discuss with you so is Friday still okay?" he quizzed.

"Yes, of course, it is. I am being picked up at 7:00. Will you be here by then? That reminds me I will get another key cut for you before Friday. Then you can come and go as you, please." she could feel him smiling down the phone and was grateful to have such a caring brother. Time was when he hardly noticed her. They were teenagers then and when their parents were suddenly killed he took his responsibilities seriously looking after her, sometimes too well.

She put the phone down realising she had forgotten to ask him what proposals he was referring to and had no idea unless it was to do with Maggie. She grinned to herself hoping he was planning to propose. He did not need her permission she grinned but the thought filled her with delight at having a sister-in-law. She made a cup of tea and retired to her study.

The church fete had raised enough money to replace the church hall roof and maybe fix the rotten floor. She had calls to make to meet builders, arrange a home visit to an elderly parishioner, not Doris this time (thank heavens) and finally a sermon to write. Appointments made, sermon written and Axis who had lain at her feet became agitated, whining and nudging her knee with his nose. Suzanne looked at her watch, almost 5:00. She turned to Axis.

"Come on then Axis, good boy let's go for a walk. I know it's almost your dinner time." He jumped up turning in circles, getting very excited yelping and letting out little woofs. Suzanne retrieved his lead, grabbed her jacket and they set off down the lane. She turned the corner only to see Hugh sitting outside of the surgery head in his hands. She hesitated to ponder if she should turn around and find another walk. *That's silly, pull yourself together there is a parishioner in distress* she told herself pulling her vicar's hat on firmly, metaphorically speaking and strode over towards him.

"Hugh, what on earth is the matter? Is Emma okay?" she felt alarmed seeing his shoulders shaking and his face as red as a tomato. She rushed to sit by him on the bench wanting to take his hand but too afraid.

"Mum is fine. No, it's just that Rex is gone he passed away in his sleep. Bertie found him and now I have to tell Molly." He shook his head without dropping his hands, sniffing.

"That dog meant everything to Molly. She will be devastated. How am I going to tell her?"

He fell silent and so did Suzanne. She sat back looking up to the sky for inspiration. She had had to deal with bereaved families in the past and in many ways this was no different but somehow it was. Rex was of indeterminate age, Molly having taken him in when he had been cruelly abandoned. This was not going to be easy. Axis pulled on his lead anxious to be going Suzanne ruffled his coat knowing that she would be devastated too if anything happened to him.

"Well, I'm sorry Hugh but there is no easy way, I think maybe let Alistair know first then he can be ready to comfort her and maybe handle the children for a while. Oh, and take a box of tissues with you." She automatically leaned forward placing a hand on his arm, Hugh didn't move, she squeezed gently feeling a frisson of electricity shoot up her arm. She didn't move her hand stuck to his skin, absorbed at the moment.

"You're right that is a good idea. I don't normally get attached to the animals that come into the surgery but Rex was different." He sat up staring deep into her eyes. Suzanne couldn't move to want this moment to last forever. He looked down at her hand. She snatched it away, the heat of a blush creeping up her neck getting, hotter and hotter.

"Well, I must be going. I will leave you to call Alistair but if you want to talk you can always ring me… any time." She chewed her lip feeling decidedly self-conscious and made to move away.

"Thanks," called Hugh "Thanks again; I… I might just do that… if it's not too much trouble?"

"No, not at all. Right, I must be going. I… I'll pop in to see Molly tomorrow." She turned to walk down the lane feeling his eyes on her but she dared not turn around to check.

That gorgeous tingle still swirled through her body making her feel alive and sexy… yes, sexy.

Suzanne tentatively knocked on the barn door of Molly's home. She could hear all kinds of noises from inside; babies shouting, another squealing with joy, the radio competing to be heard. She stepped back staring up at the sign over the door proclaiming that this was the Madhouse. Maybe this wasn't the best time to visit. She made to leave just as the door opened. Molly stood there, her curly red hair tousled with one wayward strand hanging over her eyes and a smudge of what looked like porridge on her face. Suzanne stared briefly gobsmacked before clearing her throat and turning on her usual smile.

"Hi, Molly, is it convenient to come and see you? I can see that you are busy, I could come back another time?" Suzanne had fantasised about finding 'the one' settling down, having a brood of her own. Today however she had second thoughts, living alone does have its advantages.

"No, please Suzanne; come in and save me from myself," she forced a smile. Suzanne wasn't so sure she could do that but at least they could have a chat. Suzanne followed her into the chaos that purported to be the dining kitchen. There were empty food bowls on the table, milk spilt on the floor and what looked like cornflakes scattered around Jessica. Molly had one twin on her hip, Suzanne wasn't sure which one, carrying him around as he squirmed.

The other twin was laid on the floor on a play mat gurgling to himself. The phone rang and Molly burst into tears.

"Hey, hey give me the little one, you answer the phone," declared Suzanne dropping her bag onto the floor reaching out to take hold of the squirming bundle. Molly handed him over snatched a tissue from her pocket sniffing and picked up the phone. Suzanne did her best to shush the baby she could feel that he was wet and that had now transferred to her skirt.

"We could do with a crèche at the church on Sundays, or maybe even the church hall midweek," she told the baby who was now looking at her with his big eyes. He had a tuft of golden-red hair sticking up at all angles, food had dried onto his bib and he had that indefinable smell that only babies had. She cooed at him hoping that Molly wouldn't be too long because if he cried she was at a loss to know what to do next. It was a great relief when Molly returned to the kitchen.

"I'm so sorry Suzanne. I'll just put the kettle on. I could do with a strong coffee and from the look on your face I bet you could too?" She made to move over to the kettle, fear overtook Suzanne.

"Hmm… let me make the coffee. I think this little one needs changing and I'm no good at that sort of thing," she held out the soggy bottomed baby her eyes giving her away.

Molly chuckled.

"Right, this is Oliver by the way. He is the demanding one. Elliott will play for hours just looking at his toys." Molly quickly laid out the changing mat and set to work. There was a clatter as Jessica had decided that she had finished her cornflakes and her dish landed on the floor. "Oh, no," cried Molly, "… more mess. I could have done without this today."

Suzanne switched the kettle on deciding that she would stay single forever, wondering how Molly could possibly cope with three children, her job and looking after Alistair. She shook her head. All her dreams shattered in a few short minutes in the company of Molly and her brood.

Coffee made, she placed the mugs onto the table and sat down feeling exhausted just by being in the same room as this mayhem.

"Biscuit...?" asked Molly reaching up for a tall tin perched precariously on a high shelf. "I have to keep them out of reach of little fingers," she grinned glancing at Jessica. She pushed the tin towards Suzanne who gratefully looked inside to find dark chocolate covered digestives. *Heavenly* she gasped gratefully pulling out two.

"Thank you. I saw Hugh last night and he told me about Rex. I am so sorry Molly I know what he meant to you." Molly stared at her for a moment tears welling up threatening to take over her face. She quickly shook them away as she finished dressing Oliver in clean clothes.

"He was quite old, I knew that, so it wasn't entirely unexpected news but still a shock.

I would have liked to have been with him. I don't like to think of him dying alone. I loved that daft dog, I will miss him so much." She sipped her coffee staring into space, fixed on some past memory only she could see. "Bertie is happy for us to bury him up at the farm. It's where he has always lived and would be happiest," she choked back more tears. Suzanne placed a hand on her arm.

"Would you like me to come up to the farm with you all and say a few words?" Molly turned and looked at her aghast.

"Really, are you sure, I mean do you normally do that sort of thing for a dog?"

"Of course, Rex was one of God's creatures and I am happy to do it."

Later that evening Molly, Alistair, Bertie, Lucy and Hugh all stood around the grave that Bertie had dug earlier as

Suzanne said a prayer for Rex. Molly placed his favourite toy on top of the box where Rex had been placed wrapped in his own blanket that he used to drag around the house. They all stood patiently waiting for Molly. Molly sniffed.

Everyone was silent with their own thoughts before Bertie and Alistair began to shovel the earth. They covered the grave and placed a bone on top. Molly, with Lucy for support, headed into the farmhouse; Hugh walked with Suzanne. Everyone subdued, Alistair poured out wine for the girls and gave the boys a beer. He raised his bottle.

"To Rex," he took a drink as everyone else chorused.

"… To Rex."

Chapter 19

Friday arrived with a covering of low cloud and mist over the village of Trentmouth bringing with it a chill in the air. Suzanne stood at her bedroom window looking down the cobbled street to the sea beyond, hairbrush in hand staring at a lone yacht bobbing fiercely up and down on the churning waves. She turned back into her room saying a little prayer for the poor soul being tossed about in the bay.

She looked at herself in the mirror and glanced around her elegant room. For all its beauty and comfort, loneliness came creeping up onto her shoulder whispering in her ear; a shudder passed through her. Everywhere she looked there were couples, married or otherwise but couples in love, bringing up families, doing things together? Cold gripped her heart, fear her only friend. She sank onto the bed feeling a deep sadness wrapping itself around her.

Gary Braithwaite had been at the BEEB when she had walked in on her first day straight out of Uni. He was handsome, with dark hair and even darker eyes almost black they gave him a mysterious edge; one that was instantly mesmerising. Oh everyone warned her about him and to be fair despite his flirting, cajoling and persistence she had managed to avoid him, well, apart from once at the Christmas party but that was only a kiss. His kiss was delicious, intoxicating even leaving her wanting more but knew that that road led to disaster. The research department had been left littered with broken hearts and Suzanne was determined not to be one of them.

Dragging herself back to today and with her diary cram full with – nothing – Suzanne wandered down to the kitchen to make coffee, toast and marmalade. Axis watched her, his tongue slobbering around his mouth, his eyes not leaving her toast. A drip of marmalade slid landing with a plop onto the Victorian black and white tiled floor. Axis had launched himself and licked it up before Suzanne could even think of moving making her smile.

She rubbed his ears "What would I do without you?" she said as a picture of Rex flashed before her eyes. Axis cocked his head on one side letting out a muffled woof. "Come on then let's go for a walk." She collected his lead pushed a waterproof into her backpack, writing pad, pen and a bottle of water and headed for the door. It was still early everywhere quiet except for the gulls reeling overhead screeching and swooping on the breeze. She headed for her favourite walk onto the Jurassic coast path following the cliffs that led to a bench that must have been there for many years. Now covered in lichen it had a broken slat but was a welcome sight nonetheless. She sat down pulling out her bottle of water, wishing instead that she had brought a flask of coffee. Axis wandered around sniffing at every blade of grass to see who had been there before him. With her pad and pen in hand, Suzanne let her mind wander back to Gary Braithwaite.

Gary had been the first to ask her why she was leaving the good old BEEB and to become a vicar! He was completely thrown by her revelation and more than just a bit curious.

Everyone else had shied away from the topic eyeing her suspiciously in case she was about to try and convert them or something worse.

Her choice of career seemed at odds with her shining black toy she called Ruby.

Suzanne loved her motorbike preferring it as a mode of transport especially in the city of Bristol where every day the traffic was gridlocked and parking was beyond impossible, but with a bike, you could squeeze in anywhere, almost. She enjoyed the strange looks with unasked questions, furrowed brows and whispered conversations preferring to keep her private life – well, private.

After her parents died, Suzanne had taken to visiting churches, at first in the hope of feeling closer to them, gradually the quiet stillness enveloped her own soul and she began attending services. It had been during these visits that Suzanne had become aware of the feeling that she wanted to be a vicar too, that God was calling her to his service. Dismissing the idea as nonsense, she was too young surely? And it had always been her plan to take media studies and work for the BEEB.

It had been her secret, not even telling her brother Freddie. Going to university her mind never slipped away from the church, with her parents never too far away from her thoughts. Sometimes, in the quiet of the morning, her daydreams wandered back to the stillness of the church and the definite feeling that she was not alone.

Here she was nearly twenty-nine years old and still a virgin. How embarrassing. That was another reason not to get involved with Gary Braithwaite, he would push and push to get his own way and then she knew in her heart of hearts that he would follow his old pattern looking for some other poor innocent girl to chase and conquer. Besides she wanted to wait until she met 'the one' her love was precious and Gary was definitely only in love with himself.

Gazing at the skyline her thoughts turned again to her decision to become a vicar convincing herself that she was not running away from life and people but embracing both in the knowledge that she was doing what God wanted her to do – hopefully. So why was Gary interested in her?

She stuffed her pad back into her bag having not even drawn a doodle and turned towards the boiling sea watching yet more craft bounce about on the waves seemingly in danger of capsizing. "Come on Axis, time to go." Suzanne climbed over the stile and headed back to the village and Bertie's Café. It was warm and cosy inside, a lovely bubbly atmosphere full of chatter and friends. *I must be doing something wrong* she thought. *Why don't I have a church full like this?*

Coffee and sticky custard-filled Danish ordered Suzanne sat near the door so that Axis could see her. He was tied up outside and would whine constantly if she was out of sight.

Friday was actually her day off and the last thing she should be doing is thinking about the church but as she had nothing else to do till meeting Gary later, she allowed her thoughts to drift back to her parish.

George and Alice were due to leave on their big adventure in a month's time. Maggie was organising the send-off and without Alice, Suzanne would be devoting her time to organising the harvest festival and getting ready for Christmas. She must think of something else to raise funds too but what?

"Penny for them," a voice broke into her daydreams. Looking up she saw Gary standing there with a big grin on his face. "May I join you?" A smile spread through her erupting into a big grin.

"Of course but I wasn't expecting you till tonight did I get the time wrong?" shuffling in her seat feeling decidedly embarrassed quickly glancing around to see if anyone was watching her. Relief that there was no one taking any interest in her, helping to calm her nerves, gulping at her naivety she turned her attention back to Gary.

"I was in the area and thought that I would surprise you but when there was no one at home I decided to grab a quick coffee before my next appointment." He pulled out a chair making himself comfortable.

Gary was charm personified and it was easy to see why all the girls fell for him. He was good at his job too researching bringing new ideas for programmes and then setting them up. It was hard to say 'no' to him. His career was set for the top and he knew it. All that was missing as he had told her many times before was a family but he had not found the right woman yet for the job. This always made her laugh as it felt like she was being researched herself and interviewed for the 'job' but didn't have the heart to tell him. That was another reason why he was not suitable either she was not looking to be someone else's career appendage. However, for all that he was fun, attentive and charming.

"I want to talk to you about something tonight actually," he took her hand caressing it gently.

"Oh, not another one and what might that be?" colour rising up her throat stupid thoughts flashing before her eyes, of the romantic kind.

"… Another one do I have a rival for your affections?" He shot his eyes up at her looking forlorn.

"No, silly it's Freddie he is coming tonight for the weekend and wants to talk to me about something too." She pulled her hand away picking up her fork to break into the Danish that had been waiting for her attention.

"Freddie… that's alright then; so does that mean there will be no room for me to stop over tonight?"

Suzanne coughed and spluttered almost choking on her Danish. She grabbed a napkin and pressed it to her lips trying to draw breath, tears streaming down her cheeks as she tried not to choke.

"I'm sorry, so sorry, I'll get you a glass of water," he jumped up but Bertie was already heading in their direction holding a glass and a box of tissues.

"Are you alright Suzanne, here have a drink," he carefully placed the glass into her hand and she gratefully took it taking a sip. Her head was a jumbled mess, visions of… well visions and not happy ones at that but complicated ones. Did she get the 'job'? She wanted to laugh and cry settling for misunderstanding and clearing her throat instead. She nodded her thanks to Bertie and he retreated to deal with new customers.

Gary sat down again a concerned look on his face watching her closely as she regained her composure. "Was it something I said?" he queried without a trace of irony.

"A crumb…" she pointed to her throat, "… got stuck that's all," at the same time asking God for forgiveness; it was only a little white lie. She could hardly tell him the truth;

Gary that is, not God. He already knew.

Freddie arrived right on time carrying a large folder and sporting a big grin on his face changing her own mood instantly. They hugged each other, she missed him so much.

"I can't imagine what you have to tell me but it will have to wait until later or even tomorrow, Gary will be here any minute… that look gives you away if I am not mistaken."

She grinned at him as he sheepishly hopped about on her doorstep.

"Well, yes and no, yes I think you have guessed and no, that is not the only thing I wanted to talk to you about." He dropped his bag onto the floor, pulling a small box from his pocket he opened the lid "what do you think?" Suzanne took in a sharp breath of amazement.

"Oh, Freddie, it's gorgeous," a single solitary stunning square-cut diamond shone out from its hiding place "she will love it and I'm sure she will say yes," she threw her arms around him once more tears stung her eyes and for once she let them, adding to her resolve that this would be the last time she would be "on a date," with Gary Braithwaite.

Gary pulled onto the drive tooting his horn and waving in their direction.

"He's keen…" Freddie said, "… don't be fooled, sis. I've come across men like him many times, I'd hate for you to get hurt." He pulled her to him in a possessive hug of ownership.

"I won't. See you later." She disentangled herself from him, waved to Gary before kissing Freddie on the cheek and clambered into Gary's sports car. Gary had the top down making conversation difficult as the wind tore her words away so she settled for admiring the countryside as they sped along into Wareham and The Priory car park.

Suzanne loved The Priory. It had a wonderful old world charm and ambience, even the newly built restaurant didn't take away the feeling of luxury, of being spoilt and the food was superb. She slithered into her seat overlooking the extensive well-kept gardens and admired the view of the river. A yacht slipped silently by, a man was pulling in the sails and she could see a couple of girls relaxing at the stern with what looked like champagne.

"How wonderful not to have a care in the world," she remarked pointing towards the river.

"Pardon…" Gary turned to look in the direction of her gaze "oh, yes, I see what you mean. I intend to buy a boat but I fancy a Sunseeker… one with an engine." He added as an afterthought. Suzanne chuckled at his practicality. He was a show-off and would buy a boat for prestige, not a hobby. He definitely wasn't the kind to take a boat out to sea. He was more likely to potter around the harbour with a G&T.

"I have something important to ask you Suzanne," he fixed his eyes on her making her instantly uncomfortable. Opportunely the waiter arrived and poured out two glasses of ice-cold Chablis.

"Are you ready to order, sir, madam?" he asked politely, a crisp white napkin over his arm, a black waistcoat and tie with a snow-white shirt beneath. No straggly hair or dirty shoes here. Suzanne perused the menu once more, placing her order which gave her time to get her thoughts ready to hopefully get her out of the mess she suddenly found herself in.

"I've been meaning to ask you something too Gary, it's just that I wondered what would entice you to come to church? I mean, I have been given this task of building up the congregation and well apart from the usual things, which everyone expects, I need new ideas.

So what do you think?" as she finally paused to breathe. He stared at her with a baffled look on his face. This made Suzanne smile having beaten him to it in the "I have something to ask you stakes," derailing him completely.

Gary sat back in his chair, eyes wide and slowly his lips quivered before he could keep a straight face leaving Suzanne suddenly disadvantaged, a frown replacing her smile.

This only seemed to make matters worse as Gary let out a belly laugh causing other diners to turn and stare in their direction the quiet ambience shattered.

"Gary," she hissed, "stop laughing, it's not funny," but Gary couldn't, there were even tears trundling down his face. He wiped them away with his napkin. Suzanne turned to the other guests mouthing 'sorry' before turning back to Gary who was now wiping his face with his napkin.

"… Err everything alright Sir?" asked the mystified waiter bowing slightly at poor Gary, who was desperately trying to regain his carefully cultivated composure.

"… Perfectly thank you. I'm sorry but well… never mind. Thanks again," the waiter retired quickly returning with a jug of water topped with wedges of lemon and ice cubes bobbing as he poured a glass for Gary. "Thanks," he whispered drawing a deep breath and regaining his voice.

"Suzanne, you are wonderful and I have missed you so much," he gasped, his face wreathed in smiles.

This was not the reaction she had expected and it totally threw her into a spin. Her mind whirred with possibilities. She prayed he was not going to ask what she didn't want to hear. "I... I don't know what was so funny, if you think my new career is a waste of my time then you are wrong. I love my new job. My life has been a whirlwind since I made my decision and I have never been happier." She crossed her fingers under the table. Their starter arrived and she wasn't sure if she could eat anything with the lump now blocking her throat.

"Come on, let's eat and I will tell you what was so funny," smiled Gary now that he had stopped laughing and had regained his composure. "I am sorry too as you looked like a startled rabbit sensing danger. You are so cute you know."

"Thank you, I think." She picked up her knife and fork and somehow managed to eat.

It was a delicious goat's cheese and beetroot salad with honey glazed walnuts; her favourite.

Gary topped up her glass but not his own 'driving' he mumbled. Suzanne wanted to ask him where he was going to stay tonight, but she dared not. Dinner over having covered every topic other than herself, the church and the "something important to ask you," and Suzanne having exhausted all the scenarios in her limited book of knowledge they retired to the lounge. The waiter having delivered a large pot of coffee and a plate with tiny squares of homemade shortbread finally relaxed gaining the courage to ask the question that had been burning her brain cells to a frazzle.

"So... what is it that is so important to ask me? Bringing me here and not letting me share the bill. I know how expensive it is... and..." Gary stirred his coffee.

"Right, number one it is on expenses so forget the bill. Secondly, you are a complete mystery to me Suzanne. Every time we meet I think that I have a handle on you and then you throw in a curve ball to knock me sideways again." He grinned at her "so here it is…" Suzanne braced herself having still not found the right words to let him down lightly. "I have had an idea for a new show and it involves you." He took a moment sipping his coffee becoming serious looking at her over the lip of his coffee cup. "It is twofold, one we would like you to become involved with our morning slot on the radio 'Pause for thought'. The second is much more complicated and partly answers your question to me, which I thought was hilarious by the way. You'll understand in a minute." Terrifying thoughts spun around in her brain, yes she had worked for the BEEB behind the scenes but never on air that was completely terrifying.

"This is the proposition, we would like to do a six-part series about the life of a rural church and the community but… and this is what makes it so exciting is the fact that you are so young and are female, a beautiful woman at that, you know the sort of thing. The church has always been dominated by men and often stuffy old men but the world has changed and we want to show that change," he paused, "… are you with me so far?"

"I'm… I'm astounded, I don't know what to say… the Bishop would probably have to approve and…"

"Already approved, that was my appointment this morning after I left you at the café."

"Well, I suppose it is a 'yes' then I think, I'm terrified actually. I can't believe it…"

She sucked in her breath, smiled and for the first time her heartbeat slowed to a more sensible speed.

"It would take a year to film as we want to incorporate all the seasons and ups and downs of the church and community you know the sort of thing?" they continued to talk until the waiter gave a polite cough by the door and asked if there was anything else they required.

She glanced at her watch it was late and they probably wanted to close. She couldn't wait to get home and tell Freddie all about it, relieved she wouldn't be on the end of a second marriage proposal in one night.

Chapter 20

News of the engagement between Freddie and Maggie quickly spread around the village.

Suzanne wanted to hold a celebration at the vicarage, but in the end, it was decided that the manor would be more suitable and Suzanne was thrilled to be gaining a sister even if she was technically a sister-in-law. Lady Isabel couldn't be happier, she liked Freddie very much and thought that they made the most perfect couple. He had been a constant visitor especially now that he was doing all the designs for the alterations to the house and grounds ready for it to become, hopefully, a premier wedding venue.

The morning of the official celebration arrived and Isabel decided to keep out of the way by doing some weeding in the borders at the front of the house. A task that she did not need to do but one she enjoyed. She had on her old 'working' dungarees, wellington boots and an old straw hat that would look tatty on a scarecrow. She was on her knees when she heard a crunching sound on the gravel behind her, turning and shielding her eyes from the brilliant sunshine she could see a gentleman looking lost. He was about her age, smartly dressed, thinning a little but still had plenty of rich nut-brown hair. He smiled at her and Isabel stood up pulling off her thick rubber gardening gloves.

"Can I help you? You look lost," she enquired raising an eyebrow and wiping her hands on her trousers.

"I'm just having a wander around thank you; I'm waiting for my daughter. She is discussing her wedding with… hmm," he looked skyward searching for a name.

"Maggie… I expect she is talking to Ms Chapman, she organises weddings here."

Isabel studied him a little closer. He was indeed only in his fifties. He looked to be in good shape, no excess around his middle, quite tall (about six foot at a guess), a good looking man, clean-shaven. She could smell his aftershave, citrus if she wasn't mistaken. "Are your wife and daughter making all the plans?" she embarrassingly enquired, a question she thought crass when anyone else asked such things of a gentleman. She swallowed and turned her head so that hopefully he wouldn't see her red face.

"Sadly no, she passed away two years ago after a long illness. It's just me and Daisy now." He drew a deep breath, "… soon just me."

"Oh, I am so sorry, Mr… hmm," she fumbled her words feeling guilty for prying.

"So sorry, it's Montgomery, Alec Montgomery everyone calls me Monty." He held out his hand and Isabel shook it apologising for them being grubby.

"It's a lovely place here, isn't it? As soon as Daisy heard it was now a wedding venue she set her heart on it and whatever my little girl wants she can have. Oh I know I spoil her, everyone says so but I don't care." He looked around again admiring the garden. It was in full bloom now, the air sweet with the scent of roses and the honeysuckle that was hanging heavy from the trellis. Grapes were swelling to perfection; bees were busy in and out of every flower until they swayed drunkenly, heavily laden with pollen.

"Yes, it is beautiful, especially at this time of year. When is your daughter planning to marry, is it soon?" asked Isabel searching to continue the conversation with this handsome man. Feeling intrigued it was more than a little disconcerting that her feelings were thrown into disarray.

"Next year, Daisy wanted to see what dates they have, probably in the summer. Have you worked here long?" His question threw Isabel into turmoil as she knew he didn't recognise her which was unsurprising in her gardening attire so she decided to deflect his question.

"Would you like a cup of tea or coffee whilst you are waiting for Daisy?"

"Tea please that would be lovely thank you," he made himself comfortable on the nearest bench giving Isabel the chance to dash into the house to make sure that she did not have any soil smudged on her cheek and to comb her hair. Isabel had no intention of deceiving 'Monty'. She felt attracted to him but had learnt from experience that many men saw her as an opportunity to get their hands on Trentmouth Manor. If he thought that she was the gardener then so be it. She returned with two mugs of tea and a plate of biscuits deciding that it was wiser than serving her usual earl grey in China cups and saucers.

"Thank you, just what I needed." He took a mug and a custard cream, leaning back with the sun on his face. He pulled at his tie and turned to Isabel. "Daisy's idea, the tie I mean, she said I couldn't come up here without a tie in case we bumped into the Lady of the Manor." Isabel tried so hard to disguise her smile, a little chuckle escaped as she replied.

"I'm sure it doesn't matter either way. What do you do, for a living I mean? I guess you don't wear a tie to work." She drank her tea endeavouring to be nonchalant.

"Well, actually I own a building firm, Montgomery Construction. I expect you haven't heard of us. We build new houses, remodelling, conservation work even hard landscaping anything related to buildings really and no I don't wear a tie at work no one does these days."

Just then a young couple came into view, a girl who Isabel presumed to be Daisy from the distinctive colour of her hair which was so like her father's, called out.

"Dad, there you are; it's fabulous; I'm so happy; I can't wait to tell you all about it."

"Right let's go and celebrate." He turned to Isabel, "Thank you so much for the tea and the company, hmm… I didn't catch your name," he looked at her expectantly.

"Izzie… just call me Izzie."

"Well, Izzie may I take you for coffee one day? I hear there's a lovely new café down by the sea; to return the compliment, of course."

"That would be lovely, thank you." He shook her hand holding it just a little longer than was necessary and turned to leave. Isabel watched them go; Daisy hanging onto his arm, her fiancée trundling along behind like a spare part.

Isabel sat for a long time contemplating her little deception but then it was unlikely that she would see him again. She finished her tea and returned to the house. It was time to get ready for tonight's party.

The air was soft and warm as the guests began to arrive, the Manor resplendent in bunting, balloons and fairy lights. Maggie had worked hard. She had insisted on overseeing all the work herself and it was magnificent as usual. There were many people she knew.

Suzanne with Gary, Molly and Alistair, Lucy and Bertie, Hugh and Felicity together with many she didn't know including friends of Freddie's from Oxford and some of Maggie's friends too. She was pleased that Alice and George had been invited and wondered who was looking after the grandchildren. Alice cornered her.

"I wish we could postpone our holiday Isabel what with this television thing, Suzanne will be out of her depth and I should be here to guide her. What will the Bishop think if I'm not here?" She looked quite forlorn causing Isabel to smile inwardly.

"Everything will be fine Alice. They are not filming till December in the church and before then they are doing some provisional work around the area to give a background view of the parish and Suzanne. So you must go and have your holiday, it will be wonderful, and of course, you will be back for all the Christmas events. You won't really miss anything at all."

"No, I suppose not," she admitted reluctantly, "… and if I'm honest there is always something happening, you are right, of course." She let out a small sigh tutting to herself.

"Still it's a marvellous evening and we are thrilled for Freddie and Maggie. They make a lovely couple. Any idea when the wedding will be? I do hope I won't miss it." Isabel found her friend quite amusing, she would miss her too.

"I have no idea about the wedding Alice, probably next year. They haven't said a word about it and there is so much to do before then. I'm sure they will let us know in due course. I must circulate but please enjoy some food and a drink. Bertie has done us proud as usual." Isabel moved away carefully noting that George had joined Alice carrying two drinks and guiding her towards a table.

Isabel nodded and joined in with various conversations feeling rather lonely with no one to confide in or to share her thoughts. She missed Rufus so much. They had never had children although she would dearly have loved one or two. Maggie was her sister's child who had come to live with her when her mother had tragically died giving birth to her second child. Her father soon found himself another wife with no room for Maggie and so it was that Isabel had willingly accepted Maggie and brought her up.

She wandered over to talk to Suzanne. "Freddie looks incredibly happy don't you think?"

"Yes, I have never seen him like this before it suits him. Maggie suits him…" she trailed off.

"I must come and talk to you about this whole television thing Suzanne. I need to know all the implications. It's very exciting I think." She noticed Gary talking to Felicity remarking, "… is Gary your… hmm… I don't know how to put it, your boyfriend, Suzanne?"

Suzanne shot her head around looking intensely flustered.

"Good heavens no, I used to work with him and it was his idea this 'fly on the wall', documentary but no nothing like that. I just thought that it would be a good opportunity for him to meet some villagers." She turned to observe Gary before continuing "that's a good idea actually Isabel, give me a call and we can get together next week sometime." Isabel felt a little tired herself after her busy day gardening, thoughts of Monty flashed into her head. How amusing that he thought she was the gardener. She had to admit he did give her a warm feeling, she liked him, and after all, she wasn't too old to meet someone new. She collected some food joining Molly and Lucy.

"Bertie has excelled again Lucy, the food is excellent. I wonder if he would be up for more outside catering." She bit into a tiny crumpet topped with cream cheese, an olive and a little red flower.

"Oh, he loves it, and now with me working with him full time, he has become quite creative. I'm sure he would be interested. I will ask him to call you if you wish."

"Yes, great. I was wondering what you both thought about Gary Braithwaite and his idea of putting little Trentmouth under scrutiny for the next twelve months?" They discussed the whole matter at length and Isabel found it very enlightening to hear someone else's point of view. Both Molly and Lucy thought it marvellous and it would hopefully bring business to the village like Doc Martin did to Port Isaac. The front doorbell chimed and Isabel excused herself to go and answer it assuming it to be more guests. She opened the door.

"Jeremy?" she declared in surprise.

"Yes, Aunt Isabel, I know I'm late for Cousin Maggie's little 'do' but I'm here now.

"Which room will I be staying in?" he smirked, a very unpleasant smirk making Isabel feel decidedly ill. She had not seen Jeremy for a number of years. He hadn't even bothered to turn up for dear Rufus' funeral and now here he was expecting to stay. She flustered but dare not be rude with the house full of guests, and of course, she knew Jeremy was not above causing a scene. She would just have to put up with him tonight.

Jeremy was a thin, slightly built boy well a man now at... she couldn't remember his age but he had to be nearly forty, never married. He did not look anything like his own father but rather more like his mother, with her pointed nose and beady eyes. Isabel shuddered. She showed him up to a guest room where he left his bag and followed her into the drawing room.

"Ah there's Maggie with Freddie I presume," he took a glass of bubbly from the tray of a passing waitress and headed in their direction. Isabel followed. Jeremy was always one to make an entrance and never passed up the opportunity to cause a scene. He had the habit of speaking very loudly in a manner more suited to a bull ring.

"Congrats and all that," he shook hands with Freddie "Maggie get me some food, will you? I've had a long drive, and I'm rather hungry." He glugged a large mouthful of champagne, "... and some more of this..." he said thrusting the glass in her direction.

Isabel seethed at his presumption catching Maggie as she passed by.

"That little twerp has no manners, who does he think he is? Sorry, Maggie but we will have to humour him for the sake of the guests tonight. I will get rid of him as soon as possible in the morning."

"I'm sorry I invited him now I had forgotten how horrid he could be... but he is family... and I never expected him to actually turn up," she moved away to collect some food.

Isabel hovered nearby doing her best to keep a close eye on him, feeling wretched when this should have been a celebration.

"I'm Jeremy Fitzroy de Holland," he announced to Freddie as if Freddie should know who he was, "… work in the city. I hear you are a little provincial architect working for someone else in Oxford, how low key for you but never mind we can't all be successful." He never missed a beat despite the incredulous look on Freddie's face. "Lord Rufus, the dear boy, was my dad's brother. He died without any children you know, and of course, being male naturally, I'm next in line to inherit all of this," he announced waving his arm extravagantly around the room.

Chapter 21

Molly wasn't at all surprised the next morning when her iPhone pinged with so many texts.

No one it seems could talk about anything else other than the engagement party except Alice who normally knew all the gossip, she was surprisingly tight-lipped. Molly couldn't help but laugh when Lucy invited her to the café for coffee and a chat, more gossip she grinned only too happy to join in.

It was a glorious day. She had finally managed to feed, wash and clothe three children and wander down the village to the café. She was even more grateful to find an empty table under a sun umbrella. Molly sat down heavily, exhausted from another round of 'domestic bliss'. Lucy came out to greet her carrying two lattes and two slices of lavender cake, Bertie's latest successful flavour. They kissed each other with Lucy making lots of coos and aahs at the three little ones.

"What do you make of all that last night?" she delved without preamble taking a bite of purple iced cake and looking at Molly expectantly.

"You know..." said Molly between mouthfuls, "... actually this is delicious, Stella will want the recipe!" they both chuckled, "... I feel sorry for Lady Isabel that Jeremy fellow was very rude walking in there as if he owned the place." She blew on her coffee before taking a sip and peering at Lucy.

"Perhaps he does… I certainly hope not but he seemed to think he did. I wonder what will happen now. It's funny how we have never heard of him before. Oh look here is Suzanne I wonder what she can tell us," Lucy signalled for Suzanne and Axis to join them then disappeared to collect another latte and cake.

"Good morning, ladies," Suzanne said in a less than cheerful voice, she quickly brightened when the coffee arrived, "… before you ask I don't know any more than you do," putting an end to that topic. That rather left them without any form of conversation for a few minutes instead indulging themselves in the new cake sensation and feeling rather embarrassed with each other. Finally, Lucy peered over her shoulder saying "we are getting busy and Bertie needs some help, it was nice to see you both I'll catch up later," leaving Molly and Suzanne to overcome the icy silence.

"Sorry, Suzanne, and I know you don't want to talk about it but…" she paused fixing her eyes on Suzanne giving her a chance to jump in and when she didn't Molly continued "it's just that people always come to you with a problem and you always listen, I just wanted you to know that I can be just as discreet and am happy to listen to you… if you ever want to talk that is."

Molly searched her worried face for a moment wondering if Suzanne would confide in her or be blasé and push her own worries aside. Suzanne stirred her coffee taking in a deep breath.

"Thank you, Molly; you are very kind. It would be good to have a chat sometime but not today Freddie and Maggie are coming for lunch and I need to take Axis for his walk." She stood as if to confirm her decision, forcing a smile onto her face although Molly could see tears were welling up in her eyes.

"Don't forget Suzanne, everyone needs a friend," and with that, Suzanne strolled away down the cobbled lane towards the sea a bouncing Axis by her side.

Molly turned her attention back to her own three little needs squirming in their pushchair; unable to shake from her mind Suzanne, Freddie, Maggie, Lady Isabel and the very pompous Jeremy. She pondered what all this could mean not only for her dear friends but the wider issues for the village; Isabel's plans for Trentmouth Manor, the implications went on and on. Despite the lovely day, she shuddered at the very thought of Jeremy Fitzroy de Holland becoming the Lord of the Manor.

Lady Isabel sat in the kitchen trying to enjoy her breakfast mulling over the happenings of the previous evening. Poor Maggie and Freddie had retreated to Maggie's cottage before the evening was over, their celebration ruined by her nephew. She had never liked him, even when he was a small boy he was always snivelling and whining when he didn't get his own way and despite the fact that he was her husband's family she had avoided him as much as possible. Images of past events floated up to her conscious mind replaying themselves of the many ruined family gatherings due to Jeremy. He would turn an innocent game of tennis into a battleground if he didn't win, he would throw his food onto the floor even hitting his own mother telling her she was 'stupid'. Isabel shook herself to wash the horrible images away resolving to put an end to this monster and his little game.

She picked up her pen to make some notes, first on the list to make an appointment with her solicitor followed by her bank. She scribbled down questions, dreams, plans and possibilities all to be resolved as quickly as possible. She froze, pen in mid-air as she heard footsteps in the hall quickly pushing her notebook into her pocket.

"Are… there you are Aunt Isabel why aren't you in the dining room and where is my breakfast?" She loathed him, no, loathed and detested him, the sooner he was out of her home the better. She forced an insincere chuckle from her lips.

"Good morning Jeremy we make our own breakfast here. I don't have a cook and servants, this isn't the middle ages you know." This time her smile was sincere as she saw the look of horror on his face. "If you open that cupboard over there, you will find everything you need and the fridge is that large cream coloured box next to it." She knew she was being over the top but couldn't help herself, this was fun. He recovered his composure and sat down.

"I have decided to take a walk around the house and grounds today before I head off back to London. I want to see what shape the old place is in, see what needs doing, give you a list of repairs that sort of thing. Oh and I think I will get some breakfast from that little café down by the sea." He didn't wait for a reply just glanced at Isabel and retreated outside.

She didn't know whether to be relieved that he had gone or annoyed with herself for not putting him in his place. She had never felt this lonely since Rufus had died how she longed to talk this whole thing over with him to seek his advice. She had Maggie of course to talk to but this was one thing she was going to have to deal with by herself. She took her coffee out onto the terrace trying to relax and not to let Jeremy rile her. She surveyed her garden admiring her attempts at weeding just as Monty popped into her mind, a gentle thrill stirring her, bringing a warm smile to her lips. She liked Monty; he had old fashioned manners, a gentleman, he thought she was the gardener and was polite to her, even asked her out for coffee one day. She had kept his card and began to wonder if she could be brave enough to give him a call. Maybe she mused, maybe not.

All too soon Jeremy returned from his trip amongst the locals looking rather too smug. Causing Isabel to speculate on the impression he may have given to the villagers.

Despair mingled with loathing she decided that she would never ask. He strutted across the lawn looking for the entire world as if he were measuring up the surroundings to suit his taste. Isabel merely smiled at the audacity of the man and waited.

"I have made some calls and will be returning in a few weeks with my architect from the city who is much more used to this type of specialist building. I'm rather surprised you didn't ask for my advice before. However, that maybe, we'll soon get this place fit for…" he hesitated ever so slightly and Lady Isabel cast a glance in his direction, "… hmm, organised. I'll call you, must dash," and with that, he was gone much to Isabel's relief.

Chapter 22

Hugh struggled to carry the last of his mum Emma's possessions into her new home. She had sold as much as possible having decided that a new home meant new furniture, new china, new just about everything for her new life. Hugh was beginning to wonder if he should have encouraged her to move to Dorset after all, too late now she was here and if he was honest he was rather pleased although he would keep that little nugget to himself.

It was lunchtime, the removal men having travelled down the day before were packing up ready for the long journey back to Richmond, and Emma had stayed with Alice and George. Molly was looking after the surgery this morning and he would have to get back soon.

"Do you have time to join me for lunch at Bertie's Hugh? I'm rather hungry and tired," she smiled as she picked up her handbag and keys. Hugh, having only had a slice of toast that morning, was starving and readily agreed.

Emma turned the key standing back to admire her new home. It was the little thatched cottage she had always dreamed of, a home in the country, near the sea. The front garden was filled with sunflowers; yellow scented roses climbed their way around the door hanging their heavily laden heads, bees were happily buzzing in and out of every bloom. She let out the sigh of someone content with life.

"I can't decide what to call my cottage I thought of Sunflower cottage or Rose cottage but neither seems right what do you think Hugh?" She asked her head on one side staring up at the little windows nestled into the thatch.

Hugh stared at it for a moment, "… Well looking at those windows covered in cobwebs I would say that Cobwebs would be a better name." They both chuckled as they set off towards Bertie's café just a few minutes' walk away.

"Emma!" Cried Bertie walking around the counter arms outstretched to engulf her in a hug, "… moved in safely today? What can I get you? On the house of course by means of a welcome." He let her go turning to Hugh shaking his hand. Emma had been delighted to accept the offer from Bertie to work for him full time and she couldn't wait to get started.

Bertie moved to a table pulling out a chair for her and Hugh moved to sit opposite.

"Actually, Bertie we are hoping to get some lunch. What special do you have today?"

She looked up at him and he pulled on his chin as if to be considering the question.

"I will surprise you but while you wait can I tempt you with my homemade lemonade?"

"Lovely, thank you, Bertie," Bertie disappeared as Emma turned to Hugh, "… now Hugh."

"Oh, dear, that sounds ominous Mum. What have I done or not done this time?" he teased.

"Nothing dear I just want you to bring me up to date with Felicity and any other goings-on that I should be aware of, working in a café you get to know everything and I don't like surprises, so fill me in."

Hugh considered his reply. In truth, he didn't really know anything of the "goings-on," better to ask Alice in his opinion and knowing his mum she had probably already done that.

Her true question he felt was about Felicity. What could he tell her? Well nothing, there was no him and Felicity. She was very, very nice, they were friends and that was about it.

"Well… goings-on? I really have no idea, Mum, something happened up at the manor at Maggie and Freddie's engagement 'do'. I'm not sure exactly, a nephew or someone talking loudly, a bit of a show-off I thought… You will have to ask someone else for details, not me I'm afraid. And as for Felicity, she is the kindest, sweetest person but…"

"She's not for you? I get it, so anyone else?" she threw him a cheeky grin as she picked up her lemonade just as Bertie arrived with their lunch leaving Hugh grateful that he did not have to answer his mother's question.

"I'm not staying for dessert Mum I need to get back for Molly but thank you for the lunch. I'll see you later." He bent to kiss her on the cheek, waved bye to Bertie and dashed out of the café half jogging back up to the surgery relieved to escape the inquisition.

"I'm sorry Molly…" he gasped, "… couldn't get away from Mum." He pulled deeply to draw in breath. Molly was amused.

"You should go running with Bertie… get your six packs back…" grinning at him as she ran a finger around her waistband, "… anyway everything is good here I prescribed worming tablets, stitched a cut oh and I think we need to restock our cat food because we have had quite a run on it this morning… and I've been asked for wild bird seed!" Hugh was sitting watching her, he couldn't help but admire her and how she managed to work with him; three children and a home were beyond him.

"I just might speak to Bertie about that but I am not up to his standard. Actually, if you are not rushing home do you have time to sit and have a coffee with me?" he raised an eyebrow.

"Sure…" she glanced at her watch "hmm half an hour do you?"

"Perfect."

They sat outside in the shade. It had been another glorious day with more people than usual visiting the cove, the car park was often full and today was no exception. Hugh sat patting his stomach.

"That was a delicious lunch Mum and I had at Bertie's but I should not have tried to run back… it's something Mum said that I wanted to talk to you about."

"Oh, yes? I can't imagine what that is, she only arrived this morning," she mused.

"I know but she wants to get up to speed with 'all the goings-on' around here and well, I'll be honest Molly I have no idea." He threw his hands up in a hopeless manner, "… so have I missed anything?" he turned to look at her with a helpless smirk on his face.

Molly burst out laughing.

"… And you're asking me? Why not try Alice or Felicity? By the way, how are things with Felicity?"

"Questions, questions you sound like my mum." He let out a sigh, "the thing is she is…" he found himself retelling the same story for the second time that day. There must be something he is missing here, "… and at the party last week she spent more time talking to Gary what's his name than to me."

"Did you mind? I mean you don't look too unhappy about it."

"No, I don't suppose I do; she did tell me that he was interested in seeing the beehives and might be able to use them as background in the trailer for the show. I mean what a line," he rolled his eyes skyward and chuckled. "And another thing, what was all that noise from that nephew? I couldn't understand what was going on and then the party seemed to wind down a bit."

"Hmm well, I'm not too sure myself but he seemed to be indicating that he would be taking over the manor, poor Isabel, I wonder what is going to happen next?"

Chapter 23

Alice packed and repacked her cases. Despite having bought new matching cases for their trip, the limit on weight meant that she couldn't take half of what she wanted to take and had to remove some of George's things to make room. She flopped down onto her bed staring at the mess. It was no good, she would have to start again and include George's things. Heaven knew he was taking precious little anyway, saying he didn't need all the things she had laid out for him. Alice smiled to herself excited at the trip ahead and the secret she had been keeping from George. It had taken some organising, but with the help of Isabel and Maggie, she was convinced that she could pull it off and that George didn't have a clue. The telephone rang.

"Hello, Molly, how are you, dear?"

"I was just checking that everything was okay for tonight and that George is still in the dark."

"Yes, dear, he knows we are going to Isabel's but he thinks it's just for a few send-off drinks as it were. It is getting exciting now. Although, if I may confide in you I am so limited on what I can take; I am worried about clean underwear and things like that." Molly let out a chuckle.

"Don't worry Alice, cruise ships have launderettes and so do hotels these days or at least the facility to do laundry for you. Just pack the bare necessities as you will need to save room for the things you want to bring back too."

"I never thought of that, I'm so glad I asked you, dear; see you tonight."

The evening was one of those balmy nights where all is quiet except for the cooing of wood pigeons, the cackle of the crows mixed with the occasional song of a blackbird. Alice picked up her wrap as they left the house to drive up to the manor.

"So it's just a few drinks with Alistair and Molly, is it? Only we could have done that at home instead of getting dressed up. I am rather warm, dear, in this collar and tie."

"It was very good of Isabel to offer; she didn't want me left with any clearing up to do when we are off tomorrow," nicely side-stepping the question of other guests.

They pulled up in front of the manor and parked next to Alistair's car, everyone had been asked to park by the stables out of sight. It was indeed a beautiful evening, red and gold streaking the sky with the promise of another lovely day tomorrow.

The door opened as they approached and Isabel greeted them.

"Come in, come in…" they all kissed and hugged "come through to the drawing room I have G&T lined up for you, Alice and beer George?"

"Lovely. But just one as I will have to drive later." They followed Isabel down the hall towards the drawing room. "It's awfully quiet I was expecting Alistair to come and meet us."

Isabel turned the brass knob on the heavy oak door. The late evening sun dazzled them and then there was a shout.

"Surprise..." everyone called at once completely stunning George. Isabel smiled, thrilled that they had pulled it off. Everyone mingled around them, all their friends and family together including Suzanne, Gary, Felicity and Hugh. George stared at the throng in disbelief, he shook his head over and over again, tutting and asking how everyone had been able to keep the secret for so long but Alice smiled till her face hurt.

Drinks flowed freely leaving George feeling anxious about his car saying "Alice dear I won't be able to drive. I have already had three drinks."

"Don't worry dear it's all arranged Alistair has promised to retrieve it for you and place it securely into the garage whilst we are away."

"I cornered Bertie about the garden earlier too asking how he might cope with the café, security duties at the house and the garden and he said..."

"Ahh, I think you need to talk to Alice about that there has been a change of plan so what is this 'change of plan' that I know nothing about?"

"That is your second surprise. Come along and talk with Freddie, it's all going smoothly I have been dying to tell you and I nearly did the other day." She took his arm gently pulling him towards Freddie and Maggie. "I had the idea at the church fete and asked Freddie to consider it and well he said 'yes' so... Freddie do talk to George about our little arrangement," George looked even more puzzled.

"Well, George, I was telling Alice here that I wanted to set up my own business in Trentmouth I want to get established before the wedding, anyway my problem was finding accommodation as I lived in the flat above the office in Oxford; so Alice suggested that to help us both out I could live at your house whilst you are away in exchange for looking after the garden and of course keeping everything secure, together with Alistair, of course." He paused to look at George's face. Alice watched him pull on his bottom lip which he always did when he was mulling things over.

"Excellent news," he put out his hand and shook Freddie's vigorously. "What a great idea Freddie. Thank you so much for stepping in like this." He tucked his arm around Freddie's pulling him to one side, "… now come and sit down and tell me more about this new business venture of yours."

Alice sighed with relief turning to join the girls thronging around Maggie, however, out of the corner of her eye she saw Gary chatting to Felicity so she did a detour in their direction.

"Gary…" she trilled, "… nice to see you again. I must talk to you about this little film of yours, I'm sure you are here on a fact-finding mission but as I will be away for the next three months I think that I ought to talk to you now. I'm chairman of the PCC, so naturally, you would want to liaise with me… might you have a few minutes now?" she fluttered her eyes expectantly.

"I need to speak to Hugh," excused Felicity and left them to it.

"Lovely girl," said Alice as she saw Gary watching her walk away.

"Yes, she is… her dad has bees you know and she sells the honey for him at fetes and craft shows." He let out the breath he had been holding turning his attention to Alice. Alice logged the little scene for later when she could revisit it and inspect it for its implications.

Such a pity we are going away she thought.

"Yes, Mrs Warren; you wanted to talk to me?"

"Well, yes, I just wanted to know your plans regarding the church and village. We will be back in December so I hope that won't cause you too much of a problem."

Gary quickly filled her in on the forthcoming plans. His main focus is Suzanne and her decision to become a vicar as she is so young and the difficulties she has faced; that sort of thing. And then of course he wanted to do some background on the village and its response to a female vicar as well as an overall view of village life.

"I can help you with most of that information Gary. I was wondering could you possibly delay everything until our return as you will need me to assist you with all of that naturally."

"Please don't worry Mrs Warren I have been speaking to Lady Isobel and everything is under control, so you go and enjoy your holiday and we will see you on your return. Now I have a few people I need to speak to, enjoy your evening." He bowed slightly and moved away.

Alice felt put out. She should be the one liaising with television people. She looked around to find George, he was still talking to Freddie. Felicity popped into her mind and she wondered if her radar was off as she had thought that Felicity was with Hugh and Gary with Suzanne, ah she spied Suzanne and headed in her direction.

"I'm so sorry to be leaving you in the lurch Suzanne. I was just talking to Gary explaining my position in the church and that I should be the one he needs to talk to." She paused for breath Suzanne caught her before she could continue.

"Please Alice do not worry. I would hate your holiday to be ruined, I promise that we will do our best to cope without you and run all the details past you on your return," she smiled at her.

"Oh, I suppose so my dear, George has bought himself one of those iPad things so you can still contact us if you need any help or advice. Now, changing the subject I wanted to ask you about Gary, you are a couple, aren't you? Only I have noticed that he has been paying quite a bit of attention to young Felicity and I thought that she was... hmm friendly with Hugh," she waited for a response.

"Oh, that is wonderful news Alice, we are not a couple and I would love to see him and Felicity get together and I don't think that she and Hugh were ever really a couple."

She must have seen the look of surprise on Alice's face as she continued, "... didn't you know, Alice?" Suzanne threw her a cheeky smile as she disappeared to find Freddie.

Sitting with their cocoa at home later that evening, Alice sat quietly contemplating everything she had learned as George was busy bringing her up to date with Freddie's plans.

"You know that tumbledown old fisherman's place by the quay?"

"What dear I missed that bit," she looked at him over the top of her steamed up glasses her forehead furrowed with concern.

"What is it my dear you look upset?" he asked her.

"Oh, nothing, it will keep; tell me about Freddie."

"Yes, well, he is going to turn that old place into his studio and what a marvellous view he will have too, you know I like him very much he reminds me of myself when I was his age full of ambition... Alice... you're crying," he pushed himself out of his chair and placed an arm around her, "… tell me what's wrong?"

Chapter 24

Alistair arrived home pushing the door open with his bum, his arms otherwise occupied carrying a heavy box. Molly ran to help him.

"What on earth do you have there and please tell me, did they actually get on board that cruise liner? I half expected you to be bringing them home again." She took some smaller items from the top of the box as Alistair manoeuvred it onto the kitchen table with a huff.

"Looks like the contents of Alice's fridge in here, did she not think that Freddie could use them?"

"Apparently not and yes it was touch and go but Dad would not have cancelled this trip it was on his bucket list and Mum could hardly argue now could she?" He picked some grapes from the bunch poking them out of the bag, popping them into his mouth. He pulled out a packet of chocolate biscuits.

"Fancy a coffee? I didn't have time to stop at the terminal, only just had time to drop them off, Mum insisted on hugging me as if they were emigrating forever." He laughed.

"She thinks that she will be missing out on the entire goings-on around here, I'm not sure what she thinks will be happening apart from Gary and the TV people, of course. I meant to ask you last night but how do you feel about Freddie living at theirs while they are away?"

She poured out the coffee and they sat at the kitchen table munching through the packet of biscuits.

"Saves me a job and Bertie but I will still pop over from time to time to make sure Freddie hasn't set up a commune," they both chuckled at the thought. Alistair pulled out yet another biscuit.

"We will have to have a get together when they return for Jessica's birthday and our anniversary too, two years old already," she sighed gazing into the distance.

"The boat hasn't sailed yet," he glanced at his watch, "… so can we wait till after 5:00 tonight before we celebrate our freedom and plan for their return… please?" he pleaded.

"…Anyway I must go." He turned to grab his jacket, kissed Molly and left the house.

Everything was suddenly quiet. Jess was at toddlers, the boys asleep and Molly wondered what she could do for this precious hour that she had to herself. She needn't have worried as she heard a gentle tap on the front door. Maggie and Suzanne were standing there.

Molly opened her eyes wide at this unexpected visit, her mouth momentarily dropped open before she quickly recovered opening the door wide in greeting.

"Come in, come in please, I was just going to put the kettle on. George and Alice are safe aboard the cruise ship, Alistair has left for the office and I am gratefully enjoying some 'me time'. Coffee alright for you?" she threw over her shoulder.

"Yes, lovely," they said in unison. Molly couldn't imagine why they were here, it felt like a deputation, she searched her brain but nothing came.

"We wanted to talk to you and you did say anytime Molly," Suzanne spoke for the two of them.

"Yes. Yes, I did but I am not sure how I can help?" She picked up the tray having put the last few chocolate biscuits onto a plate and carried it into the sitting room, the girls followed. They sat down opposite Molly making pleasant conversation about the weather for the cruise and the events at the party the night before.

"So... how can I help you?" Molly raised her eyebrows trying to bring the conversation around to what they wanted to speak to her about. Suzanne and Maggie looked at each other.

"Well..." stumbled Suzanne, "... there are a number of things so if I list them perhaps we can talk about them one by one?" She reached into her bag for a pad and pen.

"This looks ominous and I really don't know why you have come to me. I don't know anything about anything," she attempted a stilted chuckle. They ignored her protestations.

"So..." Suzanne drew in her breath "Firstly, Freddie has some ideas about that piece of land next to the church hall and we thought that you might know its history. Secondly, as you know Freddie is starting up on his own and converting a wreck of a place down by the quay and thirdly..." she turned to Maggie, "... you can ask Molly about that."

Molly turned her attention to Maggie, who had so far been keeping quiet, allowing Suzanne to be the spokesperson for them both finding her morning more and more intriguing.

"Do you have any more coffee please, Molly? I'm finding this rather difficult..." she raised her cup Molly obliged by refilling the coffee pot, ever more confused and wondering what terrible event could have happened to elicit this deputation.

"Right, now come on Maggie out with it? My imagination is running riot."

"At our engagement party my cousin Jeremy turned up, he is a frightful bore, it's my own fault for inviting him but I never in a million years expected him to say what he did.

Aunt Izzie has been worried sick ever since and so am I and Freddie too. We just don't know what to do. I could be homeless…" she pulled out a tissue and blew her nose. "Aunt Isabel has been like a mother to me I have lived here most of my life, there's my job too ever since I left university I have worked for Isabel. We have so many plans…" she stumbled over her words getting more and more anxious, "… anyway, enough of that. What I really wanted to tell you is that Freddie and I have decided to bring our wedding forward as we want it to be at the Manor before it's… too late," she sobbed.

Molly pulled out a box of tissues handing them to Maggie, a million no trillion thoughts buzzing around her brain. "So… let me get this straight… you think that this Jeremy could kick you and Isabel out of your home? And take over the Manor and everything that goes with it! Surely not… I… I can't believe it," she swallowed hard trying to absorb this devastating information; her head pounding with more and more scenarios, none of them good. "I can see why you would want to bring your wedding forward Maggie but I am still trying to understand why Jeremy would be taking over at all…" She sat back in her seat still confused at this information and what it had to do with her.

"I think we all need a drink… and I don't mean another coffee." She pulled out a bottle of Alistair's good brandy putting a glug in the coffee of Maggie and Suzanne with the merest splash in her own. "Sooo… first things first, when are you thinking of getting married? Not next week I hope." She grinned in an effort to lighten the mood, "… I can't help wondering where you will live and Isabel too… I'm just flabbergasted by the whole thing."

"We haven't thought that far yet, Isabel is seeing her solicitor this week and we will take it from there but as far as the wedding is concerned then no not that quick." Maggie tried a smile "no, Christmas, this Christmas and what I wanted to ask you is would you be willing to be my wedding planner and matron of honour? I'd love you to help me with everything and we would love Jessica to be a bridesmaid or flower girl too she is so sweet."

Molly was speechless she could not believe what she was hearing. There was so much to take in and of everything that Maggie could have possibly asked this was the last thing on the list. It was not even on the list of possibilities. Molly stared at her not knowing what to say. She swallowed hard stumbling over her words.

"I, well yes are you sure I mean don't you have other friends or family why me?" she flustered trying to get to grips with what Maggie was actually asking her.

"You are the only one I can trust as we are keeping it a secret for as long as possible, we don't want Jeremy finding out."

"I can understand that and it's lucky that Alice is away then…" they all burst out laughing breaking the tension that had surrounded them.

Molly got up reaching for the calendar, pad and pen of her own. "My turn to make notes so what date do you have in mind?"

"Hmm Christmas Day actually, is that alright with you? I mean we could change it as it will be busy for Suzanne too but what do you think Molly is it doable?" She fiddled with a tissue. Molly could see the anxiety on her face. She had had lots of plans herself for that day now that Jessica was growing up and more able to understand and Alice and George would be back too.

"Oh, what the hell… yes, yes, yes," she jumped up to hug Maggie and Suzanne a billion thoughts now flying around her brain. "There is one thing…"

"Oh, dear; what's that?"

"Will Bertie be catering? If he is then I can confide in Lucy, two heads are better than one and all that and Stella for your wedding cake?" She waited with bated breath as she knew she would not be able to pull this off on her own, especially with the twins to cope with on top of everything else.

"Oh, of course, but I haven't asked them yet. I wanted to make sure you were on board with it all first so after I have seen them perhaps we can all meet up and thrash out a few details."

"Great, I hardly dare ask you what your two items are Suzanne. I don't know if I can handle anything else. Tell you what, as it's nearly lunchtime how do you fancy a glass of Prosecco I always have one ice cold in the fridge."

"Lovely."

They sat down again after the obligatory toast to the bride and groom and Suzanne picked up her notebook. Molly copied her in expectation, wedding thoughts still vying for first place in her mind. She had pictures of holly, ivy and mistletoe, red and green bunting, candles and... the sound of Suzanne talking cut into her thoughts and she dragged herself back to listen to Suzanne.

"Freddie and I have been looking at that piece of derelict land by the church hall. It is an eyesore full of rubbish and overgrown with a great crop of brambles and nettles. Anyway, searching the records it would appear that it was donated by a Mr Earnshaw for church use.

The problem is we don't know who Mr Earnshaw is or was and there are no designated or defined uses attached to it, simply for Church use." She paused hoping for enlightenment.

"I know exactly who Mr Earnshaw was, he died many years ago and you know his widow very well. I'm sorry to tell you but Mrs Earnshaw is Doris, the very same lady who left the church in disgust at a female vicar."

"Oh, dear, oh, dear... oh, dear," Maggie and Molly burst out laughing at the look on Suzanne's face.

"It's not that bad Suzanne; tell me what your ideas are. I can't promise anything but let's see if they could work." Suzanne had forced a stilted laugh not convincing Molly one little bit.

"We badly need a car park for the hall so that would use some of it and if we are allowed to I thought of selling about half to a developer to build small bungalows for the elderly of the village and also a playground for the children." She drew breath looking from one to the other before continuing, "... the money we would get from the sale would then build the car park and do an awful lot of refurbishment to the church hall… What do you think?"

Suzanne gave them both a pleading look.

Molly trawled through her thoughts. She could see the sense in what Suzanne was saying, the village urgently needed housing for the elderly and a playground for the children would be wonderful. Even the car parking drew her approval. Finally, she turned her attention to Suzanne who sat quietly waiting, pen poised.

"The way I see it you are going to have to be very careful with Doris, she might just object to be awkward. She can be a wily old bird. I think that your ideas are brilliant and would be a great asset to the village just what we need. However, I think that first things first you need to talk to Humphrey Bradwood in Wareham. He's our family solicitor, to make sure of the exact wording in the bequest, to confirm that you can sell half of it just in case the wording is ambiguous."

"Right, good idea," Suzanne quickly made notes as Molly was talking.

Molly glanced at her watch "I'm sorry but I am going to have to collect Jessica and I need to wake the boys…" Suzanne jumped in.

"You go and if you like we can stay here with the boys till you get back. It's a shame to wake them up and then we can arrange another meeting, I am so grateful for your help, Molly."

Molly grabbed her jacket and dashed out of the house grateful to Suzanne and Maggie. She turned her thoughts back to Suzanne's proposal feeling excited. She had other ideas for the land too like a permanent home for the church fete. They could have the hall open in case of rain and it had toilets. She envisaged allotments, a park bench – ooh this could be so good for the village as well as the church. She collected Jessica still buzzing with ideas, that land had been an eyesore for years not to mention a health hazard, goodness only knows what may be lurking in the undergrowth she shuddered.

Plans made for a progress report, Suzanne and Maggie left after Molly had assured them that she could deal with twin boys and Jessica, their lunch and her own even though in some ways she would have welcomed the help. The afternoon passed in a whirl of excitement Molly couldn't tell anyone about the possible changes coming to the village or that she had been asked to be not only Matron of Honour but a wedding planner too. She took the children out for a walk in the direction of the village hall in order to refresh her mind about the size of the land, the state it was in and the condition of the village hall.

It was indeed a sorry sight, far worse than she had remembered. She realised that in the thousands of times she had driven past the hall she had never really taken any notice of it after all it was none of her concern, was it? Now, however, she felt differently. It had become a possible asset, in fact, she told herself she would make sure it was a concern of hers and do everything in her power to make this idea happen.

Chapter 25

Isabel sat in her study pouring over her notes. She had visited Mr Bradwood and he had been very specific with regard to her situation. He had checked the will that Rufus had drawn up, been through her finances with her and suggested a way forward. She looked up at the sound of a car coming up the drive, moving to the window to see who it was. She was expecting Freddie but could see someone else beside him she didn't recognise. It was a man and she recalled Freddie telling her that he might bring an experienced conservation developer with him to look at her plans. She darted into the hall closet to check on her appearance. Then waited for Freddie to rap on the front door before opening it with a smile.

"Hello, Freddie. Oh, Monty!" she stood staring stunned at the sight of Monty on her doorstep. "I... I... hello..." she put out her hand to shake his feeling a warm flush rise up her neck her other hand immediately feeling for her pearls, she twisted them momentarily before recovering her manners. "Please, please come in won't you," she led the way towards the drawing room trying to come up with something, anything plausible.

"I didn't realise that you two knew each other," Freddie stuttered "that makes things easier, doesn't it?" He glanced from one to the other, Isabel hoping he didn't notice the red flush now creeping up towards her face.

"Actually, Freddie we only met a couple of weeks ago when Monty brought his daughter Daisy to see Maggie about arranging her wedding. I was in the garden doing some weeding and I allowed Monty here to think that I was the gardener. I'm sorry Monty I do hope that you can forgive me?" She turned one of her most gracious smiles in his direction.

"Not at all, Lady Isobel I am the one who presumed you were the gardener and I had hoped to bump into you again today to remind you of our coffee date." They both chuckled leaving poor Freddie wondering what was going on.

"Firstly, as I said before you must call me Izzie and would you both like a cup of tea?"

She retreated to the kitchen but not before she heard the buzz of conversation from the drawing room with Freddie asking what had just happened. She left them for five minutes preparing the tea tray and composing herself, she felt quite pleased that it was Monty who had appeared on her doorstep and rather than complicating things it actually made them easier.

Freddie proceeded to explain the alterations to the house to Monty in order to turn the house into a wedding venue. There was to be a covered walkway between the house and the Chapel, an open-air venue for those warm, balmy days, a champagne reception room, restoration of the orangery and several rooms to be turned into luxurious en-suite bedrooms with four-poster beds and boutique bathrooms and the ballroom floor needed to be repaired and polished. They chattered pondering over the changes until they were both happy ensuring that Isabel approved.

"One thing I also thought of was the catering facilities. The main kitchen is big and old and I wonder if you have any suggestions about that as I am sure that there must be regulations regarding Health and Safety and so on."

"Good point Isabel, I will look into it. We may have to do some more redesigning to accommodate either an upgrade or establish a new smaller kitchen for your use or maybe both. I was looking at the old butlers' pantry that would probably make an excellent new kitchen for your personal use." Freddie looked up hopefully.

Isabel beamed "Excellent idea, it hasn't been used for many years except for storage I think that that could work very well. Come and sit down have your tea as I have something else I need to discuss with you both." They followed her to the sofas where Isabel had laid out the tea and fruit cake. She poured the tea indicating for them to help themselves to the cake she took a deep breath.

"At the end of the drive is a rather neglected Gate House, the gardener used to live there years ago and it has become rather dilapidated. I wonder if you could take a look at it before you leave as I would like to turn it into a very comfortable cottage with everything modern and up-to-date. I think that it would make a delightful self-catering cottage for two. A romantic retreat, what do you think Freddie?"

"Well, we will take a look and report back, I do like the idea, I will have to do some costing with Monty here and see if it is feasible for you."

They collected the keys to the Gate House and wandered down the drive deep in conversation. Isabel watched them admiring Monty for not embarrassing her, the perfect gentleman. She smiled wondering what it would be like to see him socially and more importantly, the thought crossed her mind if it indeed would be ethical as he would be doing all the work on the house. She didn't care what people might think she mused mischievously.

Half an hour later they were back enthused by the challenge before them on the conversion of the Gate House. They explained that it was not as bad as first thought and that it would make a superb romantic idyll for two. Freddie was anxious to get started on the drawings and Monty promised an idea as to the cost as soon as Freddie had the drawings and specifications for him.

As Monty stored away his notes and drawings he turned to Isabel "May I call you to arrange to take you out for that coffee I promised?"

A delicate smile spread across her face, she couldn't hide her delight "Of course, I shall look forward to it." With that, they left leaving Isabel to muse over the best decision she had ever made.

Chapter 26

Maggie popped in to see Molly just as she was trying to feed Elliott with Oliver hollering in the background waiting for his lunch. Molly was hot and flustered, who said that twins were easy to look after? Someone who never had twins probably, she groaned. Whoever you fed first the other would complain and she had tried and failed to feed them both together. When they weren't hungry, they were adorable, they were the image of their daddy but with her hair colouring. If she dressed them, the same other people couldn't tell them apart not even Alistair! Molly thought that was highly amusing.

"Oh, Molly, can I help? I'm not sure how but I will have a try or I could put the kettle on if you like?" Maggie for the first time since Molly had known her looked out of her depth and Molly would love a cup of coffee but opted for Maggie giving Oliver a cuddle instead.

Oliver was placated at least for a few precious minutes so that Molly could change Elliott and organise lunch for Oliver. They were both on some solids now but still mainly on milk and as Molly had not had enough milk for two she had resorted to bottle feeding in between as well.

"Thanks, Maggie; you're a lifesaver and you can put the kettle on now if you don't mind."

"No problem," she disappeared into the kitchen and Molly could hear cupboards opening and closing deciding to leave her to it, she would find what she needed. All was peaceful when she came back carrying a tray of coffee and biscuits. Oliver had fallen asleep he lay on the rug gently blowing contented little puffs and pops, Elliott fed and changed gave them a display of the biggest yawn imaginable before his eyes too began to fall. Peace reigned.

"I am so ready for this cup of coffee, Maggie; thank you for stepping in and helping," she took a deep sip closing her eyes and letting out a contented sigh of her own.

"Actually, I came to talk about the wedding if you're not too tired, Molly?" Molly's eyes shot open. She had almost nodded asleep herself forgetting that Maggie was there.

"Sorry, Maggie; of course, have you had a chance to talk to Bertie and Lucy yet?" She sat up attentively.

"Yes, everything is go from them; I need to talk to Freddie regarding the wedding reception, I know it's Christmas day but I didn't want a traditional Christmas dinner you know turkey and all that, Bertie said he would come up with some options for us to consider and I was wondering if you could now talk to your sister Stella about the cake and… you can go ahead and talk to Lucy too, she is dying to discuss it with you," she chuckled. "Oh, and I have warned them about total secrecy."

"Great, let me get my notes and we can see where we are at." Molly retrieved her notebook and settled down once more, "… I don't know about you Maggie but I haven't had my lunch yet, how about I make us some cheese and tomato sandwiches? Then we can get into the details." She looked hopefully at Maggie her stomach grumbling from lack of sustenance.

They sat at the kitchen table with sandwiches, crisps, chocolate cake and elderflower press poring over the details. Molly had written down flowers, photographer, wedding favours, colour scheme, cars or horse-drawn carriage, lighting, table decorations not forgetting the most important thing of all, the wedding gown. They chatted around each topic with no definite decisions feeling that they ought to include Freddie and possibly Bertie except for Maggie's dress. This, they decided had to be a girls' day out with a spa and total pampering.

At that moment, Molly missed Alice and her baby-sitting duties and wondered where in the world they were. The girl's day out would have to be a Saturday when she could persuade Alistair to take charge of his three children, bringing fear and pleasure to her at the same time.

Maggie left after arranging another meeting this time at her cottage one evening, she would cook and they could all chill out at least that was the plan. Molly was elated and fearful in equal measure, she had not realised until she began to sit down and take notes what a mammoth undertaking this wedding planning business was, thinking that it would be a doddle. Doddle, it was not.

She stared at the calendar with dismay, only fifteen weeks to the big day, Alice and George would be home in eleven weeks and filming started next week. *Help!* She thought recalculating the weeks to make sure she had not made a mistake. What a lot to do in so little time. She must get organised, thankfully she only helped Hugh occasionally now that he had bought her out of the veterinary practice at least that was one thing less to worry about.

Thinking of Hugh reminded her of her commitment to Suzanne and the church hall and land.

There was only one thing for it; she took out her laptop it was time to get this show on the road.

First on the agenda, a meeting with Suzanne as soon as possible, they had decided to form a committee to look at the church hall and land. It had been a good idea at the time and Molly felt enthused to be part of the team. They needed to consider who else should be on the committee, not an easy task as it was difficult to get volunteers for anything; so had decided to ask individuals as people may be more willing if asked personally.

She worked all afternoon writing a schedule including a timescale for all the different items on her now considerable agenda; culminating with the wedding but not forgetting a birthday party for Jessica and a welcome home for Alice and George too. Feeling satisfied she looked at her watch, time to collect Jessica and she could hear one of the boys grizzling in his cot.

"You're never going to be able to do all that..." this was Alistair's viewpoint when she filled him in later, "... not that I'm saying you couldn't manage it," he added when Molly had turned a stony look in his direction. "What I mean is you need a team around you, people who you can delegate to, you know and then there are the children to take care of... are you sure you are doing the right thing?" The hole he was digging was getting bigger.

"Of course I'm sure... come on Elliott open wide... I am excited about it all and daunted but... I am sure that it will be fun. That's it Elliott yum, yum." Food dribbled out of his mouth as fast as Molly could scoop it up and push it back in. He screwed up his face spitting it out once more. She gave up with that and turned to some mashed banana and custard, something she knew he would eat and cry for more.

Later that evening with all three bathed, and in bed, Molly picked up her phone to call Lucy.

"Hey, how are you?" she asked when Lucy connected.

"Fine, we were just going to sit down it has been a very busy day, the café is doing well with more and more customers every day. Actually, I'm pleased that you phoned as I need to speak to you too. Do you fancy coming over or would you prefer us to come to you?" she paused.

"Lucy that would be great, can you come over to us as I have them all fast asleep finally, there is so much we need to discuss and I'm dying to find out what you want to ask me too. Can I have a clue?"

"Nice try Molly, no you will have to wait. See you in twenty minutes okay?" She put the phone down dashing upstairs to the bathroom she felt like the wreck of the Hesperus with food stuck in her hair and her old scruffy mummy trousers on. Fifteen minutes later she reappeared into the sitting room to find that Alistair had lit the wood burner, laid out a bottle of wine and glasses.

"Wow, you look gorgeous!" He slipped his arms around her waist pulling her to him.

"We could cancel Bertie and Lucy and go upstairs." He began to nibble her lip increasing his kisses. She pushed him away gently.

"That will have to wait, they will be here any minute," feelings stirred within her, wondering if she had made the right decision tonight? There was always later she grinned.

They all settled in front of the now crackling and warming fire, Molly sighed with contentment as Alistair poured the wine; gentle piano music playing in the background, one of her favourite soothing and relaxing CDs.

"Do we have to make a plan tonight?" quizzed Lucy "I could just snuggle up and nod off it's so warm and cosy here." A yawn escaped quickly followed by another from Molly.

"Stop it, Lucy; you will have us all nodding off and we urgently need to talk. Do you know how little time we have to achieve everything on my list?" Molly struggled to pick up her laptop placing it onto the coffee table "I'm not even sure where to begin, any ideas?"

Alistair poured the wine placing bowls of nibbles onto the table too.

"Right, before we get started a toast first to your new career?" a twinkle in her eye at Molly.

"… My new career?" Molly was puzzled.

"… Village campaigner, wedding planner for starters," laughed Lucy.

"… And you don't escape Lucy, entrepreneur co-business owner, caterer and let me think… wedding consultant," they both started with fits of giggles.

"Maybe you're right we should leave it to another day but hey, I nearly forgot you wanted to ask or speak to me about something too. Oh come on, what is it?"

Lucy and Bertie looked at each other shyly.

"I'm pregnant," Bertie squeezed her hand, and for a split second, Molly was dumbfounded before she burst with excitement jumping up to hug her friend.

"Congratulations both of you," they kissed each other and Alistair shook Bertie's hand.

"Tell me more, have you had it confirmed yet, when is your scan, when is it due? I'm so excited for you. Hang on, should you be drinking any wine?" Molly said breathlessly.

"Slow down, yes it's confirmed, no date for my first scan yet and my baby will probably be due in March and I am allowed a small glass of wine occasionally." All thoughts of planning Maggie and Freddie's wedding vanished as baby talk took over.

Chapter 27

Molly delivered Jessica to her toddler's group and pushed the twin buggy up to the vicarage.

She had come armed with toys, nappies, clean clothes, expressed milk; baby wipes and even a clean top for herself in case of any accidents! She hoped that they both might fall asleep giving them chance to discuss the church hall together with all the other issues attached to it.

The walk up to the vicarage was just long enough for the boys to start yawning and it wasn't long before they nodded off peacefully to sleep. Molly felt relieved as she pushed the pram around the side of the house as Suzanne had suggested and left the pram in a sheltered corner by the open French windows where they could easily keep an eye on the sleeping babies.

Suzanne had coffee and chocolate croissants waiting. Molly felt extremely grateful as she sat down picking up her coffee.

"I see you have an agenda," remarked Molly between mouthfuls "where shall we start?"

Suzanne cast an eye over at the still sleeping babies as she picked up her trusty notebook "Right, I think we should call ourselves 'The church hall and land action group' rather than committee as many people are put off when you use the word committee what do you think?"

"I like it and I agree about the word committee but it's a bit long as we will be encompassing much more than just the hall and land as the land will have possible uses way beyond the church why not call it, let me think,... hmm... what about simply 'Trentmouth Action Group' or TAG for short because I can see wider implications and not only that many more people might be willing to get involved especially as the secret is out about the TV people filming here." Molly waited for a response.

Suzanne broke into a huge smile "Molly you're a genius. I love it 'The Trentmouth Action Group' has been born. Let me make another pot of coffee and we can start in earnest."

"Thanks, great idea." Molly checked the little ones as Suzanne went into the kitchen, they were fast asleep. She gratefully flopped back down into her chair wishing she could nod off herself.

Coffee made, they set to work.

"I have been thinking about the people who we should ask onto the committee, I mean action group as well as asking for volunteers and I wondered what you thought of Hugh..."

Molly smiled inwardly to herself knowing how Suzanne felt about Hugh, "... also Lady Isabel, Alice when she is home of course and Bertie would be good but, he is so busy now he might not be able to spare the time, Freddie as he is the architect, even Felicity as she is the local school teacher..." she paused for a response from Molly.

"Yes, to all of those, at least let's try them first and I also think that we should ask Doris... her husband did donate the land and it just might be a prudent move to get her on our side."

"Oh... yes I see what you mean... it's just that she can be so cantankerous, but never mind we will cope, yes I agree."

She appeared to be downcast at the suggestion of Doris, hardly surprising as Doris had only given her the cold shoulder and sharp shrift. She brightened quickly saying, "... and what do you think about speaking to Gary? He may want to film us and our progress. I'm sure that the thought of being on TV might encourage one or two more volunteers." Molly couldn't help but agree however contrived the plan may be.

"So, before we can approach anyone to join the action group, we need to set out our objectives, where the money may come from and what we expect our members to do."

"Wow Molly, I'm so glad that I asked you first. I'm out of my depth already... hmm do you think that I could ask you to be Chairman or Chairwoman or even just Chair! Which actually sounds quite silly, what do you think?" Suzanne clearly had not handled anything like this before and come to think about it neither had she, but with more experience in business, Molly accepted the post of Madam Chair.

The boys stirred and Molly went to check on them, they had a habit of waking each other up, but after a little gentle rocking of the pram, they fell fast asleep once more. Molly picked up her iPad.

"Firstly we need to check on the exact wording with regard to the land to ensure that we comply with the donators wishes, not forgetting Doris. She may have other ideas and we mustn't upset her." Molly paused glancing at Suzanne's distressed look. "I can see that you are not very keen on getting Doris involved Suzanne, so I am more than happy to accompany you to visit her. I think that would be better than asking Doris to come here as she may refuse without even knowing why."

"Yes, you are right. I am not much of a vicar if I can't even face an elderly woman, sometimes I wonder if I've done the right thing…" she picked up her coffee swirling the dregs, "… this is cold would you like some fresh?"

"Please…" Molly watched as Suzanne headed for the kitchen her shoulders down feeling sad for her. Suzanne didn't have anyone other than her brother Freddie to confide in, in times of difficulty and although Sandra wasn't much of a mother she had Alistair, Lucy, her sister Stella even Alice to talk to. As much as she liked Freddie talking to your brother was not the same as having a good girlie chat with a group of close friends. Suzanne came back with the coffee still looking despondent. Molly took a deep breath.

"Suzanne, I hope you don't mind me saying but I think that you are just the right person as vicar for this village, old Reverend Sykes had lost interest and did almost nothing he did not try to get new members or even try to keep the old ones. To be honest he let the place go to rack and ruin; you only have to look at the church hall and that piece of land to know that even the vicarage was neglected. Yes, you might have a mammoth task in front of you but you are not on your own, so come on pour that coffee it won't be too long before I have to go and take care of these two," she grinned turning to check on the boys once more.

"So agenda organised, campaign at the ready now all we need is for you to telephone Doris and ask if you can come and see her…" Molly knew that this was the hardest hurdle for Suzanne but the sooner she did it everything else would not only be easier but she felt sure would automatically fall into place. "Suzanne…?"

"Yes, of course, you go I can do it later." Molly hesitated to know that she really should push her to do it now. She pulled out her diary knowing that it was empty making noises as she looked at it turning the pages back and forth.

"Hmm well I could fit it in tomorrow around 11:00…" she skipped another couple of pages, "… or … hmm it's looking tough and we really ought not to waste any time on this project, hmm why not call her now then we can get this show on the road?"

"Right, if you're sure I'll… I'll do it now then." Poor Suzanne was visibly shaking.

Molly wished she could do it for her but it was one job Suzanne had to do; once she had conquered Doris life would be so much easier. She sat listening as Suzanne picked up her phone.

"Hello, Doris, it's Suzanne here… from the church…" Molly grinned as she filled in the missing blanks Doris would not be giving her an easy time of it, "… I want to talk to you about the land next to the church hall… you know the land that is full of rubbish and overgrown…"

More hums from Suzanne as she tried to jump in several times "yes, I know that Doris and yes I know that too, but that's what I want to talk to you about… yes, tomorrow about 11:00… if… if that's convenient… right yes of course I will bring some cake and a pint of milk. See you in the morning," she turned to look at Molly her face white 'Phew, hurdle one' then she began to chuckle and before long they were both laughing.

Chapter 28

Suzanne took Axis for his walk early the next morning partly to clear her throbbing headache and partly so that she could spend some time in quiet contemplation for the day ahead. She often found that walking with Axis gave her much needed solitude where she could practice mindfulness and the sea air always seemed to bolster her mood.

On her way back through the village, she called in at Bertie's grateful that the breakfast rush had gone as she needed a few minutes downtime. She tied up Axis and opened the door, that lovely tinkling of the bell never failed to lift her spirits, a smile spread across her face.

"Morning, Lucy, Bertie can I have a latte please extra hot and… let me see I will have three cherry muffins to take away and a lemon Danish to eat in… oh and can I buy a pint of milk from you too?" sounding as if it was a forlorn hope, the last thing she wanted to do was to drive to Wareham for a pint of milk.

"Ah you must be visiting Doris, am I right?" Bertie glanced at her over his shoulder as he made her latte.

"Yes, how did you know?"

"That wily old bird gets everyone to bring her cakes and a pint of milk so we keep a stock in now just for her," he grinned.

"Oh, she is wily, she knows exactly what buttons to press and I suppose everyone does exactly as she asks too."

"Yep they do…" he chuckled as he handed over her coffee.

"I'll join you if I may, Suzanne?" smiled Lucy "I could do with a sit down we have been very busy this morning," Lucy made herself a coffee and followed Suzanne to her table by the window. "Have you spoken to Molly recently?"

"As a matter of fact I have she came to see me yesterday, why do you ask?" Suzanne cut her Danish pastry into quarters picking up a small piece.

"I… I mean we have some news and I wasn't sure if Molly may have already told you?"

"No, I don't think so; what news do you have for me?"

"I'm pregnant…" she waited blushing slightly. Suzanne put her coffee down turning to hug her.

"Congratulations both of you what wonderful news, do you know when and is it a boy or a girl?"

"We decided we didn't want to know till he or she was born and our baby is due in March," she glowed, and Suzanne was truly thrilled for them even if a little envious. They chatted about babies as they drank their coffee and all too soon Suzanne knew she had to leave.

She walked back through the village to the vicarage as she wanted to change into her dog collar making the visit to Doris more formal. Her feet were heavy with trepidation courage failing fast *Thank heavens for Molly,* she thought.

Moments later Molly was standing on her doorstep, twins in tow and looking tired.

She hesitated to say, "… if it's too much for you today Molly we can always make it another day, I can call Doris as, if you don't mind me saying, you do look tired."

Molly pinched her cheeks "Oh, Suzanne, this is my normal look don't worry, nice try though," she grinned, "… come on let's go. I see you have cakes and milk." They trundled down the lane chatting strategy, prepared for anything that Doris may throw at them… they hoped.

Doris came shuffling to the door and made quite a fuss when she saw the twins, inviting them all in. Coffee made Doris return with plates, cake forks and napkins making Suzanne smile. Even the tray had a little cloth on it, a sugar basin filled with sugar cubes and a dainty pair of tongs.

"Now…" said Doris after slurping her coffee and smacking her lips, "… I'm sure that this is not a social visit vicar as you have brought reinforcements," she eyed Suzanne over her spectacles. *Wow, she called me vicar that's the first,* thought Suzanne taken aback bolstering her confidence a little in the process.

"There is something we wanted to ask you about as you are probably the only one who knows the answer," Suzanne saw Doris preen at this so obvious compliment, quickly throwing a sideways glance at Molly, she pushed on, "… it concerns the piece of land next to the church hall," she held her breath but Doris only eyed her suspiciously "I… that is we understand that it was donated to the church by your late husband," she paused again still no comment from Doris, "… and as you know it has rather been neglected over the years and well, we feel it's time to do something with it."

Doris launched "yes, it was given by my husband, God Bless his soul," she shook her head from side to side as if remembering him tutting "he foolishly thought that it would guarantee him a passage to heaven," she caught her breath, coughed and pulled a grubby looking hanky from her pocket blowing her nose loudly. Suzanne took another look at the napkin on her lap only to notice tea stains and what looked like jam or something equally undesirable, putting it down quickly, they clearly had not been washed since who knows when and could harbour germs of indiscriminate origin. She pushed down the feeling of nausea grabbing her notebook instead to divert attention away from her half-eaten cake, her appetite had forsaken her.

"Still, it was generous of him and the church is very grateful," she pulled in a sharp breath ready to unfold her plans, "... we have looked at it very carefully, naturally the first thing to do would be to clear all the rubbish as it looks as though people have been using it for fly-tipping for a very long time, rather annoyingly because as the church owns the land it is our responsibility to have all the unknown debris removed," Doris had closed her eyes, arms folded, her head back as if she had fallen asleep. Suzanne mouthed to Molly, "... is she dead?"

"No... I'm not dead young lady just listening to you and wondering when you will get to the point." She opened her eyes fixing them straight at Suzanne. Suzanne flushed deep red whispering a little prayer for help, courage and strength to deal with Doris. Was this a test from God she wondered?

Suzanne cleared her throat, "... Right. Yes. Well, sorry, Doris, I was concerned there for a minute, so that brings me to our thoughts on the use of the land." She coughed trying to clear her throat once again. "We need parking at the hall and a play area for the children would be very useful to the whole community… and as this would cost a lot of money as there are still repairs needed on the hall itself, we are considering selling off part of the land for housing…"

"No, no, no…" cut in Doris. "No, selling the land for housing, I agree to the playground and parking but that land must not be sold, my poor husband would turn in his grave." She glared at them both affronted by the very suggestion, daring them to go against her.

Molly shushed the twins as Doris' outburst had woken them up she turned to Doris.

"Hmm, any reason for that Doris?" she spoke quietly in order to diffuse poor Doris.

"Well, I… I just don't like the idea that's all. I think that the land should be for church use exactly as it was donated…" she harrumphed in satisfaction.

"We agree…" confirmed Molly, "… the thing is Doris the housing would actually be small bungalows limited to senior residents in our community and I am sure that you could be the first on the list to have one and I know that Suzanne won't mind me telling you that the little enclave would be called Earnshaw Close in honour of your loving husband…" she paused a tiny smile creasing her lips.

There was silence for what seemed like days then Doris sucked in her breath. "Well, why didn't you say so vicar? That is a splendid idea and I think that I might just come back to church now; after all, you are going to need me to be involved in all this, aren't you?"

Chapter 29

Isabel put on her apron in the kitchen ready to make her signature chocolate brownies, oh, she knew she could probably make something else but this was a special occasion, special because Freddie would be arriving with Monty. Just the thought of Monty made her hot, very hot, immediately chastising herself to turn the temperature down from sizzling to a warm glow.

They had been working on plans for the alterations to the Manor and the Gate House that she now wanted to call the Gardeners' Cottage to remind her of when she met Monty.

Isabel could hardly contain herself, she hadn't felt this good since before Rufus passed away.

She stopped spoon mid-air thinking of Rufus. He had been the love of her life, she had never been so happy. They didn't find each other when they were young, she had already turned thirty when he walked into her life and begun to think that she would turn into an old maid with a cat. She grinned to herself.

Rufus was a handsome man, tall, well-built the most beautiful pale blue eyes that bore straight through you. He was older than Isabel, quite the charmer. She didn't know that he was a wealthy man in the engineering world. She had just felt drawn to him immediately. He took her out to dinner at an expensive Italian restaurant. She had insisted on paying half the bill even though it had nearly broken her at the time. The memory of it made her chuckle.

Rufus had gallantly allowed her to pay half promptly sending her a dozen red roses the next day, making her gasp at the expense.

Theirs had been a whirlwind romance and they married six months later, much to the chagrin of his family. It wasn't until after they married that they had bought Trentmouth Manor. It was quite a task as the Manor included a large amount of land, farms and tied cottages.

It had been a terrible shock when a police car drove up the drive one morning to deliver the terrible news, she thought that she would never recover and it had taken her a long time, helped by the arrival of Maggie. She was such a sweet little girl helping her to overcome her grief at the loss of her husband followed within a matter of months by her sister, Maggie's mother.

She let out a sigh bringing herself back to the here and now and the task in hand. She glanced at the clock it was almost lunchtime and they were coming at 2:00. She had chatted to Alice on Skype that morning careful not to tell her too much even though she was anxious to know all the latest news. It was tempting to talk over her dilemma with Alice, not realising what a good friend she was till she wasn't there. So they talked about their fabulous holiday; Alice had been thrilled to see her first kangaroo and could hardly contain her excitement at being allowed to hold a koala. They had attended the opera house but Alice had drawn the line at walking over the Sydney Harbour Bridge opting for a cruise around the harbour instead. They were off to the Great Barrier Reef next before their journey to New Zealand.

Isabel made herself a cheese and salad sandwich for lunch, her stomach in too much turmoil to eat anything else except for a misshapen brownie. With time left to touch up her makeup, comb her hair and change her outfit for the third time, Isabel finally settled in the drawing room waiting for their arrival.

She jumped when she heard the knocker rap on her front door as it was not quite two and it was unusual for Freddie to be so early. She quickly glanced in the mirror, tweaking her hair, placing a warm but not too excited smile on her face. Her heels clicked across the parquet floor as she hurried to the door.

Her smile quickly disappeared as it wasn't Freddie and Monty but Jeremy with another man.

"Ahh Aunt Isabel, meant to give you the 'heads up' about this but that is as it may be we are here now. This is a very good friend of mine, Gordon Frocklington-Watts, he's an architect come to look the old place over." He pushed past Isabel. Her mouth had dropped open with shock, into the hall talking to Gordon, whatever his name was, over his shoulder.

Regaining her senses Isabel darted after him. "I'm sorry Jeremy but it is not convenient at all, not at all. I have some other guests arriving in five minutes, you must leave." She felt wrong-footed by this rude nephew whom she despised greatly, however polite she may be to his face.

"Don't worry old girl. I can show Gordon around, tea when you're ready… now as I was saying Gordon there is a lot to do before I come to take over and I need you to start as soon as possible." Isabel was ready to explode. She was so furious at the rudeness of the man, who did he think he was?

Just at that moment, the door knocker struck again and Isabel dashed to open the door.

Jeremy stopped and turned to see who else was arriving, leaving Isabel instead of calm and serene but red-faced with anguish.

"Freddie, Monty, please come in…" she opened the door wide to let them in so that the sun illuminated the hall momentarily blinding Jeremy but allowing Freddie to see exactly who it was.

"I see you already have visitors Isabel, this a planned visit? Should we leave or do you need our help?" Freddie stood his ground in front of Monty speaking to Isabel whilst looking directly at Jeremy.

"Oh… Freddie, isn't it?" Jeremy was an expert at schmooze, deflecting attention from himself in order to make Freddie feel the odd one out, "… if you could come back another day.

There's a good chap as I am showing Mr Frocklington-Watts around. I'm sure you've heard of him, a top architect from uptown you know."

By now, Isabel had heard enough, she took a very deep breath ready to deliver the speech she had been waiting for but not expecting it to be today… and in front of guests.

"Jeremy it is you who are leaving. I have just about had enough of your rude behaviour. I did not expect you to be so vulgar to my guests nor will I be expecting you to return here ever again." She paused so as to take in another deep breath. "I am also very pleased to tell you that you will not be inheriting this house or anything else from your Uncle Rufus or myself actually; you have no rights whatsoever and if you dare come again without being invited you will leave me no choice but to call the police. Now go… and take this Gordon chap with you." She pointed in the direction of the poor man caught up in this regretful little scene, holding the door wide open. Freddie and Monty both stood quietly to one side watching the scene unfold. Isabel was now quite puce in the face breathing heavily but she stood her ground. Jeremy strode towards the door stopping as he reached Isabel.

"You haven't heard the end of this Isabel. I am the rightful heir and you know it… you will be hearing from my solicitor and you had better have your bags packed…" He almost ran down the steps trailing Frocklington-Watts in his wake.

Isabel did not deign to reply. She stood by the door watching as Jeremy drove like a madman down the drive a cloud of dust following him, her heart beating so fast she felt quite sure that Monty could hear it, not something she had wanted anyone to witness especially Monty.

"Isabel my dear come and sit down can I get you a drink? A double brandy perhaps?"

Monty asked in his quiet manner, Isabel allowed him to take her arm and steer her into the drawing room where she sat down gratefully.

"I'll get it." Freddie quickly took command "I think we all need one after that little scene."

Monty sat quietly observing Isabel pulling on his bottom lip, she half expected him to say something but as he did not she let the silence prevail. Freddie returned with the brandy and Isabel proffered a weak smile of thanks.

After a few minutes, Freddie ventured to break the silence, "… if you would rather we leave Isabel, we can always look at the plans tomorrow…" turning to Monty, "… would that suit you too Monty?"

"Of course," he replied. Isabel admired him even more for his consideration especially as he had no idea what just happened and neither did his conscience let him ask.

"No. No, Freddie, please stay, I will be fine, just give me a minute. That boy has grown ruder and I am not prepared to put up with his pompous attitude any longer… Could you do me a favour and give Maggie a call as I would like her to be involved in the decision making too."

Isabel, now feeling so much calmer turned to Monty "I do apologise for what you have just witnessed. It is not something I would like anyone to see especially you…" she caught herself before saying any more, she already felt compromised and flushed, probably the brandy she convinced herself with that explanation, not Monty. "I think that it is time we had that cup of tea. Please excuse me." She rose and left the room before she could make the hole any deeper.

"Thank you," she heard him say, quickly diverting to the cloakroom to splash her face with cold water. Dignity restored she casually made the tea, laid out the brownies and returned to the drawing room with a smile.

Freddie had already laid out the drawings on the coffee table, quickly removing them when she walked in.

"I'm looking forward to seeing your designs Freddie particularly the Gardeners' Cottage." She smiled demurely as she poured the tea handing one to Monty. His fingers just briefly brushed hers sending a tingle down her spine, something she had not experienced in a very long time.

"I hope you will be pleased Isabel, I've made one or two changes that I am hoping will meet your approval. Oh and I called Maggie, she should be here in about ten minutes."

He picked up his tea helping himself to a brownie. Isabel passed a plate to Monty and he followed suit.

"Mmm… delicious, Lady Isabel, I guess you made these as they are nothing like the usual dry offerings from the supermarket, really sticky… delicious." Monty ate with a relish which pleased Isabel.

"I did make them actually Monty. It's just that I don't have many guests to bake for and I do enjoy it and please Monty call me Isabel or Izzie." She picked up her own tea taking a much needed refreshing sip.

Maggie arrived dashing straight over to Isabel, "… are you alright Izzie only Freddie said there had been a bit of a fracas with Jeremy earlier." She sat on the arm of the couch giving her aunt a hug, concern on her face.

"Nothing I can't handle Maggie dear, I will tell you all about it later. Is everything alright at the farm? And please help yourself to tea and cake," Isabel turned her attention back to Freddie and Monty mulling over her earlier decision feeling satisfied that it had been the right one after all.

Freddie explained the plans and implications with input from Monty. Isabel requested a sunroom rather than a conservatory on the Gardeners' Cottage as it would be much more usable throughout the year.

"Right, so that is everything, Isabel. Where do you want us to start?" Freddie looked pleased with himself and Monty had explained the probable costing as with all old buildings you never knew what you might find until you started a job.

"I am more than happy with everything Freddie," turning to Monty she said, "… could you start with the Gardeners' Cottage as I think that I might just escape and live there when all the work starts on the house. Less noise and dirt I would imagine." She lifted her eyes to meet his. He didn't disappoint her as his eyes gave him away as they twinkled in reply.

"Perfectly understandable and if it fits in with your plans we can start next Monday. I will arrive around 8:00 with Sebastian, my foreman; he prefers to be called Seb by the way.

Then I will leave you in his capable hands. Is that alright?" he explained.

"Perfect and please come and have coffee with me, if you're not in a hurry," she couldn't help asking with the hint of a smile.

"Right that's all sorted and I will visit from time to time just to make sure everything is going to plan." They stood to leave, Freddie folding his plans leaving a copy for Isabel to peruse.

"Oh, Maggie, Freddie can you both come and have dinner with me later as there is something I want to discuss with you, say 7:00? No, 6:30 then we can have a drink before we eat."

"Yes, that would be fine, we will see you later, and everything is alright though, isn't it?" enquired Maggie a note of caution in her voice.

"Yes, dear perfectly."

Chapter 30

Early Monday morning when all was still quiet, Suzanne opened her bedroom window breathing in deeply. The fresh breeze caught her breath as the days were turning a little chilly.

She shuddered. Autumn was threatening with the leaves on the trees singed with a hint of red and gold, the sun struggling to make an appearance. Peace invaded her soul except for the birds who were still singing on the tops of their voices; a wonderful sound to greet the day.

Suzanne looked at the clock, she just had time to shower and take Axis for his daily walk before Gary and his entourage arrived to begin work on the television series. The village still asleep Suzanne found the beach deserted, curtains were still drawn, only a few wisps of smoke could be seen curling up escaping chimneys and disappearing into the cloudless sky.

She couldn't help but grin to herself; this truly was a beautiful place, relishing the few moments to be on her own before the mayhem of the day would arrive on her doorstep. She turned back up the lane towards her home only to see the first visible signs of life. Hugh was jogging towards her.

"Morning Suzanne, can't stop but will see you later for the briefing..." he raised his arm in acknowledgement, not waiting for a response before turning the corner.

She watched him disappear out of sight, staring at an empty road as her thoughts turned to what she thought might have been. Ever since her first day in Trentmouth when she had met Hugh at the village fete she had felt stirrings within her very being. He was a little unruly with his tousled hair, rugged charm and more sex appeal than should be allowed.

Suzanne had tried very hard not to be drawn towards him, especially when he had taken Felicity out; she shrugged her shoulders turning once more towards home.

The crew arrived on time trundling into the village. Suzanne watched Gary as he set about organising the cameramen, recording teams even a catering wagon was on site. She could already smell bacon together with the tantalising aroma of freshly ground coffee making her feel hungry as she had only had a slice of toast that morning. Her nerves jangled with a mixture of fear and excitement.

"Suzanne..." called Gary indicating for her to join him, he kissed her on both cheeks and started to walk towards the enticing vehicle with mouth-watering supplies, "... not nervous are you? I hope not," he didn't wait for a reply. Suzanne knew of old that time was precious on any outdoor event, "... come and have a coffee and we can go over what is going to happen today." She duly followed graciously accepting a coffee and warm chocolate croissant. They sat down in his makeshift studio, Suzanne relishing the warm melted chocolate in her mouth and Gary biting into his bacon roll, a spot of tomato ketchup dribbling onto his chin.

"Right, now here's the plan. Today we are concentrating on background work, setting the scene so what I need you to do is walk from the vicarage to the church in your, your…" he stuttered.

"… Cassock," supplied Suzanne, "… and my surplus I presume," she smiled.

"… Err yes and can you carry a bible or something?" He actually fumbled for a moment. "This is all new territory for me but we will get there. Is that okay?"

She patted his arm. "Of course, it's new territory for me too." They continued to run through the schedule with the first briefing at lunchtime and another at the end of the day as some people were working.

"So basically today we are going to film around the village from various locations highlighting the school, vets, Bertie's, Trentmouth Manor, the seashore and finally the church with you walking across to the church as if you were about to start a service… Then as the other people, we want to interview arrive for the briefing we will let them know when we need them. Is that all okay so far?" he quizzed.

"Fine, so I can go and write my sermon, leave you to it, for now?" She rose with relief in order to retreat into the vicarage.

"… Sermon! Oh, that would be a good shot. You go and get started then I'll come and find you when we are ready." He shuffled his papers making a note of this extra idea he wanted to include.

Suzanne gratefully walked back to the house. This working Gary was someone she had not witnessed before, she used to do research and a lot of the background work not go out on assignment with him. Her main interaction with him had been in the office when he was being flirtatious with all the girls when he needed some information about his current project, this Gary commanding, organised, and professional was a new creature and one she now admired.

She made a camomile tea and headed for her study settling down in her usual position ready to start work. There was a loud crash outside, Suzanne shot to the window there were people milling around but she couldn't quite see what may have happened. It was then that she spotted a large flower urn on the ground smashed to pieces with its flowers scattered all around. She let out a heavy sigh, it was inevitable that something would go wrong. She hesitated, should she be the one to go and sort it out? Deciding against it as she could see Gary pointing to two men, clearly in control, she sat down once more. Completely unable to fix her mind on writing a sermon she wondered what to do instead when the phone rang.

"Good morning Trentmouth Vicarage may I help you?" delighted at the distraction, she waited. "Oh, Alice, is everything alright? Is George alright?" She could barely hear her.

Then she chuckled when she realised that Alice, from the other side of the world, was checking up that everything was going okay with the television people and did she need any help with anything?

"Alice that is very sweet of you but they only arrived this morning and are still setting up to do some background shots today but rest assured if Lady Isabel or Molly can't help me with anything I will ask to Skype you." Knowing that she would not be doing anything like that as Alice was on holiday and even if the church roof had fallen in or anything else equally catastrophic she would manage somehow without her. There was a tap on her study door and Gary popped his head in, a cheery smile on his face.

"Can we do you now, if it's not too much trouble? Only I heard you on the phone." Suzanne grateful to say 'goodbye' to Alice put her phone down. "Do you think that I could ask you to put your hmm... garb on too?" He was treating her with care and respect, she liked this Gary.

"I will put my dog collar on Gary but I would not sit writing a sermon with my full regalia on." She threw him a "what do you know?" look rising to go and change.

"Oh, right. Whatever would be normal for you, as I want it all to be as authentic as possible, please."

The rest of the morning flew by with only a few retakes of her sitting in her study and she was reliably informed may still end up on the cutting room floor; that was show business.

Lunchtime arrived and there was mayhem around the food truck. You could have burgers and chips, salad and quiche, a curry, a sandwich and there was quite an array of cakes and even ice cream. As tempting as it all was Suzanne decided on a sandwich with some salad and no cake as cakes were the one thing she could rely on from her parishioners, too much actually but hey ho that's life.

A few more villagers arrived including Hugh, Molly with the twins in tow and Felicity even managed half an hour before she was due back in school; Lady Isabel together with Maggie and Freddie. They all availed themselves of something to eat, always a good ploy, ensuring maximum attendance.

Gary gathered the attention of them all as they tucked into free food, explaining his aims for the week, who he would be visiting and what he needed them to do or not do. He was keen to show a glimpse of each of them going about their usual routine, followed in a few weeks by an in-depth interview. The main aim he explained was to show a busy parish for the new vicar and her everyday tasks. The ups and downs of coastal life as it intertwined with the church.

Everyone sat listening and when he asked if there were any questions he was met with a wall of silence. Suzanne inwardly grinned as Gary's pep talk sounded like sheer gobbledegook. A sharp intake of breath could be heard around the group with sideways glances and raised eyebrows.

Suzanne stepped in, "… thanks for putting us all in the picture Gary. I'm sure that we will think of things to ask later when your chat sinks in. However, I would like to ask, as we are all busy people if you could give us an overview of the expected timetable? I mean are you going to be here every day and what events you would like to cover?" The general sound of agreement rustled through the group with vigorous nodding.

"Right, thanks for that Suzanne. Yes. Well, it is our intention to cover any and all events if we possibly can between now and Christmas, just the usual ones. Please don't invent something for us and it might seem mundane to you but not to us. We want warts and all." There was a ripple of laughter, "Okay, thank you for coming, and please help yourself to anything else you would like from our catering van and I will be in touch with you all and see some of you later." He grinned and turned to Suzanne "I hope I haven't made a big mistake with this idea. They don't seem very forthcoming." He sighed looking more than a little downcast.

"Oh, don't worry; it's quite a shock being invaded like this. It seems more otherworldly at first but they will come around... honestly," Gary's face did not seem to match her enthusiasm. "Come into the house, if you have time as I want to give you a rough timetable of our events and maybe a few more tips about the residents."

"Great..." he hesitated "because I need to speak to you too... about Hugh." He looked down his nose at her from his lofty six feet two, she felt tinier than ever.

Chapter 31

Suzanne tapped the table, "… quiet please everyone, we are thrilled to have such a turnout. It is most gratifying that so many people have come forward to volunteer their services…" she glanced around the room recognising most people from her congregation and a couple of newcomers too.

"Our purpose this evening is to establish a steering group to look at all the options regarding the land, so kindly donated by Mrs Doris Earnshaw's late husband," she nodded towards Doris who was sporting a satisfied grin, "… the quite sizeable piece of neglected land is approximately two and a half acres and is directly adjacent to the church hall. Once we have this group up and running it will be their responsibility to consider all the suggestions from the community and eventually come forward with recommendations. These will then be put to the whole community to decide," she cleared her throat, picking up a glass of water. She may be used to standing in a pulpit in front of the congregation but having a television camera pointing at you and your every word recorded… well that was different.

"So I am going to ask Mrs Molly Warren to speak to you as she has agreed to be the Madam Chair of the Trentmouth

Action Group," there was a ripple of polite and not very enthusiastic applause.

"Stop... stop, hold it there, I've heard more noise when a new flavour ice cream is announced..." grumbled Gary as he walked to the front of the hall waving a sheaf of papers in the air, "... this meeting is going to be on TV folks we need a bit more enthusiasm, this is something important for the village. It could mean housing, a playground, car parking; things the village desperately need..." he let out an exasperated sigh, "... now Suzanne can you introduce Molly again please and let's hear some enthusiastic applause."

The meeting continued with ideas being bandied about, some well thought out as a skateboard area for the teens, others such as a communal park with water fountains and a fishing lake! No one volunteered to look into this proposed fishing lake and fountain though; still, Suzanne duly noted it even though she knew that the land wasn't big enough and even if it was the idea was a complete non-starter.

The time arrived for anyone interested to step forward to be part of the action group. Suzanne asked Lucy to pour tea and coffee for everyone, inviting people to stay and chat and enjoy some cake. She looked at the group of volunteers and predictably apart from herself, Molly and Doris the team consisted of Lady Isabel. Maggie was willing support together with Freddie when he was available, Hugh, Emma and finally even though he was very busy Bertie. The group she would have chosen anyway. She sighed in equal measure of relief and pleasure.

On a misty Saturday morning, the Trentmouth Action Group (TAG) met for the first time in the church hall. Bertie and Emma were busy in the café so Lucy came along to add her support in their stead. Despite Suzanne having put the heating on, it was still chilly and everyone kept their coats on.

"This is just one of the reasons we need the money from the sale of the land." Suzanne attempted to blow some warmth into her cupped hands. The water heater sputtered and popped as it struggled to heat enough water for everyone to have a coffee. She had remembered to pick up a packet of biscuits, only digestives, milk and a jar of coffee. "It might be better to knock this place down and start again…" she sounded forlorn even to herself.

"Actually, Suzanne that's not a bad idea," Molly enthused looking at the assembled group with a grin as she stood rubbing her arms in an attempt to warm herself. "Can you imagine what a difference a brand new building with its state of the art insulation and heating would make, it could even have a stage and who knows how many new groups that could attract and revenue for the church." She was now getting excited at the prospects for the future. The rest of the group stared at her and before Doris who was busy spluttering could speak, Lady Isabel cleared her throat turning to the bewildered faces.

"A lot of work and money has already gone into upgrading this building Molly and I don't think that finances would quite stretch that far as enticing as it sounds." She returned to her coffee leaving a mumble of chatter around her. Suzanne noted that Doris was nodding approvingly dipping her third biscuit into her coffee.

"Well, I don't think that at this stage we can rule anything out. We need more blue-sky thinking so that when we invite Mr Montgomery along he can advise us as to the potential income we will have from the development of the housing and what our wish list might cost."

She hoped that would cover everyone's thoughts and rescue Molly who had dropped her shoulders in despair.

"Right if everyone has a hot drink let's get some thoughts down on paper and look to the future." She smiled encouragingly at the gathered throng thinking that next time they could meet in the vicarage where it was warm and snug. Hugh had been sending her furtive glances when he thought she wasn't looking making Suzanne feel warm, sending shivers of delight down her spine. She wondered how to give him an encouraging sign but today was not the day.

Molly tapped the table and suggested that each person put forward their thoughts not only on what they should do with the land but to include wider thoughts to support the village in general. Much chatter ensued with suggestions bandied around, the volume within the room rising and certainly heated words especially from Doris who couldn't help reminding people that she was the only person present who was born in Trentmouth and that it was her husband who had donated the land.

Molly tapped the table once more "Right, as Chairman of TAG I am going to ask Lady Isabel to start us off please and perhaps I could ask Lucy to take the official notes for us if you don't mind, Lucy? So please quiet everyone… Lady Isabel."

All eyes turned in the direction of Lady Isabel. She coughed politely looking from one to the other. "Firstly I would like to say that it is time something was done about that land, I didn't realise the size of it or the fact that it even belonged to the church but that as it may be we have a duty to clear it and do something with it for the benefit primarily of the church naturally but also the whole village. We can think up all sorts of suggestions and I like most of the ones already put forward but until we know how much money we will receive from the sale of part of it I would suggest that we concentrate on clearing it, defining our boundary and…" mutterings had started to ripple around the room and Molly had to tap the table to regain control, "… and produce a flyer to inform the villagers of the current situation asking for support and to be honest whilst the ultimate decision will be ours. You never know who might emerge to help us or even produce a plan we hadn't thought of." She looked at Molly who looked at Lucy who had written the word flyer in her notebook.

Molly pulled in a deep breath filling her lungs "Thank you, Lady Isabel. It had been my intention to ask each and every one of you for your comments, however, after hearing what Lady Isabel has suggested I think with a show of hands we press on with a flyer, find out when Monty, Mr Montgomery, can join our meeting and sort out a day to start work on clearing the land first and foremost; are we all in agreement?" All hands shot in the air and Molly declared the meeting closed.

Hugh shrugged into his coat and hesitated to look across the hall at Suzanne. She smiled her most encouraging smile in his direction wondering if he was about to ask her out at last. He just smiled in return raised his hand muttering a farewell.

Suzanne dropped down onto the nearest chair cupping her face and wept.

Chapter 32

Lucy left the meeting battling the turmoil in her mind, panic coursing through her veins. She walked down the lane beside Molly chatting about the meeting; its aims and Doris, of course, who was now firmly, back in the fold much to everyone's amusement.

"Do you think that you will pull this off, Molly? You have taken on a massive task and Maggie's wedding too. Rather you than me if I'm honest." Lucy was feeling decidedly overwhelmed, probably being pregnant didn't help; there was a time when she would not flinch at anything that came her way. Since opening the café and the safety net of her salary removed she saw threats everywhere.

"I know it's exciting, I also think that with the TV people here this will really put us on the map, should bring you extra business too…" they plodded on enjoying the late autumn warmth, "… pity to go back home so soon I think I'll come down to the café with you and have a proper coffee," they both laughed. Lucy fell silent ruminating on whether to mention something to Molly that was bothering her or not, she was her best friend and they usually confided in each other but this seemed different somehow. Try as she might she couldn't quite grasp the excitement that Molly clearly had.

"I have to tell you Molly that I think that this whole TAG thing could actually hurt us…" Molly turned to look at her more fully. She looked mystified.

"What on earth makes you think that, Lucy?" Molly was clearly aghast at the thought.

"Well, the thing is we are considering allowing groups to meet in the café, especially in the winter you know things like 'knit and natter' or 'book' clubs that sort of thing and I am more than a bit worried, to be honest with you… if the church hall is looking to put itself up for hire that could scupper our plans." Lucy stared down the road at the ocean avoiding Molly's startled gaze. She pretended to watch a ship or a gull the tears stinging her eyes.

"Right I see… I don't think that there is a conflict of interest at all, in fact, they could complement each other. The groups you are talking about would be half a dozen people who are more likely to enjoy your café where they don't have to pay a fee to meet up and don't forget they would also have to bring their own tea, coffee and so on at the hall… you are readymade, no room to hire and if there are only one or two you are most definitely better suited. I think that the church hall is likely to be used more for yoga classes, scouts, talks, birthday parties much larger gatherings is what I see for the church hall. Does that answer your question and stop you from panicking?"

Lucy grinned, "Bertie always says that I worry for nothing," turning and linking arms with Molly, "… come on Bertie has made a new cake with mango and lashings of cream we will have to taste it for him to ensure the quality is up to standard," they chuckled.

The doorbell tinkled as they entered still laughing suddenly stopping when they saw Bertie bent over someone on the floor. Lucy was there in a flash only to find Emma slumped on the ground blood oozing from her head, she was deathly white.

Lucy felt her pulse, it was faint but it was there. She turned to Bertie attempting to keep the urgency from her voice. "Have you phoned for an ambulance? We need to get Emma to hospital as soon as possible," Lucy felt faint knowing that there was probably more to it than just a trip and a bang on the head with Emma but as she wasn't a Doctor she kept it to herself. "Molly can you telephone Hugh to get him down here straight away." She turned back to her patient endeavouring to make her more comfortable, trying to keep calm so that she didn't frighten anyone. Within minutes, Hugh came rushing in through the door dashing to his mothers' side.

"Is she going to be alright, Lucy? Please tell me she's not dead?" His voice was strangled by the terrified lump in his throat.

"I think she fainted but I'm not sure why so she should go to the hospital just to be on the safe side, she is still unconscious. Try not to worry an ambulance is on its way." Lucy attempted to calm Hugh, but in her heart, she knew that something was seriously wrong.

"Thank God for that," he turned to Molly "I have locked up but there are some more appointments booked… do you think that you could take over for me please? I… I don't know how long I will be," he looked back to his mother he was distraught, patting and smoothing her hand; not waiting for an answer from Molly.

Molly glanced at Lucy shrugging her shoulders mouthing 'sorry' but Lucy didn't mind they could catch up later.

In fact, Lucy had an idea to surprise Molly with as soon as the rush was over. The ambulance disappeared back up the lane having established no broken bones, just a rather nasty gash to her head that would need a couple of stitches and an x-ray to ensure nothing more sinister going on in her head.

Lucy watched as Molly actually trudged back up the lane towards the surgery first popping home to see Alistair and the children before attending to sick animals that needed her attention too.

It was two hours later that Lucy packed a basket of goodies to take to Molly. The lunchtime crowd had dwindled and as she made some rolls and cut some of Bertie's latest cake creation she finally had the chance to talk to Bertie about the meeting.

"… So it seems that we probably don't have anything to worry about where the church hall is concerned and I even thought that we might branch out into more outside catering if Molly is right about parties and meetings." She made two lattes adding them to her basket, "… I do hope that Emma is alright I think she might be overdoing it working here full time, don't you?"

"Hmm it's funny but I thought the same thing, I don't want to hurt her feelings and she is excellent with the customers. She certainly knows her stuff, I'm not sure that I could cope without her but I think that I will have to talk to her about working part-time. What do you think my darling?" He put his arms around her leaning in for a kiss.

Lucy extracted herself "later… yes I agree and now I must go and see Molly." She pulled on her jacket "I could do with a sit down myself," she kissed him once more, "… back in an hour," and left leaving poor Bertie on his own.

Lucy was now three months pregnant her scan showed that everything was normal making sure that she didn't see what sex the baby was; that would be a surprise for them when her baby was born. No pink or blue room for them.

She made her way slowly up the hill panting a little as the basket was quite heavy.

She pushed the door open to the surgery the bell tinkled her arrival. A flustered looking Molly, hair dishevelled, appeared from the back office.

"Lucy, thank goodness it's you, I can't believe how busy we have been this afternoon.

I had just put my feet up for five minutes… what have you got there?" she sniffed, "… I believe I can smell caramel latte," Lucy laughed, she could never fool Molly.

"Yes, you're right and sandwiches and cake…" she handed the basket to Molly and they retreated to the office.

"My tummy is rumbling. You are a lifesaver do you know that?" Molly uncovered the basket pulling out her favourite latte and taking a long gulp "hmm… how's Emma have you heard?"

"Yes, Hugh phoned to say that she has had some stitches in that nasty gash but she is still unconscious. He is quite worried. They are going to keep her in for observation and more tests. Hugh will be home later and said to thank you for stepping in at a moment's notice." Lucy sat down with a thump exhaling loudly and turning to look at Molly "I hope that Emma will be fine. I thought that she would be awake by now unless they have put her under sedation… it's possible… anyway let's tuck in I'm starving." She gratefully bit into her cheese and salad roll realising that she was very hungry indeed.

"So what happened then, why did she faint?" Molly was about to start on her second roll already perked up from her sudden workload, feet up onto the desk relaxing.

"Apparently the ambulance crew think she may have passed out from low blood sugar. It can happen if anyone doesn't eat regularly and have a sit down occasionally." Lucy announced rather pointedly at Molly still keeping her fears to herself. "Anyway… Bertie is going to suggest that she works part-time in future; God only knows how he will manage without her. She is a marvel. I have brought some scones she made today, they are truly scrumptious." Lucy opened the basket to reveal sultana scones, butter pats and a small jar of strawberry jam.

Both now totally full and rubbing their stomachs, Molly stretched both arms above her head and yawned.

"… To think that I agonised about giving up the business, I should not have worried, and today has shown me that I am very pleased that I did…" she dropped her arms chuckling at some hidden thought.

"This last year has been a bit of a nightmare, hasn't it? For all of us but things seem to be working out for the best… mostly anyway." Lucy suddenly had pictures sliding into her consciousness of the fire, her mother's dementia, her wedding, giving up her career and Bertie's business venture, "… yes it certainly has had its moments." She let out a deep and agonised sigh.

"Hey, come on Lucy, it's not that bad. You sound like you have all the troubles of the world on your shoulders," she hugged her friend. "I think we have only just discovered what life can throw at us and it's exciting to think what might come our way next." Just then the doorbell tinkled "I take that back." She grinned as she went to investigate.

"Oh, hello, Suzanne; is everything alright with Axis?" she smiled.

"Yes... thanks... sorry Molly I was looking for Hugh," she looked flustered.

"Oh, didn't you know he's at the hospital, Emma collapsed in the café and..." before she could finish her sentence Suzanne turned and rushed out leaving Molly and Lucy staring after her.

Chapter 33

Hugh stayed at the hospital all night by the side of his mother, holding her hand and fighting sleep that threatened to overwhelm him. There were tubes, machines, buzzes all attached to her and she had not yet regained consciousness. He had hesitated in calling his brother Clive in the States as he was still unsure exactly what had happened to Emma but decided at God knows what time it was, to call him. It had clearly been late at night but Clive was still awake.

They decided to wait until the Doctor came to see Hugh in the morning before deciding if he should get the next plane over. Clive had a successful advertising agency employing twenty people, recently winning a major new contract and didn't want to fly back if Emma had just had a nasty bang on the head. Hugh understood his dilemma, he was in the States and not just up the road but still… He promised to call again as soon as he knew what was wrong with their mother.

Hugh fell asleep in the chair exhausted. He woke with a start forgetting where he was for a minute as a trolley was being pushed around noisily down the corridor and he could hear nurses swishing curtains and chatting, cups of tea being poured, sugar being stirred vigorously, spoons clattering. Hugh blinked a few times and rubbed his face as the memory of the day before hit him and he shot to his mothers' side. Nothing had changed.

He glanced at his watch it was only just 7:00 still very early and despite the warmth of the hospital he shivered. He began to talk to Emma telling her that he had spoken to Clive and everyone sends their love. He tried his hardest to stay upbeat relaying tales of the animals brought in to him including the antics of the owners. He told her about the TAG meeting and what he had committed himself to even though he didn't really have the time. He laughed as he gave a description of old Doris who looked very smug and proud of her husband as if she had become the saviour of the church and village.

A nurse came in "Mr Gilmour would you like a cup of tea or coffee?" she busied herself picking up the chart from the end of Emma's bed making notes, checking her pulse and temperature.

"Please, if it's not too much trouble I would love one." She made to leave then hesitating she turned back to him "oh, and there's a message for you from someone called Suzanne she asks you to text her or give her a call regarding your mother."

"Thanks… I will. Oh, and do you know what time the Doctor will be coming to see Mum?" He looked expectantly at her. Her face softened and she came back into the room.

"He comes on duty in about an hour and he will be in to see you as soon as he gets here. Now let me get you that coffee, sugar and how about a slice of toast?" she smiled.

"Thanks, one sugar, and I would love some toast." The nurse bustled out leaving Hugh with the sound of the oxygen machine slowly clunking up and down.

He pulled out his phone to find messages from Molly, Lucy, Suzanne and Felicity. He scrolled through them stopping at Suzanne's toying with what to reply. He smiled lovingly at his mum remembering their last conversation about Suzanne. Emma liked her very much, encouraging Hugh to ask her out. He had dismissed the idea saying that he wasn't ready for another relationship and if he was being honest he was terrified. He picked up her hand once more.

"I have lots of messages Mum from Lucy, Molly, Felicity and Suzanne, they all send you their love and hope you get better soon." A tear stung his eye dribbling down his cheek and running off his chin. He sucked in his breath trying to stem the tide of tears and still his trembling voice. He pulled a tissue from the box on top of the cupboard removing the evidence so his mother wouldn't see him cry, wrapping his arms around himself in an effort to hold back the pain now coursing around his tired body.

The nurse came back "here you are Mr Gilmour." She placed the coffee and toast on the side and if she saw his distress she didn't mention it. "Dr will be here soon." She left hurriedly leaving Hugh to regain his composure. He tried to eat the toast but it stuck in his throat threatening to start him sobbing again. The coffee was hot and sweet but tasted like dishwater. He toyed with the idea of throwing it down the sink but drank it hoping that it would in some way revive him.

The door opened and in walked a doctor, a nurse in dark blue and an entourage of others, presumably students. Hugh immediately fretted that they would poke his mum about.

"Mr Gilmour I'm Doctor Sharp..." he took a deep breath, "... we have the test results back including x-rays and a brain scan and I'm afraid the news isn't good." Hugh just stared at him dumbfounded.

"Sister, will you kindly escort Mr Gilmour to the relative's room and I will be along in a moment to explain things further."

"Yes, doctor. Come with me would you Mr Gilmour and nurse..." she glanced over her shoulder, "... bring Mr Gilmour a coffee straight away." Hugh followed the sister in a daze he wasn't sure what he had just heard, his head felt as if it was full of cotton wool, feeling guilty remembering that he hadn't replied to Suzanne.

He looked up expectantly as the Dr bustled in "All the tests show that your mother has suffered an embolism and I'm sorry but there is no brain function..." The Doctor looked kindly and sympathetically at Hugh, his words fading into the ether as the awful truth struck him that his mother was not going to survive. Hugh thought that he was going to throw up.

He clutched his stomach trying to process what the Doctor was saying to him, the sound just disappeared into oblivion. All he could feel was a cold numbness creeping its way through him and the pain... the pain was excruciating. His heart beat faster, his head pounding from the unbelievable pain, he thought that he would be sick. He attempted to pull himself together.

"Do you have any other family Mr Gilmour?" a silence registered with Hugh that someone was waiting for him to speak, his mouth was dry refusing to let any sound out.

He swallowed... hard.

"Hmm, yes my brother Clive lives in America, our dad died some years ago..." he trailed off.

"May I suggest that you ask him to come over as soon as possible? We need to ask you to consider switching the life support off to your mother." Silence fell around them. The Doctor was still talking but Hugh had disappeared into a dense fog that he couldn't see through. He felt as if he were falling off a cliff, not even trying to save himself.

"This can't be happening... she was fine yesterday, you must have made a mistake, please tell me this is a mistake." He began to sob uncontrollably, sniffing. The sister passed him a box of tissues, Hugh blew his nose loudly.

"I'm so sorry Mr Gilmour there is no mistake your mum will probably never wake up and even if she did she would... let's say not be the same anymore. Can I suggest you contact your brother and let us know when he will arrive and I think too that you should go home, get some sleep and come back later? Nothing will happen to her when you are away we will keep a close eye on her." He stood up whispering to the sister and left the room.

The sister sat down again "Do you have any questions Mr Gilmour? Can I get you another coffee?" she stood and went to make him more coffee regardless pushing the mug into his hand. "You can go and sit with Emma if you like... it would do you good to go home, get some rest like Doctor Sharp suggested and we will see you later." Hugh stood in a blurred world where nothing made any sense allowing himself to be led back to Emma's room.

Everything was the same but now oh so different, still, machines whirring, some flashing, and his mum completely still.

Hugh got a taxi home where he called Clive who insisted that nothing happen to their mum till he arrived. He had already enquired about flights and could be in London within twenty-four hours and Dorset soon after.

Hugh fell into bed completely exhausted. He felt empty, wracked with pain, so alone.

Chapter 34

Suzanne pulled on her jacket with a heavy heart. This was one journey she thought she would never have to make. She looked at herself in the mirror her head full of questions not finding any answers. Finally, she picked up her bag and bible ready to walk down to 'Cobwebs', Emma's cottage.

Clive had arrived from the States and together with Hugh made the agonising decision to turn off Emma's life support. Clive had wanted a second opinion even suggested they fly her to the States where he was convinced that the Doctors there could do more. He was angry. Why, why, why?

Suzanne pulled herself up tall, took in a deep breath and knocked on the door. To her relief, it was Hugh who answered. He looked terrible. Her heart went out to him. She wanted to hug him, take care of him but knew she could not. She followed him into the neat little sitting room where Clive was leaning against the inglenook. They were so different it was hard to believe that they were brothers. Suzanne already knew a little about him from Emma, she had been very proud of her boys. Clive was two years older than Hugh and assumed an air of authority.

"Thank you for coming, Suzanne." Hugh struggled to talk managing to offer her a cup of tea disappearing off to the kitchen to make one.

Suzanne turned to Clive "I am so sorry for your loss Clive, Emma was truly a lovely lady and a member of the church here in Trentmouth. May I ask if you have had any thoughts regarding the funeral service?" She politely enquired just as Hugh walked in carrying a tray laid out with three mugs and a plate of biscuits.

"If it was down to me, I would just go to the crematorium, none of this mumbo jumbo claptrap that people like you spout," he spat angrily. Suzanne let out a gasp squeezing her bible as she felt the sudden abuse hit her.

Hugh was shocked choking on his tea "Clive… please don't speak to Suzanne like that and you know very well that Mum loved going to church. She saw herself as a Christian and she deserves a proper Christian funeral, it's what she would have wanted." He turned to Suzanne "I'm sorry but as you can see Clive does not hold with anything religious." Clive had turned his head away drinking his tea.

"I understand Hugh that not everyone is a believer in God or a higher power.

However, as you quite rightly pointed out we are here for Emma. Now I have made a few notes as I am aware of some of Emma's favourite hymns, do you have any you would like?"

She opened her writing-case ready to jot down any ideas that they might have.

"To be honest Suzanne can we leave it up to you, I can't even think at the moment, you know what's best. I just want to say a few words about Mum that's all." He looked down at his hands, they were shaking, it had been an enormous shock for him and everyone. Bertie had been distraught imagining that it was his entire fault. Suzanne had convinced him that it was nothing to do with her working at the café, it could have happened any day at any time but he still felt guilty and had closed the café the day she passed away.

"Let's get this over with, if you don't mind, I need to get back home. I can't stay away from the business too long and I have my family to think of too." Clive had moved to Boston many years ago where he met and married Cleo, they had three children and had a very successful company. His trips back to the UK had been far and few between, he didn't see the point. Emma had visited a few times but she really did not like flying. Now Clive just wanted to tie up all the loose ends and get out of there.

"How soon can we have the funeral? If there is any chance of a day this week, I would appreciate it." He fixed his eyes on Suzanne unblinking making her shrivel inside. He was so rude and so completely different to Hugh.

She pulled herself together having not expected Clive to be so cold "Yes, of course, what about Friday?" she opened her diary, "… morning around 10:00 or a little later if you prefer?" She looked up at him pen poised.

"Fine, 10:00 is fine." He downed the last of his tea, "… now if you will excuse me I'm going out for a walk. You can deal with this Hugh can't you?" And with that, he pulled on a sweatshirt and left.

Hugh stared at the closed door for a moment clearly embarrassed by his brother's rudeness "I'm so sorry Suzanne, Clive has always been a bit of a loner not having much contact with me or Mum. He just doesn't like anyone making decisions without him, and of course, he wants to know what is in Mum's will." He took a sip of tea "oh, dear, this is cold."

He put his mug down "let me make a fresh one for you Suzanne and I'm sorry... again. I keep apologising I just can't seem to stop." He gulped, picked up the tray and made it for the kitchen.

Suzanne so wanted to comfort him, he looked so lost. He had dark shadows under his eyes his face had lost its sparkle and Suzanne's heart was heavy that she couldn't help him.

She felt completely inadequate in this situation. Yes, she had conducted funerals before but this was different, so very different.

"Look, Hugh, if you prefer me to come back another day I quite understand, you do look tired."

"No, no please stay I would like to talk to you and anyway Clive will be annoyed if I haven't sorted the funeral when he gets back..." he broke off staring blankly.

"Right well, I will choose some hymns maybe ask Isabel for her input too and you would like to do the eulogy..."

"No, no I can't do that Suzanne please will you do it I just want to say a very brief few words about Mum, she was a brilliant mum and I loved her. It just seems so... so stupid for her to die like this and so young... she had only just moved here and really loved... it's so unfair," he broke off once more. "Please tell me why my mum had to die. I can't understand it, Suzanne." He took hold of her hand searching her face for answers, answers that she couldn't give. She couldn't pull her hand away even though she thought that she should.

"Hugh I don't know the answer to that question, no one does, and all I can tell you is that your mum was very happy to move to Trentmouth, she loved the café and all her new friends. She told me that she was thrilled when you agreed she could move here and well, this cottage was a dream come true."

"That's what I mean, she had it all planned out, she had been out painting up on the cliffs, had planned to turn her garden into a vegetable plot, make jam…" his voice caught in his throat, he shuddered before continuing "she was even going to ask you about becoming a churchwarden… and now… and now," he swallowed hard, "… and now, well now… nothing."

He rubbed his hand over his face, shaking his head in despair.

"It's important to remember all the good times, everything that your mum loved and if you could tell me a bit more about her life and all the family I will put a eulogy together to honour her with." Suzanne gently extricated her hand from his grip opened her pad once again poised to take down some notes. Hugh talked and talked animated at times, it was clear to see the love he had for his mum shining from his face. He recounted tales from when they were young boys growing up in Richmond, the death of his father and Clive's departure to the States. He had so many stories to tell and Suzanne wished she had had more time with Emma herself, she was a wonderful lady always ready to help someone, always smiling. She had such a joy in living, in life itself.

The door burst open "Oh, you still here?" Clive looked her up and down with a look of disdain but Suzanne knew when not to engage the 'enemy' instead she smiled as sweetly as she could possibly manage.

"I think we are finished for today, I will start work on the service and then ask for your confirmation before we go to print the order of service. Oh, and do you have a picture or two for me please that I can use? That would be very helpful." Although, she didn't see what Clive did she heard him sneer wondering how on earth he could be Hugh's brother.

Hugh jumped up "let me grab my pullover and I'll walk you up the road, I could do with some fresh air actually." He smiled as he struggled into his chunky jumper that had seen better days and followed Suzanne out of 'Cobwebs'.

They walked slowly up the road in silence for a few minutes passing the veterinary door prompted Suzanne to ask "I presume Molly is taking care of things for you at the moment Hugh, she is a godsend, isn't she?"

"Yes, she certainly is and I am so sorry. Sorry. I'm saying sorry again. Oh dear, let me start again." They both let out a stilted chuckle. "Molly has been great, I don't know how I would have coped without her and you know what? I do not know how she does everything she does, she's a miracle worker. And I do sincerely apologise for Clive. You see Mum and Dad thought that they couldn't have children and so adopted Clive when he was just a baby and then quite naturally I came along two years later. Clive has had a chip on his shoulder ever since believing me to be the golden boy, the favourite when the truth was that Mum and Dad treated us both exactly the same. I didn't get any favours at all, I'm not complaining you understand. When they told us we were in our teens and everything changed, Clive grew sullen, introverted and angry, still is really and so after graduating he took himself off to the states and if I'm honest he never literally looked back."

Everything clicked into place for Suzanne. "That answers many questions explaining why he wanted you to wait till he got here and his main reason being to find out what has been left to him, he thinks that Emma may have cut him out of her will."

"I guess so, but he needn't have worried. Everything is split fifty-fifty as it should be.

In fact, I am going to buy out his half of 'Cobwebs' and move in myself. It's time I left the cottage up at the farm and after the funeral has been paid for there will be very little cash left.

Clive doesn't want anything from the cottage saying I can do what I like with it, so once this is over I'm not sure if I'll ever see him again."

Suzanne's heart went out to Hugh, his story certainly gave her an insight into the family dynamics. They arrived at her gate Suzanne turned to speak to him "Thank you for walking back with me and sharing what must have been a difficult story to tell Hugh. I'll get back to you as soon as I can, have you ordered flowers for Friday?"

"Yes, yes, I will, and thank you, Suzanne," he bent forward kissing her on her cheek.

Suzanne immediately blushed bright red stammering.

"Oh, well, yes, no problem. Oh and Hugh if you ever want to talk... you know where I am." She pushed open the gate walking briskly up to her front door not daring to look back.

Chapter 35

It had been several weeks since that awful day when Emma had died and Trentmouth was beginning to get back to subdued normality. It had been an enormous shock to everyone.

Hugh still blamed himself finding no consolation in anything.

Clive had returned to the States promising to visit again soon but with the thought of a big fat cheque going into his bank account before too long, Hugh was not inclined to believe him. So with a heavy heart, he was busy packing up the cottage at the farm ready to move to 'Cobwebs' his new home.

Suzanne shivered to tug a bobble hat tight over her ears; Axis was jumping up and down in anticipation of his walk. She let out a long sigh collecting his lead as she opened her kitchen door; the sun was low in the sky bravely attempting to shine. Mist clung to the hills; the cold caught her breath, nothing seemed to deter Axis. She had reluctantly pulled on her boots grabbed a scarf and gloves; autumn was already here with winter not far behind.

Winter was not her favourite time of year.

Head down Suzanne made for the cliff path, Axis pulling on his lead. She couldn't help but replay the last few weeks unable to avoid the nagging question in her head concerning Hugh. He was a super guy, gentle, kind, thoughtful, handsome she had to admit and well, she liked him… a lot. However, did he have any feelings for her? He had kissed her cheek… her hand automatically swept up to touch where his lips had caressed her face, the memory still burning in her heart. He would be moving into the village at the weekend and be an almost neighbour, she let out a sigh. Despite her suggestion of an open door if he would like to talk, he had not taken her up on the offer. She climbed the hill not seeing the view, dragging her feet through the mud, praying for some sort of guidance.

An hour later Suzanne trudged back into the village feeling refreshed, thankfully the wind had dropped leaving the sea calm and the fishing boats were out on the waves once more. She raised her hand in greeting Freddie who was busy working in his new office down by the sea deciding to call in on Bertie today in the café to see what news he might have.

"Suzanne… so lovely to see you," he hugged her pressing a kiss onto her cheek. "Your usual caramel latte and a toasted teacake?" he grinned.

"Oh, yes please, and can you make it extra hot? I am cold through to my bones." She pulled off her coat, hat and gloves and sat on the couch by the wood-burning stove letting the welcome warmth soothe her aching body.

When Bertie had installed the couch by the stove, everyone thought it completely unnecessary to take up space for another table but he had insisted and how right he was.

The soft comfy couch had become a premium spot and you were lucky to get it!

It was quiet in the café this morning, too early for lunch but just right for Bertie to grab a few minutes break and join her. He pulled out a chair sitting down heavily; positioning himself so that he could easily jump up when another customer came in.

"How are you, Suzanne? You look... a bit... dare I say it... tired? Please tell me to buzz off if I'm being impertinent." He had a deliciously warm and encouraging smile. She couldn't be cross with him, everyone loved Bertie.

Suzanne threw him a quick smile in reply "Thank you for pointing that out, Bertie; I am actually worried about Hugh and you too... How are you coping without Emma?" She neatly turned the conversation from herself, not wanting to tell him her real troubles; after all, people were supposed to come to her with theirs.

"Well..." he toyed with his black coffee avoiding her gaze, "... I miss her... we all do," he paused for several minutes "Emma was a breath of fresh air, happy, really enjoyed her job.

She had ideas for the café too, even suggested we turn the storeroom, which leads through to the house into a community shop where people could sell local crafts to the grockles!

Thinking about it that's not a bad idea at all, maybe we will just do that and call in Emma's Crafty Cave or something..." he let out a chuckle "but on a more serious note, I will have to find another member of staff soon as I can't rely on Lucy. She has had awful morning sickness and is feeling guilty that I am here on my own most of the time," he trailed off staring into the distance.

"If I think of anyone, I'll let you know but no one springs to mind I'm afraid," she bit into her teacake "Hmm have you seen Hugh since his brother left? I was wondering if he was alright," she said pretending to take great interest in the raisins in her bun.

"He's okay I think he's moving in at the weekend. I said that I would give him a hand on Saturday night, I can't during the day and Alistair is helping too. Molly came in yesterday, she had to contact Alice and George about Emma and predictably Alice was distraught saying that they would come home immediately until George put his foot down saying they would be home soon enough and she could pay her respects then," he grinned "that is so typical of Alice."

"It is, but she couldn't do anything if they had flown home. I wondered if Molly would tell her but knowing Alice she would have been more upset if they hadn't I'm sure," she drained her coffee. "You know Bertie, I could drink another one of those please."

"Coming up," he leapt into action returning with another caramel latte, extra hot.

"I have been thinking Bertie, well, two things actually…" she took an appreciative sip.

"Oh, yes, and what's that?"

"I like the idea of Emma's Crafty Cave or Emma's Craft Studio…"

"Hmm I like that and you've given me another idea but it will keep. Go on…"

"I was thinking on Saturday night after you have all been helping Hugh to move house why don't you all come to me for supper? Bring Molly and Lucy of course, I will make lasagne with salad and French bread, nothing fancy but then no one will have to cook. What do you think?"

"Great idea and I will bring dessert and I'm sure that we can all supply some wine."

"Brilliant, right now I must go I have a lot to do," she stood to wrap herself up again in her warm clothing, Bertie kissed her cheek and she collected Axis to make their way home.

Saturday dawned all too quickly; Suzanne had a TAG meeting to attend in the morning before she could head into Wareham to pick up supplies for the evening's meal. The meeting went well, they had made a lot of progress. The ideas had been narrowed down and with the help of Freddie and Monty, it was time to make some decisions.

"Our objective today…" began Molly, "… before we put our plan to the community is to make a firm decision on what we want the land to look like so that Freddie can draw up a plan of the area showing how it would all fit into the landscape and village life." People were nodding with enthusiasm as Molly opened a large sheet of paper with the landmarked out on it including the existing church hall plus cut-outs of each idea so that they could fit them into place or discard them.

"Now the most popular ideas after the bungalows and car park are a small play area, allotments and a grassed area with seats where we could have a permanent home for the church fete plus any other fund-raising events that the church would like to put on…"

"Would it be big enough for a marquee, Molly?" asked Suzanne ideas flowing through her mind like a harvest festival get together, a Christmas play and carols and lots more fizzing her brain. She knew from experience that if people are reluctant to come into the church then the church must go to the people.

"Well, it would if we don't have the allotments... I was thinking that most people have a veggie patch in their gardens these days and would there be enough call for allotments?"

The conversation trundled on with how many cars to accommodate and how big the play area should be.

"Do we know yet how much we can sell the land for and exactly what we can afford to do with it?" asked Lady Isabel.

"No. That is the next step. If we are agreed to forget the allotments we can go to Freddie and he will liaise directly with Monty. We should have some figures to work with at our next meeting. Anyone else want to comment?"

"I was just wondering if six semi bungalows are enough, shouldn't we have 8 or 10?" Doris was anxious to have a little enclave to fuss over Molly knew and pondered for a moment before replying.

"I will put it to Freddie but the danger is to get more homes in they would have to make them smaller with less garden and possibly remove the parking spaces too. Let me come back to you on that Doris," Molly was convinced that that would change her mind.

"I didn't think of that Molly, you are quite right and six I'm sure will make for a very nice little community," she smiled indulgently nodding as if it was her idea.

"Right that's it for today I will give everyone a call to arrange the next meeting when I hear back from Freddie. Thank you, everyone," they all started to disappear and Suzanne approached Molly.

"Come into the vicarage and have coffee with me Molly, if you have time?" she encouraged trying not to sound needy.

"I would like that, catch you up in 5, okay?" Suzanne dashed home to put the kettle on. She was fizzing with her plans for dinner that evening with her friends. The vicarage was cold and lonely most of the time and she considered the idea that as she was a single person that probably left her out of most people's equations as an even number worked best, for dinner parties anyway.

She had just piled up a tray when there was a rap on her door, she dashed through her hallway with a smile already fixed ready to welcome Molly... but it wasn't Molly to her surprise it was Hugh. Her smile dropped as she suddenly felt anxious tripping over her own tongue.

"Hugh! What a surprise, I mean won't you come in? Please," she added as an afterthought. Her brain raced unable to think straight and doing her best not to reveal the panic in her voice. She looked up to see Molly coming through the gate.

"I see you have another visitor Suzanne, I'll go and catch up with you later. Alistair is waiting for me and if I know him he will be totally frazzled by now desperate for rescue," she chuckled as she turned to leave.

"Molly..." called Suzanne "I'm... um... sorry but see you tonight?" she endeavoured to sound normal knowing she was failing miserably.

"Sure... can't wait..." she trailed off closing the gate and ducking under the Autumn withered honeysuckle.

"Come in Hugh, I've just made coffee. Would you like one? I wasn't expecting you but pleased nonetheless and how are you? You know since..." she knew she was gabbling but couldn't help herself she had been taken by surprise feeling completely flummoxed.

"Love one thanks. I didn't realise Molly was popping in. I hope I'm not interrupting anything," he followed her into her study which had far the prettiest view from the house. It was cosy, more intimate. The smell of freshly ground coffee wafted in from the kitchen.

They sat down and Suzanne poured the coffee before asking "How are you Hugh? It was a huge shock losing your mum like that and..." she hesitated to see the lost look in his eyes. He had changed since Emma had died. He seemed... she couldn't quite put her finger on it trying to second guess how he must be feeling.

"I just wanted to talk to someone... you don't mind do you?" He looked at her with big doe eyes "I didn't know who else to turn to..." he trailed off.

"Of course, my door is always open to any member of the parish." She tried to sound nonchalant as a blush rushed to her face and Hugh's eyes shot up at her in surprise.

He fumbled with his hands "I... um... came more to see a friend rather than the parish vicar..."

Suzanne felt stupid, totally put in her place, she was devastated "I... I'm so sorry Hugh it's just that... look I don't know how to say this and I am so out of my depth here but..." she paused for a long moment "look the truth is... the truth is... this is so much harder than I imagined it would be, it's just that... I'm so sorry Hugh I just don't know how to say it."

Suzanne looked down at her own hands feeling a total fool wishing the ground could swallow her whole.

"Let me try," a tiny smile played on the corners of his mouth struggling to lift his spirits however slightly. "I've agonised over something for a long time and it's eating me up inside…" he let out a long breath "and I feel that if I don't say something now I will never have the courage to say it again so here goes… please feel free though to show me the door at any time," Suzanne felt fear run through her veins turning her icy cold, was he ill? Was he leaving to go back to Richmond? Did his ex-fiancé want him back? Her mind raced with the worst imaginable options. She instinctively leant forward taking hold of his hands. "Tell me, what is it?" This time he didn't pull away.

"It was something my mum said actually and I never really answered her and well… when she passed away I felt I owed it to her to come and see you so that I can get something straight once and for all." He stopped to take another deep breath.

"Oh, dear Hugh, I do hope there is nothing wrong? I can't imagine what this is all about." She stroked his hand in a non-committal way endeavouring to help him say what he wanted to say and at the same time hoping that he would forget what she was trying to say earlier.

"Ever since we met at the church fete when you thought that I was Alistair," he gave a slight chuckle.

"Yes, I remember and you suggested I bring Axis in for a check-up." She was warming to the memory her mind floating back to that wonderful moment when she first saw him.

"That's right anyway; I instantly felt drawn to you. I had never met anyone like you before and well ever since I've wanted to ask you out but… I never had the courage because you are a vicar and I wasn't sure, am still not actually, well what I am trying to say is… is will you have dinner with me? If that's appropriate, I mean if it isn't you only have to say and I'll be out of here and I won't bother you again." He paused finally to draw in a deep breath shaking.

Suzanne stared at him her eyes rapidly filled with tears, of all the things he was going to say that was the one she had not thought of. Her throat constricted as she searched his face.

Was she hearing correctly? She jumped up "I would love to… yes, yes, yes."

Hugh jumped to his feet throwing his arms around her, he just couldn't hold back any longer. His lips found hers kissing her over and over again. Suzanne had never, ever been happier in her whole life tears streaming down her cheeks delirious with joy.

They pulled apart "Oh, Hugh, I… I thought that you didn't like me. I tried so hard to encourage you I have loved… um… I, I fell in love with you the day we met…" she looked deep into his eyes the words had tumbled out before she could stop them, She had said it and it couldn't be taken back. She loved him; there that was it out in the open.

Hugh's arms were around her hugging her close, so close, "… and I love you too," he whispered.

Chapter 36

After Hugh had moved to Trentmouth village, Bertie and Lucy found themselves struggling for income. The rent from the cottage had been keeping them afloat now that Lucy wasn't working and the café was still establishing itself.

Bertie pinned a notice up outside the café advertising a cottage for rent on a long term basis. They had considered holiday letting which could be more lucrative but the changeover every week and the cleaning and washing of the linen made that a non-starter.

Bertie stood back staring at the sign hoping that the perfect tenant would turn up soon.

He held his chin with one hand, the other perched on his hip-deep in thought. He dare not let this venture fail and although they had many ideas, thanks to Molly and Emma – Emma, he still missed her terribly – but how and where to start?

"Hey... penny for them," Lucy had slipped her arms around his waist hugging him tight and resting her head against his back. He turned to return the loving hug, rocking her slightly and kissing the top of her head. He never stopped contemplating how he became so lucky.

"They are not worth a penny my love just silly nonsense." He squeezed her more tightly wanting to tell her the truth but also wanting to keep it from her. There was no way he could risk upsetting her at this point in her pregnancy, his heart still ached from her miscarriage earlier in the year.

"Come on I know you better than that, something is bothering you and you must tell me I'm your wife we share everything good or bad." She lifted her face to him and he laid a gentle kiss on her lips.

"Let's have a coffee as it's quiet and I promise to tell you what is on my mind… deal?"

He kissed her again not wanting to let her go.

They sat, holding hands under the table, staring at the empty lane leading to the beach.

It was a crisp sunny day, the sky that watery blue that looks as if it can't decide if it is going to rain or not. The wind had a chill to it that told you autumn had definitely arrived.

"I don't want to upset or worry you darling but the rent we used to get from Hugh is going to leave a hole in our finances and I was pondering what we could do to raise our income…" He looked downcast; his shoulders slumped even though he tried not to "I could go to the bank for a loan, I might have to actually what do you think?"

Lucy turned to him her eyes full of concern, his heart nearly broke he so desperately wanted to care for his precious wife and unborn baby. He felt wretched.

"Things are not that bad surely?" Her eyes seemed to bore a hole into him, he wanted to take back what he had just said and take care of things himself but then they were a team; he couldn't and wouldn't leave her out.

Lucy took hold of his hand squeezing it "I can always ask Dad, he would help us."

"No," snapped Bertie more sharp than he had intended, "... sorry darling but no, it's a good idea if all else fails but I want us to stand on our own two feet. He has helped us so much already and I want to do this on our own, prove that we can do it. You do understand don't you?"

"Yes, I do, and I do love you... so, so much." Bertie could see it in her eyes, he wanted to whisk her home and make sweet, tender love to his beautiful wife.

"I love you too. However, we can have a brainstorming session till we get customers and see what we can come up with."

They spent the next half an hour endeavouring to consider what ideas could bring in the customers, it seemed longer as the wind whipped up the lane from the sea and the storm clouds gathered and no one in sight. Bertie jotted them down, however bizarre, and they had put together quite a list when the doorbell tinkled startling them and in walked a man in wet weather gear carrying walking poles. He stood grinning at them, water dripping off his bucket hat.

Lucy gathered up their paperwork and mugs as Bertie turned to greet their customer.

"Good morning, what can I get you on this horrible wet day," Bertie enthused.

"Thankfully you are open; I panicked for a second there. Can I have a coffee and something hot? What do you recommend as I am starving."

He was as tall as Bertie with an unruly mop of sandy coloured hair. He pulled off his sunglasses pushing them into his pocket as he retrieved his wallet. Bertie couldn't help an amused grin as it was pouring with rain and this man had been wearing sunglasses. He shrugged to himself.

"How about an egg and mushrooms in a bun or we do have homemade Cornish pasties, cheese and onion or vegetable? I can soon warm one up for you," Bertie wondered who this man was? He hadn't seen him before perhaps just a coast path walker.

"I'll take the egg and mushrooms please and a vegetable pasty to go, thanks."

"Coming up…" Bertie disappeared into the kitchen as the customer made himself comfortable by the window. Bertie had an idea. He could advertise 'Winter Warming' lunch specials. He would have to look through his cookery books and check out the web for ideas.

Something old fashioned like vegetable stew and dumplings in a carved out cottage loaf; followed by steam pudding and custard or blackberry and apple crumble. He was thrilled that this man had come into the café this morning igniting his brain with yet more ideas. He resolved to engage him in conversation to try to find out about other cafes along the coast and do some research. He would not be beaten by this little setback.

Bertie deposited the burger with a dish of tomato relish and another filled with pickles onto the table before asking "Have you walked far today?" He placed cutlery and a napkin beside his plate.

"No, not really, I had hoped that it would clear up but it looks as though this squall is in for the day unfortunately," the man glanced out of the window in dismay before turning to Bertie once more, "… could you recommend a good B&B by any chance as it looks as though I might be stuck here for a day or two." He looked up hopefully before spooning some relish onto his bun and popping a gherkin into his mouth. "This is great by the way," he grinned.

"Hmm, well thanks but nothing springs to mind I'm not sure if anyone does B&B you might have to go into Wareham... you could try asking in the vet's, Hugh might know of somewhere. We have a cottage that has been let out long term. It's empty at the moment, we are looking for a longer let than a couple of nights but if all else fails we would consider it."

"Okay, thanks; can I let you know?" He picked up his burger and took a big bite before licking his lips as the relish squeezed out dribbling onto his chin.

The morning was quiet with a few brave wet stragglers popping in mainly for hot drinks and toasted teacakes. The heavy rain eased into a drizzle with occasional breaks in the clouds and the promise of some brightness that never came.

Lucy had been busy giving each table a deep clean, replacing the packets of sugar and topping up the salt and pepper pots.

"I think that we should invest in some more pretty gingham cloths in different colours Bertie, brighten up the place and the walls are a bit bare too. What do you think?"

Bertie pondered on the expense as he glanced around the café, she was right, of course. He let out a sigh, "... I wonder how much they would cost," he tapped his lips; it was becoming a habit so he put his hand into his pocket instead.

"Oh, Bertie..." Lucy chuckled "I can buy the material and make them myself that would be so much cheaper and anyway if the café is bright and cheerful then that would in itself entice customers in," she smiled indulgently.

"Sorry, I can't help it always calculating the cost… I was wondering about making scones today, I don't want them to be a waste, but on the other hand, if we get a rush on we won't have enough."

Lucy scanned the sky before replying "what about making Mediterranean muffins instead they will at least freeze and maybe a few scones just in case. I can chalk them up as a special if you like?" she raised her eyebrows at him.

"Good idea, I'll get to it right away." He threw her a smirk grateful that Lucy was a glass half full sort of person when he often wasn't.

The sky cleared a little at lunchtime with the odd spot of sunshine peeping through the clouds, and with it, a few people started to trickle into the café putting a smile firmly back onto Bertie's face.

Mid-afternoon saw Molly coming in with the twins fast asleep in their pushchair.

She looked drawn and tired very much in dire need of a pick-me-up.

"I have some free time before collecting Jessica so I thought that I would have a coffee and cake with you… if you have time, Lucy?" Molly waved a hand at Bertie behind the counter glancing quickly around the café.

"Great… I can manage that as we are not very busy today… sadly." She pulled in a deep breath "would you like a scone as we seem to have too many left and what sort of coffee do you fancy?"

Molly glanced at the chalkboard "Ooh Mediterranean muffins! I don't think I have had those before. I'll take four to go and a sultana scone now please, oh and a flat white."

She made herself comfortable taking off her raincoat and pulling out her iPad.

"Looks as though you have come to work, Molly? You should relax more." Bertie grinned wishing he could take his own advice, "… What are you up to anyway?"

"Thanks, Bertie, well, I have been working on the changes to the land by the church hall which has taken up a lot of my time and I am still sorting the arrangements for Maggie and Freddie's wedding. That reminds me who is going to be his best man any idea?"

"No, sorry. Why?" Bertie slipped into a chair next to Lucy taking hold of her hand in his.

"I have been looking at options for a hen night for Maggie and it suddenly dawned on me that I don't know who he has asked and I urgently need a guest list too." She tapped her iPad adding that to her ever-growing list of things to do.

"Also I know you don't normally open in the evening but how would you feel about having the hen night here? I had thought of canapés, the fizz of course and do you have a licence for music?"

"Whoa, let me get my iPad I need to start making notes and no we don't but yes we will open in the evening for Maggie but that has also given me an idea too. Give me a minute." Bertie dashed out to the back to retrieve his iPad; ideas now taking hold in his head, they were not going to fail in fact he couldn't wait to tell Lucy about the thoughts now racing around his brain. There was only one problem; with Emma gone, he couldn't do this on his own.

Chapter 37

The film crew were settling into a routine rolling up with the food wagon in tow and handing out freebies to the villagers taking part on any particular day. Today however was the decider for the land. The church hall was packed, standing room only. Molly had put together a PowerPoint to demonstrate the various options open to them and there were paper copies for anyone wanting to take one for closer scrutiny. Finishing with the TAG group preferred option.

Gary and the film crew had followed the proceedings from the beginning of TAG documenting all the twists and turns of planning including the now notorious Doris having another tantrum. Molly had assured him that she was not putting on an act for the camera, this was Doris being Doris. Gary had imagined in the beginning that this would be a nice, warm little documentary to slot into the early evening schedule. Instead, it was turning out to be quite a feisty village full of characters, not the sleepy little seaside cove he at first expected.

He had filmed the well-attended harvest festival although many people had turned up in the hope of being on TV. He was used to life in the smoke, not the community life he now found himself being drawn into. Felicity had been a big part of that draw, she was different, homely, understanding and more carefree; he had been used to sophisticated females, independent and demanding. He pulled himself back into the moment his eyes searching for Felicity he smiled at her, beginning to feel more at home in Dorset asking himself if that was dangerous?

The crew set up at the back of the room when suddenly there was an almighty cracking sound everyone fell silent staring around and looking up at the ceiling, was the roof about to fall in? It turned out to be a crack in a floorboard, a dangerous looking splinter had emerged, no one was hurt and Suzanne with the help of Hugh quickly roped the area off with some chairs.

Gary was delighted in a bizarre kind of way as it made great TV, even though luckily it turned out to be only a few splintered floorboards, no harm done, but it brought home the need for funds and urgent action. Gary couldn't have written a better script if he tried.

Molly brought the meeting to order and someone dimmed the lights as Molly explained how much money there would be from selling the land for housing, which brought a murmur of surprise around the room. She pointed out the various options and ideas that had been suggested before finally arriving at the one that the action group had settled on. At this point, she switched off her computer and with the lights back on introduced Freddie and Monty.

People wanted to know who the bungalows would be for, was a car park really necessary, the land should be used for a community garden and play area but as Molly explained the land was initially for church use and the needs of the church had to be considered first and foremost. Finally, Monty stood to take the floor.

"As some of you know my company Montgomery Construction has put forward the offer to buy the land and build the much-needed homes here in Trentmouth. I am pleased to announce to you that, if acceptable to Madam Chairperson and the action group that my team have taken a close look at this existing church hall. Now I know that it has been here for many years built of wood and a corrugated iron roof," he drew in a deep breath, "… but as demonstrated earlier when some of you could have fallen through the floor…" a chuckle went around the room, "… it has passed its sell-by date. Now I can see that efforts have been made to keep the place up together and I can assure you that we will re-use whatever we can but…" he paused again scanning the room. Doris was on the edge of her seat the room hushed. "I would like to announce that should you approve the plans today as the team have set out then my company will build you a new church hall free of charge," he smiled scanning around the room. There were gasps as people began to take in what Monty had just said and then someone somewhere in the room began to clap then one by one people began standing up and applauding, whooping and whistling.

Molly was on her feet too together with Suzanne and the rest of the action group. She attempted to get people to sit down again, waving her arms up and down and calling for hush.

Finally, she gained order around the room "That was quite a shock from Mr Montgomery I have to say. However, can I have a show of hands to accept the preferred plan as we have shown you tonight together with the kind offer from Monty to build us a new church hall?"

Shouts of aye went around the room and almost everyone raised their hand in a unanimous showing of acceptance. Only Doris looked glum as she had been one of the founder members who had built the original church hall. Gary had captured it all on camera and was busy congratulating his team. The crowds began to disperse and Suzanne quickly called the team together with Freddie and Maggie to join her back at the vicarage as soon as everything had been cleared away and locked up.

It was with great excitement that everyone crowded into the vicarage drawing room.

Suzanne opened bottles of wine and the few beers that she held in reserve for when Freddie visited, although these days he hardly had time for a cup of tea and stayed with Maggie in her cottage on the estate.

Suzanne tapped her glass for quiet "I hardly know where to start, what a tremendously successful evening. I am overjoyed," she gushed "a lot of hard work and effort has been put into this project and I am sorry that Doris felt she couldn't join us tonight but hey ho… nevertheless, and of course, mostly down to Molly," there was a ripple of applause "I would just like to say that this is only the beginning… now the real work begins. Can I ask you to raise your glasses to, Molly?" A cheer went up as everyone toasted their thanks to Molly.

The congregated team began to chat and split into small groups. Lady Isobel caught Monty's eye and he wandered over excusing himself from talking to Freddie.

"That was wonderful of you Monty, we would never have been able to afford to replace the church hall even though it was in desperate need of replacing and I'm sure that the whole community will be grateful, including Doris… eventually." She smiled.

"Well, to be honest, a lovely new cul-de-sac of bungalows next to the eyesore of a rundown old building isn't the best way to encourage buyers and I had already calculated the cost. To tell you the truth it was a pleasure to see the look of surprise on everyone's faces," he grinned "so Izzie when can I take you out to dinner?"

Gary found Suzanne, "Tonight has been fantastic Suzanne even the floorboards cracking, I am going to talk to my editor as soon as I can as I envisage a mini-series coming off the back of tonight not just a one-off documentary, what would you say to that?" He was grinning from ear to ear hardly able to contain his excitement.

"I don't know, if you think so Gary, nothing really happens here we are just a sleepy little backwater, a forgotten corner of Dorset." She sipped her drink feeling embarrassed.

"You are kidding me?" he sounded incredulous "I can't tell you how fascinating this place is and the characters make it a 'what on earth happens next?'" he raised his hands indicating inverted commas, "… event more like Emmerdale or Corrie and I love that title, I can see it now," he stared up towards the ceiling waving his arms across an unseen vista, "… A forgotten corner of Dorset, Suzanne, you're a genius. See what I mean?" He held her hands seeing stardom in his own.

Chapter 38

Monty had insisted on picking Lady Isabel up at home for their dinner date, she had managed to get an appointment at the hairdresser's, even had her fingernails and toes done, something she normally did herself but well this was a special occasion. Maggie had helped her choose what to wear. She had changed her mind dozens of times from a neat but boring turquoise suit that shouted 'business' into a rather snazzy and predictable little black evening number, before settling on a red woollen fitted dress with a matching jacket set off by her precious diamond necklace. Precious because Rufus had bought it for her to wear on their wedding day and until now she couldn't wear it without shedding a few tears. She wanted to give the air of interest and interest without being desperate because she wasn't was she? Well for good company and after that who knows she trilled.

Monty had booked a table at The Priory knowing that was Isabel's favourite restaurant. The Priory as its name implied was an old Priory, a delightful old stone building situated on the river banks at Wareham. It had extensive gardens where in the summer you could sit and have afternoon tea watching the boats sail by, sipping ice-cold champagne.

The staff, always on just the right side of friendly, efficient, smart and knowledgeable greeted her by name taking her wrap before sitting them at a table with a lovely view. Monty had arranged for champagne to be waiting on ice, a warm buttery yellow rose to set the scene, the waiter lit the candles and discreetly melted into the background.

"I must say you look beautiful tonight Isabel, just beautiful," his full lips lifting into a tiny but visible smile, his eyes twinkling in the candlelight. Isabel couldn't remember when she had felt so at peace as though everything was right, where it should be.

"Thank you," she managed before lapsing into a contented silence wondering what else to say she was not used to such occasions. She picked up her glass hesitating then allowing a wide smile to take over her face in an attempt to hide her trembling voice 'cheers' was the only word she was able to utter.

"… To a lovely evening," Monty touched her glass with his, "… and enchanting company," he took a sip.

The waiter arrived with their starters and they lapsed into chatter talking about silly things like the weather and his business keeping well away from anything remotely personal.

By dessert, they had covered the situation in China, the floods in Somerset and the fires in Australia. The whole world had been covered avoiding anything appertaining to them.

"Actually, Monty I would like to ask you about the Gardeners Cottage, I'm sorry if it's too much like a business when we are having such a delightful evening but I hardly get a chance to talk to you when we are at the house."

A waiter arrived "would Sir and Madam like to take coffee in the lounge? There is a lovely fire burning in there and it is very comfortable?" he politely asked.

"That's a good idea," he stood to leave offering his hand to Isabel, "… shall we?"

He was very gallant and irresistible; a small smile teased her lips 'lovely' she managed.

Monty turned to the waiter "do you have any of those delicious petit fours by any chance?" he raised his eyebrows whilst casually looping Isabel's arm through his. "Coming up, sir," the waiter bowed almost indiscernibly and disappeared. Monty led the way into the lounge where there was indeed a warming fire crackling in the grate. They sat opposite each other Monty unbuttoning his jacket and Isabel wanted to slip her shoes off but protocol dictated otherwise. The coffee and delicious looking petit fours arrived and the waiter disappeared discretely.

Monty did the honours passing Isabel a coffee offering her the first choice between a dark chocolate confection with a sliver of cherry on top, a white chocolate dainty square and two others all of which looked absolutely laden with calories. They sat back luxuriating in the tastes, smell of the rich coffee and the warmth of the fire enveloping them as if no one else in the world existed.

"Mmm," Monty said at last, "… you asked me about the Gardeners Cottage Isabel it is coming along nicely, in fact, I will be on-site on Monday and will give you a personal tour, and see if everything is to your satisfaction? Actually, the upgrades you have requested will make it quite luxurious, a very nice place indeed as a holiday let…" he paused, "… are you quite sure that is what you want?" He poured another coffee before demolishing the last chocolate.

"Quite sure and I shall look forward to seeing it on Monday," she sipped her own coffee tempted to tell him the truth but decided that it can wait for another day; after all, there was no hurry… yet.

"Tell me about Daisy, is she your only child?" Isabel neatly turned the conversation away from herself curious to know all about Monty and his family.

"Daisy…! Where to start, she is my only child I would have liked a son but…" he shrugged his shoulders, "… but it never happened and well when Daisy started courting Seb I was very pleased, he is a good man." He drank more coffee pinching the bridge of his nose as if he was hesitating too on how much to tell her. "I would have loved for Daisy to come into the business learn the ropes and take over one day," he sighed, "… as it turned out she has no interest in construction and went to catering college. She wants to be a chef, run her own restaurant. I am encouraging her as there is no point trying to get her to consider my business, the problem is she comes out of college and thinks that she can open up to the public with no actual experience." He raised his hands in mock horror "young people; you know how it is, I am trying to persuade her that she should get a job in any catering establishment to see how it all works before she sets her sights on her own place."

"So what is she doing at the moment?" Isabel was curious to know.

"Nothing… well actually that's not quite true she is planning her wedding, shopping and spending my money…" they both laughed at that. "However, Seb now, Daisy's fiancé, he is a great guy and I am going to train him up to be able to run the business and who knows they may have a son or a daughter who will want to follow their old granddad," he chuckled.

Isabel was feeling tired, it may be the warmth of the fire or the excellent meal, not to mention that last brandy, her eyes began to drop as she was enjoying a quiet moment.

"Will you excuse me, my dear?" Monty left her alone for a few moments returning with her wrap having settled the bill. Isabel allowed him to place her wrap over her shoulders his touch sending unexpected shock waves through her making her whole body tingle, waking all her senses even the ones she thought had disappeared forever.

On the doorstep back at the Manor, she turned to him "Would you like to come in for a nightcap?" as a smile danced on her lips.

"As wonderful as that sounds I shall reluctantly decline," he took her hand caressing her fingertips before kissing them tenderly. Isabel felt a surge of absolute delight coursing through her veins not wanting him to stop there, he lifted his head and leaning forward placed a soft kiss on her cheek waved 'goodnight' and disappeared.

Chapter 39

Molly burst into the café looking more fraught than usual, "Lucy I need your help…" she pulled out the nearest chair dragging her scarf from around her neck putting it onto the next chair together with her hat, gloves and coat. Lucy watched her in amusement as Molly made herself at home.

"Coming up…" grinned Lucy "shall I make that a double espresso?" not waiting for a reply she turned to the coffee machine, it hissed and gurgled into life. Lucy made herself tea as coffee strangely tasted horrible since she became pregnant. "I'll be with you in a minute," she turned to Bertie who raised his eyebrows in acknowledgement, they were getting used to Molly and her panic attacks, needing help. They grinned at each other.

"Is everything alright at home?" she quizzed, "… nothing wrong with Alistair or your three gorgeous children is there?" Molly shot her a startled look reaching for her phone and placing it on the table. Lucy exhaled as Molly didn't smile "Oh, oh not a good start Molly you had better tell me what's going on." She pushed a slice of lemon drizzle cake in front of her and Molly ate without tasting it, she gave the impression that the whole world had just landed on her shoulders.

"Well, it's six weeks to Maggie and Freddie's wedding and I still have a whole list of things to do, I have to arrange a birthday party for Jessica… I think she is having the terrible two's early…" Molly downed her coffee and Lucy nodded and pointed at Bertie to quickly get her a refill before Molly imploded. "On top of that, Alice and George are due back in ten days and Alistair thinks that it would be a great idea to throw a welcome home party…"

Molly nearly choked on that last one, "… and then… and then it's our wedding anniversary next week and… I haven't even begun to think about Christmas and presents… and everything," she started to sob.

"Hey, hey it's not that bad. Let's take it one at a time and tell me how I can help okay?" Lucy had jumped up to comfort her friend, lucky the café was empty so no witnesses.

"I presume Alistair is on babysitting duty?" she enquired passing Molly a box of tissues.

"Yes, yes he is," Molly wiped her eyes. "God knows I will be pleased to see Alice and George, especially Alice, as she does help out with the children. You know I never realised how much I would miss them and well it is a good idea to welcome them back… I just don't know how I am going to fit it all in?"

"Right, first things first, book an evening out for you and Alistair on your anniversary and we will look after the children."

"Are you sure?" asked Molly sniffing and pulling out another tissue.

"Quite sure, how hard can it be? No, don't tell me I will find out for myself," she held up her hand just as Molly sucked in her breath to launch into another tirade of explanation.

"Next," continued Lucy "what do you think about holding Jessica's party here in the café or we can just cater and deliver the food to you? And come to that you could host the welcome home for George and Alice here too as your place is way too small," she chuckled.

"Lucy, you're a lifesaver," she squealed, "what a brilliant idea! I will speak to Alistair and let you know." Molly returned to her cake looking like a different person.

"The last two on your list might take a bit more thinking about. I think that a meeting is needed with you Freddie, Maggie and probably Isabel too. Oh and Bertie of course and I don't know if I can help at all with Christmas but I will if I can." Molly grinned at her best friend.

"I did get a bit carried away didn't I?" she sniffed as a grin erupted.

"Better?" asked Lucy.

"Better."

Chapter 40

Alice grumbled as the taxi pulled up outside their front door "I thought that Alistair could have at least come to pick us up at the airport George, I am so tired and he's not even here to greet us now," she struggled out of the taxi rather crossly as George paid with a generous tip "and another thing I want to hear all about what is going on with only titbits from Molly I must be way behind on all the gossip... and poor Emma... I must speak to Hugh give him our condolences, find out how he is coping..."

They dragged their cases up the steps to the front door. George fumbled for his keys, "Alice, darling..." he turned weary eyes in her direction his shoulders slumped "we are not even through our front door and you want to rush off and be the Good Samaritan." He let out a sigh "please dear can we have a cup of tea, sit down and relax first? We are seeing Alistair and Molly later but till then we can sort ourselves out, have a look around the garden and well, just... just relax my dear, maybe even nod off for half an hour ready for tonight."

Alice knew he was right, but she had missed so much and she hadn't even mentioned the television people, the church hall and land, the vicar and Lady Isobel, they all needed her attention; she had no real idea what was going on. She dropped her shoulders heading for the kitchen to make a cup of tea leaving George to move the cases indoors.

The house felt warm and cosy enveloping her in its familiar scents and sounds.

Someone had at least attempted to dust the furniture as she appreciatively sniffed the scent of polish. She walked into her kitchen half expecting it to be a mess with dishes piled into the sink and crumbs on the floor as Freddie had been house-sitting for them whilst they were away, instead, she stopped stock still as what greeted her was an enormous vase of flowers and next to them a tin with a note propped in front. She smiled feeling better, they hadn't been forgotten and the kitchen was immaculate. She picked up the note; it was from Freddie thanking them for the kind loan of their home telling them that he had moved in with Maggie, the cake had been made by Molly and he hoped that they would enjoy the flowers. Alice smiled to herself; he was a lovely man, so considerate. She lifted the lid of the cake tin to find a lemon drizzle, their favourite and set about putting the kettle on.

A few minutes later she carried a tray into the snug where George, bless him, had already nodded off gently snoring. He looked so peaceful she didn't really have the heart to wake him so she sat down to drink her own tea and reminisce not only about their truly wonderful holiday but everything that must have happened whilst they were away. She knew about Emma, of course, and Molly had sent regular emails keeping her abreast of the goings-on with TAG but apart from that she knew little else. Maybe nothing to report! She chuckled to herself. That couldn't possibly be true; she hoped to find out this evening. Thinking back Molly had been right not to tell her too much she knew she would have fretted, and in any event, they were having a meal together tonight why at Bertie's she couldn't imagine but the young ones always did everything differently these days.

George stirred "Alice my dear ah a cup of tea, lovely," he sat up pulling at the belt around his trousers "I shall have to get back to my walking football… I wonder if they are still playing now that it's winter," he thrummed his fingers on the arm of the chair and picked up his china cup and saucer. "I thought that we might take an amble around the garden whilst we still have some light, I want to see how Freddie and Bertie have coped, check on the vegetable patch too." He beamed at her then leaning over took hold of her hand "we have had a magical holiday my dear, one never to forget, but I am happy to be home… with you."

A tear stung her eye, Alice sniffed pulling out a handkerchief dabbing away the tears "We have darling, I'm happy too I just love living here in Trentmouth I couldn't imagine living anywhere else on earth," she squeezed his hand "I'll get my coat and we can take that walk you mentioned around the garden and then I think that it might be time for sherry."

George pushed himself up wrapping his arms around her hugging her close placing a tender kiss on her lips.

Back indoors Alice shuddering from the cold pulling off her hat and gloves, she hung her coat in the hall cupboard pulling out her slippers. "How quickly we fall back into the same routine," she threw a grin at George, "… and I don't want to sound ungrateful but wouldn't it be nice to stay in tonight, see everyone tomorrow?"

George folded her in his arms "It would sweetheart, you know what? I love you… so much"

"… And I love you too… forever…"

"… And a day," they both chorused.

It was 6:30 when they finally pulled on their coats once more set off to walk the short half a mile to Bertie's café.

"I am surprised that we didn't get any calls this afternoon… but then again maybe they weren't sure what time we would be home." Alice snuggled up to George linking her arm through his.

"Probably, but I really don't mind. It was just perfect to have you all to myself." He grinned. They walked down the lane like loved up teenagers; George had remembered to bring a torch to light their path, as the only street lights were near the church and harbour.

They walked hand in hand through the village chatting about their plans for the next few days "Nothing has changed has it?" declared Alice. "There is no reason that it should, it all looks the same but I feel different somehow and you know what? You're right George," continuing without waiting for a response from him "I should take more of a back seat and let the young ones take over. We have many more adventures to plan." George merely squeezed her hand.

"Oh, look there's no light on in the vicarage, how strange, everything is so quiet. I suppose we have gotten used to the hustle and bustle of a cruise ship." They continued in silence for a moment or two before Alice drew in another breath "You don't think they have forgotten it's today that we were coming home do you?"

"I certainly hope not I'm starving," George quipped; Alice lovingly laid a gentle push on his arm giggling.

They reached the café, it was dimly lit and they could see Molly and Lucy laying up the table.

"They haven't forgotten us, dear; come on let's go in."
They climbed the short steps to the front door, George clicked
it open allowing Alice to enter first. The lights flashed on full
as an excited crowd burst out from the kitchen.

"Surprise…" they all chorused at once.

George and Alice stood momentarily stunned by the lights
and the noise before gasping with delight. Alice put both
hands up over her mouth agog at the sight in front of her, tears
welled up and she couldn't fight them as they trickled their
way over her cheek forming pathways through her make-up.
She snatched a tissue from her bag furiously dabbing them
away turning to George who looked just as surprised.

Everyone began talking at once demanding to know about
their holiday, where did they go? What did they do? What will
they remember forever? So many questions and Alice didn't
know who to speak to first. She could see Alistair at the back
of the room his arm around Molly, he was grinning at her as
Alice tried desperately to get to her son her arms longing to
hug him. Alistair signalled for a drink and Alice nodded her
face hurting from so much smiling. She manoeuvred her way
through the crowd her arms out to both Alistair and Molly.

"I've missed you all so much but what a wonderful
holiday we have had and so happy to be home. Tomorrow
Molly can I come and see our gorgeous grandchildren? If
you're not too busy," she threw a pleadingly glance at Molly.

"Of course, you can, it will be lovely to catch up when
you haven't got all these people clamouring for your
attention."

Alice was thrilled, and for the first time this evening, she
managed to look around the café properly. There was a banner
proclaiming 'WELCOME HOME' above the counter,

coloured lights strung around the windows and lots of bunting everywhere.

She made her way back to George handing him a glass of beer "I'm going to get something to eat before I faint and I want to talk to Isabel and I haven't even spoken to Hugh yet or Lucy and Bertie… isn't this wonderful dear?" she was delighted looking around and with her plate filled with quiche and salad, French bread and chutney she managed to find Isabel and sit down.

"Hello, Alice, you do look happy to be home," declared Isabel.

"Oh, I am; we have had the most fantastic time. I don't know where to start but I was hoping to hear what has been happening here with the church and the TV people…" Isabel cut her short "Oh, please Alice, time enough for a catch up later, enjoy your evening and if you're free to come over tomorrow afternoon for a cup of tea and I will show you what is happening up at the Manor alright?" Isabel returned to her supper and Alice knew that was the best plan. She could hardly expect Isabel to talk about private matters this evening when you didn't know who might overhear.

Alice and George managed to talk to everyone even fleetingly, finally catching up with Lucy who was taking the weight off her feet in a corner. She had pushed her shoes off and rather than wine was sipping a good cup of tea and nibbling at her food.

"Lucy dear how are you? You do look tired this evening and I must thank you for a wonderful spread, everyone is enjoying the food and we appreciate it very much." She patted Lucy on the arm, she could see the tired lines around her eyes.

"Thank you, Alice, but it is mainly down to Bertie and Molly," she rubbed her belly "this little one is playing for England in there and I must admit I do get very tired sometimes."

"You must take care of yourself dear, sit down more oh and how are your dear mum and dad? I thought that they might be here… are they alright?" she queried.

"Mum has good days and some bad days as you would expect she doesn't know what's going on half the time but it is my dad who is really suffering. He is afraid to leave her on her own and he is exhausted."

"Oh, dear, I will go and visit in a few days' time to see if I can sit with her to give him a break, what do you think?"

"That would be wonderful Alice thank you so much I will let Dad know, now tell me about your big adventure."

Isabel stood by the counter to collect her gloriously fattening lemon dessert and another glass of wine. She pondered over the chocolate swirly cake, fruit cake, scones, fruit and cream looking from one to the other hesitating over such a delicious display; the chocolate looked inviting.

"You can have more than one Isabel if you wish," said Bertie creeping up on her.

"Bertie, you made me jump I was miles away just then and thank you but I think I will treat myself to the chocolate concoction. I usually avoid chocolate cakes but not tonight."

Bertie sliced the cake placing it onto a plate together with a fork and napkin.

"Tell me how are you managing without Emma?"

Bertie looked down at the floor scuffing his toe as if he was carefully considering his reply "Actually, Isabel with Lucy being pregnant and not able to do as much I really, really miss Emma…" he let out a deep sigh "she was a godsend she made all sorts of cakes, marvellous with the customers. I desperately need another member of staff but… anyway don't let me burden you with my problems. I hope you are enjoying your evening?"

"I have an idea, Bertie, I can't tell you about it at the moment so can you leave it with me? I'll see what I can do."

Chapter 41

Things were happening so fast and furiously now. Alice was marvellous as Molly knew she would be, wanting to be a good Grandma taking care of the children as much as possible and Molly was grateful; being careful not to show too much gratitude.

A meeting had been arranged at the vicarage to run through the final preparations for Freddie and Maggie's wedding. Molly talked on her phone as she walked up the lane through the village. It was a crisp, cold morning; the sun was shining in a clear azure blue sky failing to warm her, her breath forming clouds as she spoke. Preparations were finalised for Jessica's birthday party, invitations accepted and she had left one very excited little girl at home with more energy than a bouncing kangaroo.

Gary thought that the meeting today would make a very good viewing poll on his now approved mini-series, a wedding on Christmas Day, he could hardly ask for more. However, not all the crew agreed preferring to be home with their own families; so when Gary had announced double pay plus a bonus he had found plenty of volunteers!

She scurried up the road glancing at her watch as her phone rang again.

"Hi, Stella, I'm just on my way now is everything alright on your end?"

"Morning Molly, yes fine I thought that I would just let you know that Jessica's birthday cake is ready and I'm sending you some pictures of the wedding cake for approval with Maggie today."

Stella now had a thriving business both locally and on the internet, her masterclasses were fully booked up and she had had to fit in extra dates for people wanting to learn to bake and ice Christmas cakes. She now had three staff helping her and even Tony had joined the company doing the accounts, ordering supplies, sending out parcels even doing deliveries.

Next on her agenda were fetes and festivals, Stella had calculated that getting involved with all manner of events, from church, village, sports, cheese, cultural events, music the list was endless and they all needed catering of different kinds especially delicious homemade gluten-free, nut-free, dairy-free, vegan and your usual full fat, cream-laden, fattening yummy cakes, was her next step. She was building an empire.

"Oh, and Molly… Mother rang… she wants to come over for Christmas…" Molly stopped stock still in the middle of the road, her eyes glazed over, how could she cope with a wedding, three very excited children, the film crew and her Mother on Christmas day? "Molly are you still there?" Stella sounded panicked for a moment.

"Yes. Yes, I am but I can't think about that now, can I call you later?" It would be good to see her Mother but then she would be no help at all, just another body to take care of and she wasn't invited to the wedding so what would she do on her own on Christmas Day?

"I'm sorry Stella but I feel like my head will explode at the moment; call you tonight?" She clicked off her phone as she pushed open the side gate to the vicarage trudging up the path.

Suzanne opened the door "Come on in Molly you look like you could do with a strong coffee, is everything alright?" Molly gratefully unwound her scarf, slipped off her boots placing her coat onto a stylish oak Art Deco hat stand just inside Suzanne's front door.

"Please, Suzanne. Is anyone else here yet?" she did her best to paste a smile onto her face but it slipped immediately her eyes stinging. She gulped quickly to swallow the lump that had lodged itself in her throat Suzanne clearly saw that something was wrong putting an arm around her shoulders.

"No. No one else is here come through to the kitchen and we can have a chat and that coffee before anyone else arrives."

Suzanne had settled into a very good life in Trentmouth, she was well-liked by the villagers and slowly the numbers in the congregation had increased due in part to the presence of the film crew. She had lots of good ideas even holding a service for pets when hamsters, rabbits and birds had been brought into the church as well as the usual cats and dogs.

The land next to the church hall had also won her lots of admirers, especially Doris who now championed the cause for more women vicars.

Suzanne put a mug of hot strong coffee in front of Molly "Do you want to talk about it?" she asked.

"I hardly know where to begin but the crux of the matter is that I have just spoken to Stella and Sandra, my Mother, wants to come over for Christmas and to be totally honest with you I don't think I can face it with everything else going on and on top of that I would have to put her on the couch as we are struggling with three children in our two-bedroom place as it is…" she trailed off picked up her coffee to take a soothing gulp, "… sorry Suzanne it's just that my Mother can be quite demanding and my focus should be the wedding and the children not my Mother who quite likes to be the centre of attention." She swallowed in an attempt to calm her frazzled nerves.

Suzanne took a deep breath "Well… I am rattling around this place on my own so how about if your mother stayed here with me? I will need some help in so many ways what with the carol service the crib service not forgetting midnight mass and a wedding… I could keep her occupied as the film crew will be here too." She grinned "What do you say?"

"Wow… Suzanne you have no idea, Mother will be in her element and she will think it marvellous to be relied upon. Yes. Yes, and yes," Molly jumped up hugging Suzanne just as the doorbell rang.

Everyone seemed to arrive at once and Suzanne set about making coffee and biscuits all around. Gary was the last to arrive with his usual sheaf of notes tucked under his arm.

"Do you mind if we go through my schedule first please as I have another appointment today before heading back to London tonight?" Gary was always in a hurry, gracious with it but no one was in any doubt that his other 'appointment' was with Felicity.

They all agreed quite happily and Gary opened his folder.

"Right now, sorry about this Suzanne but I need to confirm the arrangements for the other services as well as the wedding…" he glanced up at Suzanne who was pulling out a sheet of paper of her own, "… I never knew so many things happened in a church. It has been a real eye-opener, and I can see how it is a full-time job and not just on Sundays." They all chuckled at this as the look of revelation on Gary's face told its own story.

Suzanne handed him an agenda of all the upcoming events with times and locations including the Christmas Fair, probably the last event in the old church hall as it was scheduled for demolition in the New Year. They discussed exactly what Gary needed to film of the wedding, mainly beforehand, the arrival of the bridesmaids, the groom with the best man and finally the bride. He was not filming the actual wedding as Maggie and Freddie wanted to keep it more personal not share it with, the hoped-for, 5 million viewers! He would then take a few shots of the two of them setting off on honeymoon even if in reality they were staying in the honeymoon suite at Trentmouth Manor.

"Right, that's me sorted, Suzanne…" he looked at his watch "I'll see you…" he checked his agenda "Saturday week for the Christmas fete, I'm off." He bent to kiss Suzanne on her cheek before exiting quickly on his way.

"Phew," exclaimed Suzanne "right who's for more coffee?"

They worked through their individual lists. Bertie left as soon as the food for the reception had been approved and finalised. That left Freddie, Maggie, Isabel and Suzanne together with Molly.

"I still have two questions on my list… I hope you have some details for me, Maggie. I really need to know who is going to walk you down the aisle and who is going to be the best man?" she asked turning to Freddie.

"Well, I have no idea where my father is as you all know and even if I did I would not be asking him… so… as I have spent almost all of my life here with Aunt Isabel and sadly Uncle Rufus is no longer with us. I have asked Aunt Isabel to give me away and she has accepted," she turned a beaming smile in the direction of Isabel who returned it with pride.

Everyone burst into applause and congratulations.

"Freddie, I do hope that you have finalised your best man?" Molly turned a pleading glance in his direction.

Freddie shuffled for a moment "Well, yes I have, I couldn't get hold of him, to begin with, he's always off on some adventure or another, and then he needed to confirm his plans with his parents. They live in Scotland and he usually spends Christmas with them and as he's an only child he wanted to make sure they were happy! They have agreed provided he is with them for Hogmanay."

Suzanne nearly burst with surprise "Felix said yes? That's wonderful Freddie. I can't wait to see him, how is he, and more to the point, where is he? He can stay here with me for the wedding; oh I am so excited this is fantastic news." She hugged her brother with delight.

"I will fill you in later Suzanne. He wants to wear his clan tartan as he will proudly be the next Laird MacKinnon, so of course, I said yes and actually he wants to spend a month down here getting to know everyone before the wedding. In fact, he has rented Bertie's cottage already, he arrives tomorrow."

"Fabulous I will cook tomorrow night. Please all come, including you and Alistair Molly and I will invite Hugh…" she paused for rather a long moment and Molly who had been sitting in awe of what was happening around her turned to Suzanne.

"Hugh… is there something I should know, Suzanne?" all eyes turned towards Suzanne and she blushed a deep scarlet fumbling with her fingers.

"Err, well, actually Hugh and I… That is to say, Hugh asked me out and I said yes." her face turned puce.

"That's fantastic Suzanne… absolutely fantastic!" Congratulations came thick and fast from all directions.

"I always thought that you and Felix might…" Freddie trailed off "He was asking about you actually… I am thrilled for you and Hugh just the same."

"Felix and I are good friends, always have been since we were kids really, nothing more, he's like another brother to me… never anything romantic," she finished all flustered.

Molly looked at Suzanne intently, watching her squirm; she couldn't wait to meet this Felix he sounded intriguing and she wondered if they had only been friends after all.

Chapter 42

Isabel wrapped up warm to walk across to the Gardeners Cottage where she knew Monty would be waiting for her. She pulled on a pair of gloves and her Dubarry boots, having a final took into the mirror, checking her hair before setting out. The air was icy cold with a touch of frost on the grass glittering in the pale sunshine, a biting wind wrapped itself around her playing with the hair she had carefully done only minutes before. Cobwebs were delicately draped across the hedges, themselves covered in frost with not one spider to be seen. A robin hopped onto the path in front of her bobbing up and down. Isabel smiled enjoying her brisk walk pulling her coat more tightly around her.

A few minutes later she saw Monty on the doorstep, he raised a hand in greeting, she returned his wave hardly able to contain the rush of warmth she felt for him.

"Morning Isabel not too cold for you today, is it?" he rubbed his bare hands together attempting to warm them.

"I'm fine; thank you, Monty and excited to see what progress you have made." He opened the door for her where the warmth instantly hit her "Oh, I see you've lit the fire and I have to say it's wonderful." She crossed over to it immediately pulling off her gloves to feel the warmth on her fingers that were fast turning into ten white icicles.

"Actually, I wanted to make sure that it worked as it is one of the decisions I have for you today." He joined her pulling up two upturned wooden crates to sit on. "You mentioned a wood-burning stove but as this only needs the chimney swept and checked and the fireplace isn't damaged I wondered if you might like to keep it?"

"I see what you mean Monty I had thought that a wood burner might be more attractive to holidaymakers but you're right it would be wrong to remove this original fire surround in some ways, and I can just see it now Christmas tree in that corner," she pointed to the space to the right between the fireplace and the mullioned bay window, "... stockings hanging from the mantel intertwined with holly and candles... hmm," she could see in her mind's eye, a couch draped with a red and white throw, a happy couple entwined just enjoying sipping brandy, lights twinkling on the tree, snow falling outside "hmm... yes, perfect Monty let's do it," she could almost smell the turkey roasting and sweet-smelling cinnamon filling the air from hot mince pies.

"Great! Right, I'll take care of it. Sorry, I can't offer you a coffee to keep you warm Isabel I didn't think to bring a flask today." He rubbed his hands again before taking notes about the changes.

"Oh, please Monty, come and have coffee with me when you have finished here as I have something else I want to talk to you about, it will be a bit more private at the Manor," she threw him a teasing smile. The men were banging and hammering somewhere in the cottage and what she had to say was definitely for his ears only.

His eyebrows shot up with curiosity but he merely smiled, a twinkle in his eyes his only betrayal "Of course I would be delighted. Now I want to walk you around the cottage just to confirm once again your requirements before we start removing walls." They proceeded through each room as Isabel shared her vision of how she wanted the cottage to look with an open plan kitchen dining room through to the lounge with its large bay window overlooking the extensive grounds to the sea beyond.

"Right Monty, if that's it I will walk back to the house and put the kettle on." She turned to leave slipping her gloves on once more.

"I will be with you shortly Isabel I just need to have a word with Seb to make sure he is up to speed with the alterations."

She set off once more along the drive thinking that it would be a good idea to have a low stone wall built to delineate the boundary of the cottage and it might seem extreme but a garage and a carport would be very useful too. A robin was singing its heart out nearby making her beam a smile of satisfaction at her plans. As she drew closer to the house she noticed that snowdrops were pushing their way through the earth and already the air was heavy with its winter cloak.

Suddenly she stopped still, staring up at the house, her heart sank as she saw a familiar car parked by the entrance… it was Jeremy. She panicked for a minute staring around wondering if he had seen her but he must have as she saw the driver's door open. On instinct, she pulled out her phone quickly pressing the number for Monty as he was the nearest person who could help her. She put him in the picture and he promised to be there as quickly as possible. Feeling more confident she returned her phone to her pocket marching up to Jeremy who was now standing, hands-on hips, looking decidedly annoyed.

"There you are Aunt Isabel you shouldn't be out in this freezing weather." He was being suspiciously ingratiating leaving Isabel wondering what he was up to now. She didn't have to wait long.

"Jeremy," she politely responded as she pulled the key from her pocket and let them in. "Come through to the kitchen and I will put the kettle on."

"Thank you; it is perishing out there, and I have driven down from the smoke too cold to stop. And thinking about it I ought to have a key to the old place... for the future, of course." Isabel merely glanced at him, fuming inside, saying nothing.

Isabel busied herself with the kettle and mugs hesitating to ask him what he was doing here, she could bide her time when hopefully Monty would arrive. She fashioned sentences in her mind wondering how she could be more direct than she already had been. He was not inheriting a penny despite what he may think and he had threatened to return to claim what he thought was rightfully his.

Jeremy sat at the kitchen table, "... three mugs, is there someone else here, Isabel?" It hadn't taken him long to drop the polite 'aunt' from his conversation.

"Actually, yes, Monty will be joining us in a minute." She poured out the coffee and opened a packet of biscuits putting them onto a plate.

"Not that builder, what is he doing here? And anyway what I have to say is in private not for the ears of a workman," he spat derisorily. "I came to let you know that I am willing to overlook that other… umm… little lapse on your part Isabel and to talk about this sensibly."

He had some gall and it took all her time to stay calm. Isabel bit her tongue to stop herself from saying something she might very well regret; she would not stoop to his level merely saying 'Monty is my guest'.

"Look Isabel I can only stay for the weekend so our conversation will keep for later," he reached over picking up a couple of biscuits as calm as you like. Isabel's heart leapt in her chest that was the last thing she wanted she could not allow that to happen she had to think fast. The doorbell rang and she dashed to the door her head still buzzing.

Isabel let Monty in "Thank goodness you are here Monty," she squeezed his arm, "… just please go along with anything I say," she looked pleadingly into his eyes with panic rising up causing her to tremble.

"Alright…" he hesitated but he politely took his coat off, "… you're shaking Isabel, he hasn't touched you has he?" He put his arms around her, concern flooding his face.

"Nothing yet, just being here he unnerves me and he thinks he is staying the weekend," she hissed her voice rising, "… but not if I can help it."

"Don't worry I'll follow your lead," they casually wandered into the kitchen. Monty was politeness exemplified. He walked straight up to Jeremy his hand out.

"Jeremy… hello how are you?" Isabel seethed at the never-ending rudeness of her nephew as he made a grump in response ignoring Monty's hand.

"I'm afraid you can't stop here for the weekend Jeremy it isn't convenient," he shot his head up at her, a mixture of disdain and anger on his face. Isabel merely calmly topped up her coffee passing one to Monty. He smiled at her took his coffee and sat down at the table.

"Why ever not?" he sounded astounded at this announcement. "And what do you mean not convenient?" He spluttered spittle flying across the table. Isabel stood to collect a cloth to clear up the mess, a smirk crossing her face when her back was turned. "… I have things to say to you."

She swung back round to face him with undisguised anger on her face, enough was enough "Well, I have nothing to say to you and… because Monty is staying here this weekend." She crossed over to stand behind Monty placing her hands on his shoulders resting her head in a loving gesture. Monty stayed calm his unblinking eyes on Jeremy.

Jeremy looked from one to the other, "… you and him…?" He stared for a minute his eyes bulging in disbelief, "… that was bloody quick poor Uncle Rufus isn't even cold in his grave! You don't deserve to inherit this place. You're a bloody disgrace to the family." He scowled jumping up grabbing his car keys "I wouldn't stay now if you begged me to and as for you… you have no idea what you are getting into… I would be careful if I was you." He narrowed his eyes pointing a finger at Monty before he made a dash for the door pausing only to glance over his shoulder spluttering some obscenity as he slammed the front door revving his car and speeding down the drive.

Isabel let out the breath she had been holding and they both burst out laughing "I'm sorry Monty for involving you like that but I didn't know what else to do and you were marvellous."

"The pleasure was all mine," he picked up her hands kissing her fingertips "if that invitation is still available I would love to stay with you for the weekend." He cupped her face in his hands caressing her cheeks with his thumbs, placing a tender kiss on her lips, "… as a guest of course…" He must have sensed her hesitation even as her heart leapt in the air a warm rush of blood spreading through her like wildfire. She returned his kisses with an urgency that threatened to overwhelm her; pulling back feeling that it was way too soon she broke away her head taking over, she looked deep into his loving eyes unable to resist him any longer.

"I would like that very much," he kissed her again his arms around her pulling her in close, Isabel returned his embrace with the same hunger she could feel from him.

Chapter 43

"Daddy… where are you I have been trying to contact you all weekend?" Monty grinned to himself, he thought about not telling her thinking that she might take a defensive position even attack him assuming that he had forgotten about her mother. Actually, that couldn't be further from the truth, he had loved his wife dearly and was more lost and lonely than he imagined possible after she died.

He placed an arm around Isabel pulling her towards him as they snuggled in bed enjoying a lazy Sunday morning drinking coffee. "Well, Daisy, my love, I am sorry about that but I am staying at Trentmouth Manor… as a guest of Lady Isabel," he kissed the top of Isabel's head and smiled raising his eyebrows, Isabel just grinned.

"Oh…" replied Daisy.

He could hear the puzzlement in her voice quickly deciding not to enlighten her further he took a deep breath, "… actually Daisy I want to talk to you too, you know that lovely place we visited down by the sea at Trentmouth, Bertie's Café?"

"Yes, Daddy, the food was very good, why?" She was always suspicious he chuckled to himself, just like her mother.

"Could you and Seb meet me there in about an hour for coffee?" He glanced at his watch a mischievous look on his face.

"Okey-dokey… is everything alright?" there goes that suspicious nature again.

"Of course, I just thought that it would be good to spend some time with my daughter that's all."

"Right… see you later… bye," and she was gone. Monty switched his phone off turning to Isabel to kiss her very gently, she was as sweet as nectar. He didn't want to leave her, and he pushed her hair back from her forehead.

"You don't mind do you, Isabel? Only after what you told me earlier I think that I should see her on my own." Holding her face between his hands he kissed her eyes, her nose and her soft silky cheek. He exhaled loudly not wanting to but knowing he must drag himself away from her side.

"No, of course, not… I will miss you," she threw him a smile.

"What a wonderful woman you are Isabel… perhaps I could come back later? If you don't have other plans that is." He desperately wanted to see her again but was equally afraid of pushing his luck.

Isabel threw the covers back swinging her legs out of bed, he caught her hand "We need to get dressed if you are planning to meet Daisy in an hour," she grinned.

He drew her back towards him "Oh, I think we have plenty of time…" she slipped back between the sheets, Monty kissed her deeply, caressing her, cupping her dainty rounded breasts "you are so beautiful," he whispered finding her every curve feeling her shudder under his touch. He wanted to explore every part of her, delighted when she moaned his name, he needed her desperately but he could wait. He slowly explored her body tracing his fingers over her smooth skin feeling her passion building and when she arched her back ready to receive him he slid into her as they reached a crescendo of love together.

Daisy and Seb were already waiting for him when he arrived at Bertie's, he glanced at his watch, and he was late. A smile caressed his lips as he thought of Isabel, desire climbing within him again. He shook hands with Seb and kissed his daughter.

"I ordered coffee for us Daddy I hope you don't mind?" she had a petulant look on her face; he smiled knowing that she would not ask him why he was at Trentmouth Manor.

"Wonderful, do you want anything to eat? I'm starving," his thoughts took him back to Isabel in her kitchen with nothing on but a flimsy negligee, he grinned at them in an effort to concentrate and put the picture of Isabel to the back of his mind. He looked over his shoulder at Lucy who approached them pad and pen in hand.

"Hello, Monty, what can I get you?" She was radiant now sporting a definite bump, her apron just about reaching around her waist; she tucked a strand of hair behind her ear.

"I would like a toasted teacake please and marmalade, what about you two?" He looked from one to the other. Their orders were given Monty glanced around noticing the plastic sheet over the wall at one end wondering what was happening behind it, the builder in him curious at what was going on. He suddenly realised that Daisy was speaking to him and he dragged himself back to the here and now.

"Sorry, Daisy, I missed that; what did you say?" He picked up his napkin shaking it out returning his gaze back to his daughter.

"I asked what you wanted to see me about Daddy; you mentioned something on the phone." She bit into her egg roll.

"Oh, yes, can we go for a walk along the beach, if you have time, I will explain later but not here okay? This is a lovely place don't you think?" He glanced around as Lucy returned with more coffee.

"Yes, yes it is…" she sounded confused Monty grinned to himself deftly ignoring her questioning voice.

"Thank you, Lucy. What is going on over there behind that sheet of plastic may I ask?"

He buttered his teacake tipping the small jar of marmalade on top. It smelt warm and spicy full of plump sultanas he bit into it licking his lips.

"Oh, it was just a storeroom and a passage into the cottage but as we need more space we are turning it into a comfy spot for groups as we get a lot of walkers and we thought that it could double as a community shop where locals can display and sell crafts," she turned to him with a questioning look for his opinion.

"That sounds like a very good idea, excellent in fact, if you need any help please ask. I could pop back sometime just to have a look for you as you may need a lintel in there." He pointed to where Bertie had removed the old door and widened the entrance into the old storeroom.

"Thanks, Monty, that would be great. Any chance you could stop by when we are quiet between say 9:00 and 9:30 tomorrow morning? I can rustle up coffee and toast for you," she smiled.

"Yes, sure, I will just see the boys first up at Trentmouth Manor at 8:00 and then come on down," he turned back to Daisy "If you are ready we can go for that walk," he settled the bill and they set off along the promenade.

Despite the bright sun low in the sky, there was a brisk breeze blowing off the sea, the air tasted salty whipping around their faces. Daisy hung onto her dad's arm at one side and held onto Seb on the other.

"Okay, Daddy, time to spill…"

Monty took his time reliving the romantic and quite unexpected weekend he had spent with Isabel. She was indeed a woman a man could lose his head over, not just beautiful and she was beautiful but the kind of woman a man could see himself growing into old age with.

He felt his loins stir within him, he needed her, wanted her.

"Daddy…!" the sound of Daisy's voice broke into his reverie. He reluctantly and with necessity dragged himself back to the beach and his daughter.

"Yes, Daisy…" he patted her hand smiling at her. There was nothing he wouldn't do for his one and only daughter and he must be careful that she didn't find this out. "I have been thinking quite a lot about your desire to open your own restaurant."

"Oh, Daddy, thank you… thank you… thank you… I knew…"

"Hold on a minute Daisy, I didn't say anything about buying a restaurant for you in fact let me say right now that I will not be doing that," he paused to let that information sink in. He didn't want to hurt her but he knew only too well that she had absolutely no experience and that failing with your first business venture can seriously damage anyone's ego as he knew to his cost.

"You have told me yourself that you and Seb want two or three children…" she made to splutter and contradict him, he held up his hand, "… and I would love nothing more than to be a granddad but… you have your wedding next year and I know how much work you are putting into that, it will be everything you want it to be. So with that in mind, I have done a little research…" he thought it best not to mention that it was actually Isabel's idea at least not today.

"You know that delightful café down near the sea "Bertie's?" he paused waiting for a response. Daisy nodded. "He recently lost his right-hand woman, a lovely lady called Emma, anyway he is looking for a new member of staff, someone who can bake and cook light lunches, someone who can be relied upon, be innovative and I thought of you my darling."

"… But Daddy I want to run my own restaurant, I don't just want to be a waitress…" she wailed pouting at Monty. He let out a sigh glancing over her head at Seb looking for support.

Seb took the hint and pitched in, "… sounds good to me Daisy you will get loads of experience and Bertie isn't just looking for a waitress although it would be good to tackle all areas of a business from the ground up as I did with your dad so that you understand it better for when you do have your own place." He sucked in a deep lung full of negative ions off the sea and launched again "I like Bertie, he has some brilliant ideas… already he is the go-to cafe for veggies and vegans making quite a name for himself… Why don't you think about it?" He put his arm around her shoulder pulling her in close, kissing the top of her head, "… and don't forget I want to see us with lots of children too."

Daisy was quiet for a few moments then she sucked in a deep breath before launching with "I suppose I could put some of my ideas forward too, try them out see what works… I do like the place, a lot actually… I even thought that we should become vegan Seb," her eyes lighting up beginning to get some enthusiasm together "I might just have a chat with him see if I think that we could work together." He kissed her head once more throwing a wink at Monty. In reply, Monty mouthed 'thank you' back at him with a grin.

They made their way back towards the quay Daisy huddled against Seb to keep warm and chat happily about all the things she could do to improve the business for Bertie and Lucy. Monty wisely said nothing.

Chapter 44

Trentmouth was covered in a blanket of snow, it looked magical, the sky heavy with more snow to come. Alice shivered. She stood at the French doors staring out at her garden. The holly and yew were both heavily laden with scarlet berries, melting snow dripped from the tips of leaves. The roses she hadn't had time to prune looked forlorn struggling against the cold wind that blew wisps of snow piling them into corners.

"I wish we could stay in by the fire," moaned Alice as George came in carrying a tray of coffee and crumpets. She turned to look at him dropping the curtain back in place.

"Now you know you don't mean that and anyway Molly is relying on you to help her today at Jessica's party," he put the tray down in front of the log burner before pulling her to him in an affectionate hug. "We are so lucky you know, Alistair and Molly make a good team and the children are such a joy," he laid a gentle kiss on her lips.

"I know it's just so cold and do I miss Australia…"

George burst out laughing "I never thought that I would hear you say that Alice, it took me two years to persuade you to go to Oz and now you miss it…" he shook his head chuckling even more "I do love you, Alice…"

"Oh, you know what I mean, of course, I love our home and everything but it was sunny and warm in Oz every single day… and I suppose that could get boring too." They sat drinking coffee and munching their crumpets listening to the radio.

"What time are we due at Bertie's for Jessica's party dear?" asked George looking up from his paper.

"Not till about three, I said that I would help her set up the bunting and lay the tables.

You could help blow up balloons George I'm sure Alistair would appreciate the help. I am so grateful that Bertie is doing the food and that new girl, Daisy her name is, seems quite pleasant. She had lots of suggestions for food and decorations and I couldn't help notice the look from Bertie as he rolled his eyes… but she was quite right you know, food for children should look like fun so that they will eat it."

"I think that you like this new girl, Daisy, I shall enjoy meeting her." he shook his paper out picking up a pen for the crossword. Alice turned her attention to the garden once more letting out an enormous sigh. At the sound of George folding his paper, she allowed a smile to crease her lips knowing that that was the sign for more conversation.

"You have been very quiet dear is anything the matter?" George had infinite patience and Alice relished the opportunity in letting him tease out of her what was really on her mind.

"No…"

At this, George twisted round in his chair sitting up straight. His piercing deep blue almost black eyes directly trained on her more delicate periwinkle blue ones, she fluttered them ever so slightly.

"I know that look only too well so you might as well tell me what is on your mind?"

Alice had him "I have been thinking, especially since our return home, that maybe we could do more travelling… the only thing is…" she clasped and unclasped her hands a signal to George that here comes the big one.

"What have you been thinking my darling?" he took her hand smoothing his thumb back and forth in a soft way that always sent a tingle through her even after forty years of marriage.

"I have always loved this house and never wanted to leave it… I somehow feel closer to Christopher here… I know it's silly and I often wonder how he would have turned out as an adult…"

"My darling I think about him too and he would have made us just as proud of him as Alistair has. Come here…" they stood up clinging to each other in a loving embrace, he kissed her head squeezing her tightly. "You are my world sweetheart and I do love you… so much. What has brought all this on?" He pulled back holding her at arm's length looking into her crinkled face.

"I was just thinking that maybe now is the time to downsize, we don't need this big house, we would be much better off in a smaller property…" she gulped down her worries, "… you mentioned moving into Wareham a couple of years ago but… I don't want to do that, I, I know what you said about the bank and the shops but that doesn't bother me. What I really want to do is stay here, in Trentmouth, be near the grandchildren." She searched his face for a clue as to what he was thinking; he had placed a finger onto his lips tapping a few times. Alistair did that too she grinned.

"Hmm, you could be right my dear, why don't we consider those new bungalows that Monty is going to build next to the church hall and…" before he could finish Alice had grabbed him and was kissing him all over his face.

"Brilliant idea, I had thought about that too but wasn't sure how you would respond, yes, yes let's do that but we must keep it to ourselves at the moment."

"Good idea, I will have a quiet word with Monty then we can plan our escape to more exotic places, the world is ours." He grinned.

"Oh, George, yes, I am so excited I could burst…" she placed both hands on her face trying to stop the grin as it threatened to stretch her face out of shape. She chuckled, excitement rushing through her veins.

"Me too… in fact, I have a cure for all that pent up energy," he took her hand leading her out of the snug and up the stairs.

Chapter 45

The party for Jessica was deafening with so many excited children racing round and round.

There were whoops of joy, bumped heads and bursting balloons galore. The café had been transformed into a little girl's pink palace with twinkling fairy lights, pink streamers, pink tablecloths; pink paper napkins even the little gift bags for the guests to take home were pink naturally, and tied with pink ribbon.

"Bertie this is fabulous." Molly was enthused when she managed to find a moment of peace to corner him. The children were all sitting eating star-shaped sandwiches with bits of star-shaped cucumber, tomato, pepper and carrot. For a few minutes, at least, they were all munching away happily without causing a riot.

"Don't thank me. This is all down to Daisy," he encompassed the room with a sweep of his hand. "I have to say I was a little bit dubious about taking her on, she is a bundle of energy and her ideas for this place are never-ending… however, she got this right. She made me take down all the Christmas decorations saying that they would spoil the birthday atmosphere, and of course, she was right… again, the only thing is I will be up late tonight returning the café back to normal and putting the Christmas tree back up… ready for breakfast tomorrow."

Molly turned to him, "… look as this was all done for Jessica I'll get Alistair to help you restore the café and then when you are finished come up to us for a proper drink and some supper. Lucy can help me with the children; hopefully, Jessica will not be sick or too hyper from too much sugar to sleep then we can all chill out. What do you say?"

"Fabulous, we would love that, you're on."

Molly turned her attention back to the party wandering over to George and Alice.

Alice looked quite red in the face which concerned Molly as she didn't like to think that Alice was overdoing it.

"Everything alright Alice you look quite flushed?"

"Yes, yes everything is just wonderful Molly dear, it's just quite warm in here don't you think?" Alice threw a smile at George who nodded saying nothing, simply returning her grin.

"Okay, if you say so, Alice," she shrugged leaving Molly mystified, perhaps their holiday had done them the world of good which was just as well as Molly would have to talk to them soon about the changes in the village. She had to discuss the television schedule, all the progress with the church hall as Alice had missed all the meetings, not to mention the changes at the church… however, it could all wait till after the wedding which was now less than a week away.

Molly stood in the kitchen preparing supper. Alistair and Bertie were still busy at the café and Lucy was happily engaged reading a bedtime story to Jessica. She took a deep sip of her favourite Australian red wine relaxing in its warmth as it slid deliciously down her throat.

She tipped her head back, closing her eyes reviewing the last three months.

A whirlwind had happened and she was definitely left whizzing around herself. She toyed with the idea of setting up a Wedding Planning business, she could do it she knew there was no doubt but a few questions gnawed at her. Most importantly she was a mum with three small children, who to be fair needed her full-time attention. She had promised to be a locum for Hugh; that brought its own problems as she had to keep up to date with new drugs, rules and regulations, procedures... she let out a sigh. Then, of course, there was Alistair; he had taken a dim view of her involvement with the church hall project and all that that had entailed and if she were honest there was far more to it than she had imagined.

She stirred the tomato sauce having decided that a simple mushroom pasta dish with a green salad, fresh bread with fruit to follow was a quick and easy option after such a hectic day. Her thoughts were shattered as Alistair and Bertie fell through the door having clearly started their evening early already a little tipsy. She put a finger to her lips shushing them.

They tiptoed in like two naughty schoolboys flopping down onto the sofa. She listened as they continued their chat in more hushed tones.

"I don't know how you do it Alistair working full time plus taking care of Molly and three children..."

Molly almost choked on her wine as she mused over poor Alistair. He was not doing the nurturing, cooking, cleaning, shopping and a thousand and one other jobs that all vied for her attention but to be fair he did stack the dishwasher... when he remembered... she couldn't help but grin to herself.

"Molly, I have to confess, does most of it mate… but I do support her and do my bit, we are a team after all." Alistair was sprawled across an armchair one leg over the side looking for all the world like a man who thinks he is in charge.

Only two men could have a conversation like that and believe it she chuckled leaving them to it she set the table and popped up to find Lucy. Jessica was fast asleep and poor Lucy had nodded off, the book still open on her lap. She carefully closed the book shaking Lucy to wake her. She woke with a start. They crept out of the room to find the boys draining her precious bottle of red.

"Hey what about us," called Molly whisking up her glass for a top-up.

"Not for me," said Lucy lovingly patting her stomach with a grin.

"Right let's eat," Molly placed the dishes onto the table, exhausted they all tucked in.

Alistair stoked the dying embers of the fire adding a couple of logs as Molly poured out hot chocolate long after Bertie and Lucy had gone home.

"I'm worried about your mum, Alistair," Molly said nonchalantly as she pulled a dark chocolate mint out of its box. Alistair whipped his head round in her direction.

"Oh… why is she ill?" his tone taking on the immediate concern.

"No… no, I don't think so; she just looked flushed to me and I wondered if looking after the children was too much for her that's all." She picked up another mint popping it into her mouth relishing the smooth chocolate as it slid down her throat.

"I'll pop round tomorrow to make sure everything is alright." He sat on the sofa next to her placing his arm around her shoulder pulling her close, toying with a strand of her hair.

"That was a brilliant party today, Jessica loved it." He kissed her head lightly before moving down to nibble her ear nipping it between his teeth. Molly laid her head on his shoulder snuggling closer.

"Yes, it was, I am so grateful not to have done the work myself," she let out a moan, melting into him.

Alistair pulled her up to standing sliding his arms around her waist pressing her into him "You are the best Molly I love you so much and I'm sorry if I don't say it often enough," Molly traced a finger across his lips "apology accepted, however..." she softly touched her lips to his letting her tongue tease his ever so gently.

"... However...?"

"However... you could show me exactly how much..." she began to unbutton his shirt slowly drawing out the pleasure of sliding her hands over his taut chest.

In a second, he had his shirt off and lifted Molly's top throwing it onto the floor. Molly grabbed the blanket from the back of the sofa, throwing cushions onto the floor she wanted him and wanted him now.

Chapter 46

Molly sat on the floor surrounded by heaps of brightly coloured wrapping paper, tinsel, ribbons and sticky tape. She tied a parcel she had covered with bright red glittery paper with an equally bright red glittery bow. She held it up admiring her work of art before placing it under the tree.

Lucy had come to help leaving Bertie assisting Monty in the café. A lintel had been installed, plastering done and now they were painting the new community room extension to the café. Bertie had insisted that he could do it himself but Monty had pointed out that it would be quicker with two in exchange for lunch and a beer. Bertie couldn't refuse.

Molly and Lucy had put up a huge Christmas tree which was threatening to swamp the room even though the rafters opened up to almost a double-height room. The fairy on top of the tree touched the ceiling with her magic wand giving the whole room a magical atmosphere. The tree was festooned with twinkling white lights, red and green baubles spun and shone throwing sparkling shapes and shadows around the sitting room and across the ceiling.

"Thank goodness Alice and George have Jessica and the twins still take an afternoon nap or I would never get this finished," Molly gasped with exhaustion. It was December twenty third and Molly had been determined not to put the Christmas tree up and wrap presents till after Jessica's birthday wanting to keep the two occasions separate. A decision she was beginning to regret arguing that birthdays are precious especially to little ones and she didn't want to muddle the two. Although next year, she decided the tree could go up much earlier.

"Can I make you a coffee, Molly?" Lucy struggled to stand up with both hands rubbing her lower back to help ease the pain "No one told me that backache was this bad," she moaned.

Molly shot her a grin "how do you think I felt carrying twins? And yes to the coffee, please." She watched Lucy waddle towards the kitchen giggling at the memory of her own days with, at times, excruciating backache as she picked up the last present to wrap.

Tomorrow would be the final run-through for the wedding; she had the hen night at the café later although thankfully Daisy had it all in hand especially as Bertie was painting.

She only hoped that Daisy had stuck to her plan not adding other things she thought would be great for a hen do like silly string… I mean how old does she think we are? She pondered shaking her head. They had music, Prosecco, food, love and laughter – what more could they possibly need especially as that is what Maggie wanted.

Lucy returned carrying a tray with one hand still perched on her lower back. "Are you alright, Lucy? I mean I know my back used to ache like mad but you are only just about six months," she tried to hide the note of concern in her voice.

"No, I'm okay, honestly, I think I've overdone it that's all. These last few weeks since Emma… well you know have been full-on. Daisy has been a godsend; she is just what we needed." She sat down on the comfy sofa and Molly retrieved a footstool for her. Lucy gratefully raised her feet up. They sat together drinking coffee and munching chocolate digestives when Alistair walked in.

"I thought that you were busy this afternoon," he joked kissing Molly and smirking at the two of them.

"Just finished actually, what do you think?" Molly waved her hand in the general direction of the huge Christmas tree.

"Whoa… magnificent," he took his coat off scooping paper and tinsel onto the table so that he could sit down. "Where is everyone?" he scanned the room just as a sound could be heard from the baby monitor. "I'll go…" he pushed himself up from his chair disappearing into the boy's room.

"Well… that's our tea break over, let the mayhem begin!"

"Right and I think that is my cue to leave you to it, Molly. Happy days…"

"It will be your turn soon enough…" she chuckled as she picked up her coat and hat.

"Don't suppose you fancy walking me down the road, do you? I need a rest before tonight. I was going to go home and glam up for later but do you think that I could stay like this?" she looked down at her navy trousers and voluminous top.

"Of course, you look lovely, maybe just add a bit of lippy. Just let me get my coat and let Alistair know where I am going."

They walked down the lane arm in arm at a slow pace chatting about the evening to come. Lucy and Bertie had decided to have Christmas dinner on Christmas Eve with her mum and dad as her mum couldn't really go anywhere now or do very much and she didn't want to leave them completely on their own.

"Bertie will cook, of course, shame really as he doesn't even get Christmas day off!

He says he would rather cook. He will prep everything tonight as we will be at the wedding and then Dad only needs to pop it in the oven. That reminds me have you met this Felix yet?"

"No, I haven't, is he gorgeous?" they both laughed.

"Actually, he is. I found out that he mainly travels the world having amazing adventures. He says that it is all in aid of research for the books he writes. He's been trekking in Nepal, bungee jumping in New Zealand, take a canoe up the Amazon, even attempted the frozen Antarctic... he is really nice and at the moment he is hunting for fossils on the Jurassic coast."

"Wow I can't wait to meet him; perhaps you can introduce me tomorrow at the rehearsal." "Sure..." Molly glanced at her watch "Oh, no look at the time, I must get back I've still so much to do and my mother arrives tonight." She wailed with dread etched on her face. "See you later." Molly turned and trudged back up the road trying to think what order to do the myriad of things still vying for her attention. She needn't have bothered as a taxi was pulling up outside their front door as Molly turned the corner, her heart sank.

She watched her mother get out of the taxi like a Matriarch bestowing her presence on her adoring family, oops wrong programme she beamed at the naughty thought, biting her tongue. Her mother had always had a... a supercilious attitude, expecting everyone to conform to her wishes, fall into place with her plans and for a quiet life they mostly did.

"Mum… you're here earlier than we thought," Molly held out her arms as Sandra bestowed an air kiss on her daughter. "Let me help you with your bags and get in out of this cold wind," she picked up a suitcase immediately regretting it, "… this case is definitely overweight for the plane Mum what on earth have you brought with you, all your worldly goods?" She forced a chuckle to lighten the mood hoping that she was entirely wrong.

"Christmas presents for all my Grandchildren and of course a wedding present for Maggie and Freddie. I forgot how cold it could be in Dorset in the winter," she shivered to pick up the smallest bag.

Molly opened the door to see Alistair's face change from shock to amusement when he looked at her, raising his eyebrows. He had both boys in their highchairs trying to feed them, with little success as more food was on him and the floor rather than in the open mouths of two very hungry and protesting infants.

"Sandra…" he exclaimed, "… let me help you," he strode over to her taking charge she acquiesced easily.

"Alistair how lovely to see you and these two gorgeous boys, where's Jessica?"

Molly took charge of feeding the twins; Alistair could always charm her mother. "She will be back any minute she spent the afternoon with George and Alice."

Sandra muttered a very insincere "Lovely… I have a birthday present for her in my case if you don't mind opening it for me Alistair… and what are the arrangements for my stay, Molly?"

Molly glanced at her Mother *nothing has changed* she thought. "Well, as soon as I can I will take you up to the vicarage as you are staying with Suzanne but tonight you can either spend the evening here with Alistair or come to Bertie's for Maggie's hen party with me and Stella," she opened two yoghurts and began to spoon more food into the wide-open mouths in front of her. "Alice will be there, Isabel and a few others you may know."

"Yes, I see of course that would be lovely, any chance of a glass of wine Alistair?"

Molly was shocked at the audacity but then again not too surprised; her Mother had always liked a glass of wine I mean who doesn't? She asked herself but it was a bit early even for her Mother. And since when had everything been "lovely," she wondered.

At last, children in bed, Molly changed into her glad rags, lippy on, Sandra ensconced at the vicarage leaving her time to look over her checklist one more time. Her phone pinged with a text from Suzanne to let her know that they were just leaving the vicarage. Molly closed her iPad and checked herself in the mirror before finding Alistair.

"They are on their way darling," she leaned in for a kiss, "… I have my phone if there is a problem with the children." She let out a sigh, the hen night she was looking forward to but her Mother could be a nuisance at the best of times and the last thing Molly wanted was for her to spoil the evening. Somehow Sandra had even wangled an invite to the wedding; she shook her head in despair. A knock on the door brought her back; she quickly grabbed her coat and hurriedly left.

You could hear the music from Bertie's at quite a distance; the café was a blaze of coloured flashing lights with balloons flapping in the breeze and streamers hanging from the rafters. It looked and sounded wonderful, not everyone might agree, leaving Molly hoping that no one would complain. The three of them chatted excitedly about the evening to come, a Christmas Day wedding and the forthcoming celebrations.

Maggie was already flushed when they arrived. Daisy was serving drinks, the tables had been re-arranged to leave an area to mingle in the centre of the café with a long table along one wall now heaving with plates of food. It looked fabulous, the evening was a fantastic success and Molly gratefully let out a sigh of relief giving a huge tick in her mind to one more item off the list.

All too soon Bertie and Freddie arrived to put the café back in order ready for the next day. Isabel escorted Maggie home, everyone was tired even Sandra who had moaned about jetlag – from Spain! Molly couldn't help but laugh.

Chapter 47

Christmas Eve dawned finding Suzanne already up and in her study. She had made a pot of coffee but with no sound coming from Sandra's room she had buttered toast and marmalade taking it into her study with her. She stood by the window drinking in the view, she never grew tired of the sight of the sea in the distance, nothing moved. She took another bite of toast before settling down in front of her computer looking at her diary for today.

It was going to be a very busy one with the wedding rehearsal at 11:00, the Crib service at 15:00 and finally the midnight service at well actually 11:30. She sat back wondering when she would find time to eat never mind sleep ready for her first Christmas Day early morning service followed by the family service and the wedding in the afternoon.

Axis whined at her door so Suzanne abandoned her review of her sermons, thankfully they were already written and checked but she liked to look over them one more time.

"Come on Axis, let's go for that walk," Axis bounced along beside her as she pulled on her boots, coat and woolly hat. She quickly scribbled a note for Sandra, picked up her phone, unhooked the lead from the back of the kitchen door and set off.

It was bitingly cold this morning; Suzanne shrank back into her coat shivering. There was a fresh fall of snow overnight as yet untouched. Suzanne let her memory guide her into thoughts of Hugh as they passed the veterinary practice causing a smile to spread across her face. He was charming and cautious around her treating her almost like a china doll.

There was already smoke curling out of the chimney at Molly's despite the early hour, she trudged on pausing outside 'Cobwebs' Cottage wanting to see if Hugh was up but thinking better of it she turned to continue towards the sea.

"Suzanne…" a voice came from behind her she turned to see Hugh running down the lane his scarf flying in all directions, "… hold on, I'll come with you." Hugh was panting when he stopped by her side.

"You're out of condition," she grinned.

"Cheeky…" he leant in laying a gentle kiss on her lips before reaching down to ruffle the fur of an excited Axis. "Right, where are we going?" he asked raising his eyebrows.

They set off down to the sea taking the coast path up onto the top of the cliffs where Suzanne let Axis off the lead. He shot off in all directions stopping and sniffing at every blade of grass or tuft of dead brambles, the snow covering his paws.

"Do you fancy stopping at Bertie's for coffee before you go home?" Hugh quizzed as Suzanne looked at her watch.

"As wonderful as that sounds… better not, the rehearsal is at 11:00 and I need to check on Sandra."

"Oh, yes, I forgot about Sandra, everything alright, is it?" He hugged her tightly to him and Suzanne laid her head on his chest feeling fragile after the hectic and deafening hen night. She reluctantly pulled herself away from him.

"Yes, everything is fine but I must go, see you at 11:00 and maybe you could stop and have lunch with me," she turned to walk up the lane wishing she could have had that coffee. Snow began to float down once more making her hurry.

Hugh lifted his hand to wave after her calling, "… great, see you later," to her retreating back before he wandered into the café for breakfast. Suzanne watched him go feeling miserable forcing her mind to contemplate her schedule for the next two days.

Sandra had in turn left Suzanne a note saying that she was going down to see Molly and would be back in time for the Crib service. Suzanne felt relieved that was one person less to worry about wondering if she had been right to offer a room to Sandra as she had tried to take over already. She made another pot of coffee collecting her thoughts and notebook ready to go into the church, it was already 10:15.

The rehearsal over people began to wander away. Isabel was standing with Monty his hand gently resting on her waist.

"Maggie dear would you and Freddie come and have lunch with us as there is something I want to tell you?"

"Oh, I think I can guess, Izzie," she grinned nodding at Monty.

Isabel chuckled "No, it's not about Monty I think you know all about him already," she couldn't help but grin, "… so, if you could come along about 12:30, I… I mean we will have champagne waiting on ice, I thought that it would be good to have you to myself before you become Mrs Martin tomorrow."

Isabel was busy at the stove making a hotpot; she wanted to make something simple and easy with just an apple pie and custard to follow.

Monty hooked his arm around her waist "Are you sure that you want to do this today?" he nibbled her ear sending shivers down her spine.

She dropped the spoon with a clatter turning into his arms, "… quite sure," she kissed him lightly and he pulled her to him kissing her deeply arousing her, wanting more, "… and it must be today, I want them to start married life knowing my decision."

There was a rap on the front door and Monty moved to let them in. Maggie and Freddie wandered into the kitchen which despite the size of the house with its formal dining room, the kitchen was always where people congregated.

"Shall we eat in here?" Isabel motioned to the old farmhouse table already placing the cutlery into the middle throwing Maggie a grin.

"Great, I'll set it for you, what's so special that you want to see us today Izzie?"

Maggie busied herself pulling out placemats and the condiments setting them onto the table, "… only you look very happy with yourself," Isabel just smiled "Monty is clearly doing you the world of good," she whispered conspiratorially. Isabel blushed; she glanced over at Monty with deep affection.

"All in good time; Monty will you open the champagne please?" Monty wrapped a tea towel around his arm and with a flourish popped the champagne cork pouring out the golden foaming liquid into delicate crystal flutes.

"Congratulations to you both…" toasted Isabel taking a deep sip of champagne letting it slide down her throat before quickly returning to the stove, "… lunch is ready, come and sit down."

The men had been talking business as usual. The renovations to the Gardeners Cottage had come to a halt partly due to the snow but also it was customary for the building trade to take a longer break at Christmas. The main work was complete leaving only the kitchen to be installed, decorating and the finishing touches to be done by Isabel as she had her own ideas of how she wanted it all to look.

"I think we will take coffee in the sitting room today, it's cosy in there as Monty lit the fire earlier," announced Isabel standing to clear the table. "If you boys don't mind checking the fire for me and we will be along shortly oh and Monty…" she gave him a little nod and without a word he disappeared out of the kitchen, a man on a mission.

The sitting room was a much more private room, cosy and intimate unlike the formal drawing room now being used as a reception room for weddings, a room that Isabel had kept for herself.

They finished their coffee and tiny squares of pink and white coconut ice-covered in dark chocolate as Isabel leaned across the table picking up a large brown folder. The room fell quiet as Isabel pulled out the original plans for Trentmouth Manor together with the two farms, three cottages and various outbuildings. She spread them out carefully onto the table.

"These are the original plans that came with the deeds when we bought the place all those years ago," she smoothed out the plans as they were folded, crinkled and even some brown sticky tape in places that were now falling off. They all clustered around for a closer look at the now faded drawings.

"Here is the boundary of the estate marked in red and if we look at the new drawings that Monty has had marked up for me you will see…" she pulled out crisp new drawings placing them on top for them all to see, "… here you will see a new red boundary around Gardener's Cottage encompassing this little odd-shaped piece of land at the rear together with the new drive with its own access onto the lane."

"Is that so that the holidaymakers can come and go without entering onto the estate?" asked Maggie head down scrutinising the plans without looking up at Isabel "… you don't think that's too much garden do you for a holiday?"

"Not quite Maggie. Let me show you this document," she picked up a hefty envelope from under the table pulling out a bound sheaf of papers to which were attached some more plans. "These are the deeds separating Gardeners Cottage from the rest of the estate," she opened up the paperwork for Maggie and Freddie to see watching the puzzled look that passed from one to the other feeling thrilled knowing what comes next.

"Right… but I don't understand why you felt the need to do that. Surely it's just another part of the estate and as far as I can see it will make a very profitable part too, the cottage is divine." She turned her eyes to Isabel who by now couldn't help herself as a grin spread over her face.

"That's exactly what I wanted as you see Maggie and Freddie, I have decided to live in Gardener's Cottage permanently…" she paused to let that information sink in.

"I still don't understand, is it because the house will be more like a hotel and not private anymore when the weddings start next year? I know that most of the house will be transformed with lots of people in it but there will still be a private wing away from all the guests…" poor Maggie looked shocked and a little forlorn. Isabel could hardly contain her excitement and the news any longer.

"No," she let out a chuckle glancing at Monty knowing she was doing the right thing.

"No, that is not the reason because…" with a flourish she pulled out another document headed Deeds, handing it over to Maggie and Freddie with a huge beaming smile.

Maggie took it and began to look at it curiosity on her face, her forehead furrowed.

Isabel threw a look at Monty a smile creasing her face, butterflies dancing in her stomach.

"These are the new deeds minus Gardener's Cottage and as a wedding present I have signed over the whole estate to you both," Isabel grinned at their shocked faces as it took a few seconds for them to assimilate this turn of events, "… from tomorrow, on the occasion of your wedding, the whole thing is yours to run and own and deal with exactly as you wish and I am going to retire into my new home."

Maggie leapt to her feet with a squeal of excitement hugging her aunt, tears began to roll down her cheeks "I don't know what to say, we don't know how to thank you, this is beyond our wildest dreams," she turned to Freddie "I… I can't believe it, Freddie, Trentmouth Manor is to be our new home and business venture all rolled into one. Thank you, thank you, thank you. But hang on a minute what about Jeremy? We thought that…"

Isabel gave a loud guffaw "It has absolutely nothing to do with Jeremy, never has, he just didn't know it," she laughed

327

some more and they all began hugging and kissing each other with joy.

It had been a wonderful day and Isabel was thrilled with her decision knowing that it was the right one. Snow began to fall softly outside and the fire crackled as Monty put on more logs. Yes, it was a perfect day she smiled contentedly.

"Monty this calls for a celebration to Mr & Mrs Martin the new owners of Trentmouth Manor let's break out another bottle of champagne."

The End